Paul B. Du Chaillu

Stories of the Gorilla Country

Narrated for young people

Paul B. Du Chaillu

Stories of the Gorilla Country
Narrated for young people

ISBN/EAN: 9783337428396

Printed in Europe, USA, Canada, Australia, Japan

Cover: Foto ©Andreas Hilbeck / pixelio.de

More available books at **www.hansebooks.com**

STORIES

OF THE

GORILLA COUNTRY.

NARRATED FOR YOUNG PEOPLE.

By PAUL DU CHAILLU,

AUTHOR OF "DISCOVERIES IN EQUATORIAL AFRICA," ETC., ETC.

With Numerous Illustrations.

NEW YORK AND LONDON:

HARPER & BROTHERS, PUBLISHERS,

1897.

PREFACE.

My dear Young Folks,—

My publishers, thinking that you would like to hear of Friend Paul, have just published specially for you this new edition of his travels in Africa in five little volumes—*Stories of the Gorilla Country, Wild Life Under the Equator, Lost in the Jungle, My Apingi Kingdom* (for the Apingi people made Friend Paul their king), and *The Country of the Dwarfs.*

When Friend Paul returned to New York he found the young folks his devoted friends; they believed in him and his books.

They believed in the great forest and jungle where he spent five years.

They believed in the horrid gorilla, and in the encounters he had with that huge monster; they believed, too, in the other apes that he had discovered, the Nshiego Mbouvé, the Kooloo-kamba, and Nshiego Nkengo. Some of them saw the great gorillas and the other apes at the famous publishing house in Franklin Square. They believed in dear little Tommy, and Fighting Joe; also in the wonderful animals, insects, and snakes Friend Paul described.

They believed in all the tribes of wild men with whom he had lived, and who were friends of his; in the cannibals; and in the dwarfs. With him they loved King Ranpano, Quengueza, and Obindji, and also his hunters, Igala, Fasiko, Niamkala, Malaouen, Kerlaouen, and others.

The young folks believed in Friend Paul, for he was one of them, a lad nearly eighteen years old, when he went to Africa the first time.

When he lectured to the young folks they came by the thousands, girls and boys, to proclaim loudly that they loved him and believed in him ; and when he put ou the clothes he wore in Africa, with all his weapons, their enthusiasm knew no bounds. They rushed on the platform, and boys and girls shook hands and kissed him. Oh, how happy it made Friend Paul ! And many of them are his friends to-day.

Since he has been in Africa he has travelled in many lands, and written other books for old folks. One of these lands he has called "The Land of the Midnight Sun," and soon he is going to write for the young folks his adventures in that wonderful couutry where the sun shines night and day. There he hunted bears, wolves, and other animals, aud in winter used reindeer for horses, and long snow-shoes to walk with.

Since he wrote about the dwarfs many of the young folks have become mothers and fathers ; and it is for their children that this new edition is published.

Friend Paul himself is still a bachelor, and he wants the young folks of to-day to love him as their parents did.

Your faithful friend,

PAUL DU CHAILLU.

NEW YORK.

CONTENTS.

CHAPTER VIII.

CHAPTER XVII.

CHAPTER XVIII.

CHAPTER XIX.

CHAPTER XX.

CHAPTER XXI.

CHAPTER XXII.

CHAPTER XXIII.

LIST OF ILLUSTRATIONS.

PAUL DU CHAILLU IN HIS AFRICAN COSTUME.

STORIES OF THE GORILLA COUNTRY.

PRELIMINARY CHAPTER.

I HAD passed several years on the African Coast before I began the explorations recorded in my first book. In those years I hunted, traded with the natives, and made collections in natural history.

In such a wild country as Africa one does not go far without adventures. The traveler necessarily sees what is strange and wonderful, for every thing is strange.

In this book I have attempted to relate some of the incidents of life in Africa for the reading of young folks. In doing this I have kept no chronological order, but have selected incidents and adventures here and there as they seem to be fitted for my purpose.

I have noticed that most intelligent boys like to read about the habits of wild animals, and the manners and way of life of savage men; and of such matters this book is composed. In it I have entered into more minute details concerning the life of the native inhabitants than I could in my other books, and have shown how the people build their houses, what are their amusements, how they hunt, fish, eat, travel, and live.

Whenever I am at a friend's house the children ask me to tell them something about Africa. I like children, and in this book have written especially for them. I hope to interest many who are yet too young to read my larger works.

MY RECEPTION BY THE KING.

CHAPTER II.

ARRIVAL ON THE COAST.—A KING AND HIS PALACE.—DANC-
ING AND IDOL-WORSHIP.

ABOUT the year 1856 a three-masted vessel took me to a wild country on the West Coast of Africa, near the equator.

It was a very wild country indeed.

As we came in sight of the land, which was covered with forest, canoes began to start from the shore toward us; and, as we neared the land, we could see the people crowding down on the beach to look at the strange sight of a vessel.

The canoes approached the vessel in great numbers. Some of them were so small that they looked like mere nutshells. Indeed, some of the men paddled with their feet; and one man carried his canoe ashore on his shoulder.

At last the natives came on board, and what funny people they were! I could not discern one from another; they seemed to me all alike.

What a queer way of dressing they had, too! You would have laughed to see them. Some had only an old coat on. Others had an old pair of trowsers which probably had belonged to some sailor; these wore no shirt or coat. Some had only an old ragged shirt, and some, again, had nothing on except an old hat. Of course none of them had shoes.

How they shouted and halloed as they came about the vessel! They seemed to speak such a strange language. No one on board appeared to understand them. They made so great a noise that I thought I should become deaf.

One of them had a fowl to sell; another brought an egg or two; and another a few bunches of plantains.

Our captain knew the coast, for he had long been an African trader, though he had never been at this place before.

The ship cast anchor. It was not far from a river called Benito.

I left the vessel and went ashore with some others. As I landed I was surrounded immediately by crowds of natives, who looked so wild and so savage that I thought they would kill me at once.

I was led to the village, which stood not far from the sea, and was hidden from view by the very large trees and the great forest that surrounded it. On one side of the village was a prairie.

I shall always remember this village. It was the first African village I had ever seen, and it was unlike those built in Southern Africa.

Don't think for a moment that I am going to speak to you of stone or wooden houses! No! These wild people lived in queer little huts, the walls of which were made of the bark of trees, and were not more than four or five feet high. The top of the roof was only about seven or eight feet from the ground. The length of these huts was about ten or twelve feet, and they were seven or eight feet wide. There were no windows, and the door was very small. They immediately took me to one of these houses, and said they gave it to me. They meant that it was mine as long as I would stay with them. It belonged to the son of the king.

So I went in. But where was I to sit down?

There was no chair to be seen.

Patience, thought I. These people had probably never seen a chair in their lives. It was so dark I could not see at first. By-and-by I saw how the hut was furnished. There were some calabashes to hold water, and two or three cooking-pots. There were some ugly-looking spears, an axe, and two or three large and queer-looking knives, which could sever the head of a man at one blow. Of course I looked for a bed: I need not tell you there was none; but, instead, there were some sticks to lie upon. The very looks of this sleeping-place made me shudder; I thought of snakes, scorpions, and centipedes. The dark hut seemed the very place for them. Shortly after the king's son came. If I remember well, his name was *Andèlè*. He told me that his father, the king, was ready to receive me.

The king ready to receive me!

This was a great announcement. I must dress.

But how?

2

There was no washing-basin to wash myself in; bo sides, I had forgotten my soap.

I was glad I had no beard at that time, for I do not know how I could have shaved.

In short, I resolved to go and see his majesty as I was.

The sun being very warm, I took my umbrella with me. The people conducted me to the royal palace.

What do you suppose a palace to be in the Benito country? The king's palace was made of the same material (bark of trees) as the houses I have just described to you, and it was only about twice as big.

As I entered I went toward the king, who was seated on a stool. Another empty stool was by his side.

I may say that Apourou—such was the king's name— did not come up to my ideas of a king. In fact, I should have laughed at him had I dared.

His costume was composed of a red soldier's coat, and he wore a little bit of calico round his waist. That was all. You must understand he had no shirt.

He was a tall, slim negro, with gray hair, and had large scars on his face, and his whole body was covered with tattoos. He wore large earrings. He was smoking a big ugly pipe.

He looked at me, and I looked at him.

The room was full of people, and the king had several of his wives around him. The queen was there. Would you believe it? in that country a man marries as many wives as he chooses!

The king looked at me for a long time without saying a word. Finally he opened his mouth, clapped his hands, and said I was a funny-looking *fellow.*

He next said he was very glad to see me, and would

take care of me. Then he touched my hair, and said I must give him some. He would like to have me remain with him always. At this the people shouted, "We want the *ntangani* to stay with us!"

What do you think he did next?

He quietly proposed to me that I should get married to some of his country-women; and added that whom-soever I should choose would become my wife. The suggestion was received by all the people with a tre-mendous grunt of approval, to show that they thought just as their king. Then they shouted, "The girl he likes he shall marry!"

I said, "I don't want to get married; I am too young." I did not want to tell him that I would not, for all the world, marry one of his people.

It was getting very warm in the hut, and there was a strong odor. The people were packed so close together that they reminded one of herrings in a barrel, and you must remember I said the house had no windows.

Then the king presented me with one fowl, two eggs, and one bunch of plantain; and as I went away he said I had better give him my umbrella. But I went off as if I had not heard what he said. I thought it was rather too much for a king to ask a stranger to give up his um-brella. I had just begun to learn what African kings were.

The people followed me every where; I wish I could have understood their language. One man could talk English, and I am going now to give you a specimen of his English.

When he thought I must be hungry, he said, "Want

chop? Want chop?" When he saw that I could not understand what he meant, he made signs with his hands and mouth, which at once explained to me that he had asked me if I wanted to eat. I said "Yes;" and after a while, some cooked plantains, with some fish, were brought to me. I did not care for the plantains; it was the first time I had ever tasted them.

After my meal, I walked through the street of the village and came to a house, in the recess of which I saw an enormous idol. I had never in all my life seen such an ugly thing. It was a rude representation of some human being, of the size of life, and was made of wood. It had large copper eyes, and a tongue of iron which shot out from its mouth to show that it could sting. The lips were painted red. It wore large iron earrings. Its head was ornamented with a feather cap. Most of the feathers were red, and came from the tails of gray parrots, while the body and face were painted red, white, and yellow. It was dressed in the skins of wild animals. Around it were scattered skins of tigers and serpents, and the bones and skulls of animals. Some food also was placed near, so that it might eat if it chose.

It was now sunset, and night soon set in over the village. For the first time in my life I stood alone in this dark world, surrounded by savages, without any white people near me. There was no light in the street, and only the reflection of the fires could be seen now and then. How dismal it was!

I looked at my pistols and my guns, and was glad to find that they were in good order.

By-and-by the people began to come out of their huts, and I saw some torches lighted, and taken toward the large *mbuiti*, as they call the idol, and there placed on the ground. The large drums or tom-toms were also carried there, and the women and men of the village gathered around. The tom-toms beat; and, soon after, I heard the people singing. I went to see what was the matter.

What a sight met my eyes!

The men had their bodies painted in different colors. Some had one cheek red and the other white or yellow. A broad white or yellow stripe was painted across the middle of the chest and along both the arms. Others had their bodies spotted. Most ugly they looked! The women wore several iron or brass rings around their wrists and ankles.

Then the singing began, and the dancing! I had never seen such dancing before. It was very ungraceful. The drummers beat on the tom-toms with all their might. As they became warm with exertion their bodies shone like seals, so oily were they.

I looked and looked, with my eyes wide open; I was nearly stunned with the noise. As the women danced and sung, the brass and iron rings which they wore struck against each other, and kept time with the music and the beating of the tom-toms.

But why were they all there, dancing and screeching around the idol? I will tell you.

They were about to start on a hunting expedition, and they were asking the idol to give them good luck in their sport.

When I found it was to be a hunting expedition, I wanted to go at once with these savages, though I was only a lad under twenty years old.

I retired to my hut with a valiant heart; I was going
to do great things.

If you had been in my place, boys, would you not have
felt the same? Would you have left the gorillas alone?
I am sure you all shout at once, "No! no!" Would you
have left the elephants go unmolested in the forest?
"Certainly not," will be your answer.

And what about the chimpanzee, and the big leopards
who carry away so many people and eat them, the huge
buffaloes, the wild boars, the antelopes, and the gazelles?

Would you have left the snakes alone?

Perhaps you are all going to say "Yes" to that; and I
think you are right, for many of these snakes are very
poisonous, and they are numerous in these great forests;
for the country I am telling you about is nothing but an
immense jungle. When a man is bitten by one of these
snakes he often dies in a few minutes. There is also to
be found in those woods an immense python, or boa, that
swallows antelopes, gazelles, and many other animals. I
shall have a good deal to tell you about them by-and-by.

So I resolved that I would try to see all these native
tribes; that I would have a peep at the Cannibals; that
I would have a good look also at the dwarfs.

I am sure that, if any one of you had been with me on
that coast, you would have said to me, "Du Chaillu, let
us go together and see all these things, and then come
back home and tell the good folks all we have seen."

Yes, I am certain that every one of you would have
felt as I did.

FIGHT WITH A BUFFALO.

CHAPTER III.

Now, boys, fancy yourselves transported into the midst of a very dense and dark forest, where the trees never shed their leaves all at one time, where there is no food to be had except what you can get with your gun, and where wild beasts prowl around you at night while you sleep.

I found myself in such a place

Immediately after we arrived in those gloomy solitudes we began to build an olako to shelter us from the rains.

I must tell you that Benito is a very strange country. It is situated, as you have seen by the map, near the equator. Of course you know what the equator is? There, at a certain time of the year, the sun is directly above your head at noon, and hence it is the hottest part of the earth. The days and nights are of the same length. The sun rises at six o'clock in the morning, and the sunset takes place at six o'clock in the evening. There is only a difference of a few minutes all the year round. There is no twilight, and half an hour before sunrise or after sunset it is dark. There is no snow except on very high mountains. There is no winter. There are only two seasons—the rainy season and the dry season. Our winter-time at home is the time of the rainy season in Equatorial Africa, and it is also the hottest period of the year. It rains harder there than in any other country. No such rain is to be witnessed either in the United States or Europe. And as to the thunder and lightning, you never have heard or seen the like; it is enough to make the hair of your head stand on end! Then come the tornadoes, a kind of hurricane which, for a few minutes, blows with terrible violence, carrying before it great trees. How wild the sky looks! How awful to see the black clouds sweeping through the sky with fearful velocity!

So you will not wonder that we busied ourselves in preparing our shelter, for I remember well it was in the month of February. We took good care not to have big trees around us, for fear they might be hurled upon us by a tornado, and bury us all alive under their weight. Accordingly, we built our olako near the banks of a beautiful little stream, so that we could get as much water as we wanted. Then we immediately began to fell trees. We carried two or three axes with us, for the axe is an indispensable article in the forests. With the foliage we made a shelter to keep off the rain.

While the men were busy building the olako, the women went in search of dried wood to cook our supper. We had brought some food from the village with us.

We were ready just in time. A most terrific tornado came upon us. The rain poured down in torrents. The thunder was stunning. The lightning flashed so vividly and often as nearly to blind us.

Our dogs had hidden themselves—indeed, all animals and birds of the forest were much frightened, which was not to be wondered at. How thankful I was to be sheltered from such a storm! We had collected plenty of fuel, and our fires burned brightly.

We formed a strange group while seated around the fires, the men and women smoking their pipes and telling stories. We had several fires, and, as they blazed up, their glare was thrown out through the gloom of the forest, and filled it with fantastic shadows. Though tired, every body seemed merry. We were full of hope for the morrow. Every one spoke of the particular animal he wished to kill, and of which he was most fond Some wished for an antelope, others for an elephant, a wild boar, or a buffalo. I confess that I myself inclined toward the wild boar; and I believe that almost every one had the same wish, for that animal, when fat, is very good eating. Indeed, they already began to talk as if the pig were actually before them. All fancied they could eat a whole leg apiece, and their mouths fairly watered in thinking about it. No wonder they are so fond of meat, they have it so seldom. Who among us does not relish a good dinner, I should like to know?

By-and-by all became silent; one after the other we fell asleep, with the exception of two or three men who were to watch over the fires and keep them bright; for there were plenty of leopards prowling in the neighboring forest, and none of us wanted to serve as a meal for them. In fact, before going to sleep we had heard some of these animals howling in the far distance. During the night one came very near our camp. He went round and round, and, no doubt, lay in wait to see if one of us

would go out alone, and then he would have pounced
upon the careless fellow. I need not say we did not give
him a chance; and you may be sure we kept the fire
blazing. Finally, we fired a few guns, and he went off.

These leopards are dreadful animals, and eat a great
many natives. They are generally shy; but once they
have tasted human flesh, they become very fond of it,
and the poor natives are carried off, one after another, in
such numbers that the villages have to be abandoned.

The next day we went hunting. I had hardly gone
into the forest when I saw, creeping on the ground under the dry leaves, an enormous black snake: I fancy I
see it still. How close it was to me! One step more,
and I should have just trodden upon it, and then should
have been bitten, and a few minutes after have died,
and then, boys, you know I should have had nothing to
tell you about Africa. This snake was a cobra of the
black variety (*Dendrapspis angusticeps*). It is a very
common snake in that region, and, as I have said, very
poisonous.

As soon as the reptile saw me he rose up, as if ready
to spring upon me, gave one of his hissing sounds, and
looked at me, showing, as he hissed, his sharp-pointed
tongue. Of course, the first thing I did was to make a
few steps backward. Then, leveling my gun, I fired and
killed him. He was about eight feet long. I cut his
head off, and examined his deadly fangs. What horrible
things they were! They looked exactly like fish-bones,
with very sharp ends. I looked at them carefully, and
saw that he could raise and lower them at will; while
the teeth are firmly implanted in a pouch, or little bag,
which contains the poison. I saw in the end of the fang

a little hole, which communicated with the pouch. When the snake opens his mouth to bite, he raises his fangs. Then he strikes them into the flesh of the animal he bites, and brings a pressure on the pouch, and the poison comes out by the little hole I have spoken of.

I cut open the cobra, and found in his stomach a very large bird. Andèkè packed the bird and snake in leaves, and, on our return to the camp, the men were delighted. In the evening they made a nice soup of the snake, which they ate with great relish.

I had also killed a beautiful little striped squirrel, upon which I made my dinner. I felt almost sorry to kill it, it was such a pretty creature.

In the evening, as I was sitting by the fire and looking at the log that was burning, I spied a big, ugly black scorpion coming out of one of the crevices. I immediately laid upon its back a little stick which I had in my hand. You should have seen how its long tail flew up and stung the piece of wood! I shuddered as I thought that it might have stung my feet or hands instead of the wood. I immediately killed it, and the natives said these scorpions were quite common, and that people have to be careful when they handle dry sticks of wood, for these poisonous creatures delight to live under the dry bark, or between the crevices.

A nice country this to live in, thought I, after killing a snake and a scorpion the same day!

So, when I lay down on my pillow, which was merely a piece of wood, I looked to see if there were any scorpions upon it. I did not see any; but, during the night, I awoke suddenly and started up. I thought I felt hundreds of them creeping over me, and that one had just

stung me, and caused me to wake up. The sweat covered my body. I looked around and saw nothing but
sleeping people. There was no scorpion to be found.
I must have been dreaming.

Not far from our camp was a beautiful little prairie.
I had seen, during my rambles there, several footprints
of wild buffaloes, so I immediately told Andèkè we must
go in chase of them. Andèkè, the son of the king, was
a very nice fellow, and was, besides, a good hunter—just
the very man I wanted.

So we went toward the little prairie, and lay hidden
on the borders of it, among the trees. By-and-by I spied
a huge bull, who was perfectly unaware of my presence,
for the wind blew from him to me; had the wind blown
the other way, the animal would have scented me and
have made off. As it was, he came slowly toward me.
I raised my gun and fired. My bullet struck a creeper
on its way, and glanced aside, so I only wounded the
beast. Turning fiercely, he rushed at me in a furious
manner, with his head down. I was scared; for I was,
at that time, but a young hunter; I got ready to run,
though I had a second barrel in reserve. I thought the
infuriated bull was too powerful for me, he looked so
big. Just as I was about to make my escape, I found
my foot entangled and hopelessly caught in a tough and
thorny creeper. The bull was dashing toward me with
head down and eyes inflamed, tearing down brushwood
and creepers which barred his progress. Turning to
meet the enemy, I felt my nerves suddenly grow firm as
a rock. If I missed the bull, all would be over with me.
He would gore me to death. I took time to aim carefully, and then fired at his head. He gave one loud,

hoarse bellow, and tumbled almost at my feet. In the mean time, Andèkè was coming to the rescue.

I must say I felt very nervous after all was over. But, being but a lad, I thought I had done pretty well. It was the first direct attack a wild beast had ever made upon me. I found afterward that the bulls are gener ally very dangerous when wounded.

Now I must tell you how this beast looked. He was one of the wild buffaloes frequently to be met with in this part of Africa. During the greater part of the day they hide in the forest. When much hunted they be-come very shy. They are generally found in herds of from ten to twenty-five, though I have found them some· times in much greater number.

This animal (*Bos brachicheros*) is called by some of the natives "niaré." It is of the size of our cattle. It is covered with thin red hair, which is much darker in the bull than in the cow. The hoofs are long and sharp; the ears are fringed with most beautiful silky hair; the horns are very handsome, and bend backward in a grace-ful curve. In shape, the buffalo looks like something be-tween an antelope and a common cow; and, when seen afar off, you might think these wild buffaloes were a herd of our cattle at home.

How glad the people were when Andèkè and I brought the news that we had killed a bull! There was great rejoicing. But I was tired, and remained in the camp, while they went with knives and swords to cut the buf-falo to pieces, and bring in the flesh.

What a fine place it was for hunting! The animals seemed to come down from the mountains beyond, and remain in the flat woody country along the sea-shore.

There were a great many wild boars. You know we all wanted one of these. So one night Andèké and I agreed to go and lie in wait for them on the prairie. In order to look like Andèké, I blackened my face and hands with charcoal, so that in the night the color of my face could not be distinguished.

We started from the camp before dark, and reached the prairie before night. I stationed myself behind a large ant-hill not far from the open space. There I lay; one hour passed—two hours—three hours, and still neither wild boar nor buffaloes. I looked at Andèké. He was fast asleep, at the foot of another ant-hill close by. Once I saw a whole herd of gazelles pass by; but they were too far from me. Occasionally a grunt, or the cracking of a twig, told me that a wild boar was not far off. At last every thing became silent, and I fell asleep unconsciously.

Suddenly I was awakened by an unearthly roar—the yell of a wild beast.

I rubbed my eyes in a hurry—what could be the matter?

I looked round me, and saw nothing. The woods were still resounding with the cry that had startled me. Then I heard a great crash in the forest, made by some heavy animal running away. Then I saw emerge from the forest a wild bull, on whose neck crouched an immense leopard. The poor buffalo reared, tossed, roared, and bellowed, but in vain. The leopard's enormous claws were firmly fixed in his victim's body, while his teeth were sunk deeply in the bull's neck. The leopard gave an awful roar, which seemed to make the earth shake. Then both buffalo and leopard disappeared in the forest, and the roars and the crashing of the trees soon ceased. All became silent again.

I had fired at the leopard, but it was too far off.

We staid a week here, and I enjoyed myself very much in the woods. I collected birds and butterflies, killed a few nice little quadrupeds, and then we return- ed to the sea-shore village. There the fever laid me low on my bed of sickness. How wretched I felt! I had never had the fever before. For a few days my head was burning hot. When I got better, and looked at my- self in my little looking-glass, I could not recognize my- self; I had not a particle of color left in my cheeks, and I looked as yellow and pale as a lemon. I got fright- ened. This fever was the forerunner of what I had to expect in these equatorial regions.

3

ENTICING THE LEOPARD.

CHAPTER IV.

A VILLAGE ON THE SEA-SHORE.—LYING IN WAIT FOR A
LEOPARD.

ON the promontory called Cape St. John, about a degree north of the equator, stood a Mbinga village, whose
chief was called Imonga. This was, I think, in the year
1852. The country around was very wild. The village
stood on the top of a high hill, which ran out into the
sea, and formed the cape itself. The waves there beat
with great violence against a rock of the tertiary formation. It was a grand sight to see those angry billows,
white with foam, dashing against the shore. You could
see that they were wearing away the rock. To land

there safely was very difficult. There were only two or three places where, between the rocks, a canoe could reach the shore. The people were as wild as the country round them, and very warlike. They were great fishermen, and many of them spent their whole time fishing in their little canoes. Game being very scarce, there were but few hunters.

Imonga, the chief, had a hideous large scar on his face, which showed at once that he was a fighting man. Not a few of his men showed signs of wounds which they had received in battle. Many of these fights or quarrels took place in canoes on the water, among themselves, or with people of other villages.

I do not know why, but Imonga was very fond of me, and so also were his people. But one thing revolted me. I found that several of Imonga's wives had the first joint of their little finger cut off. Imonga did this to make them mind him; for he wanted his wives to obey him implicitly.

The woods around the village were full of leopards. They were the dread of the people, for they were constantly carrying off some one. At night they would come into the villages on their errands of blood while the villagers were asleep. There was not a dog nor a goat left; and within two months three people had been eaten by them; the very places could be seen in the huts where the leopards had entered. They would tear up the thin thatched palm-leaves of the roofs, and, having seized their victims, they would go back through the hole with a tremendous leap, and with the man in their jaws, and run off into the forest.

The last man taken had uttered a piercing cry of an-

gnish, which awoke all the villagers. They at once arose
and came to the rescue; but it was too late. They only
found traces of blood as they proceeded. The leopard
had gone far into the woods, and there devoured his victim. Of course there was tremendous excitement, and
they went into the forest in search of the leopard; but
he could never be found.

There were so many of these savage beasts that they
even walked along the beach, not satisfied with the woods
alone; and when the tide was low, during the night, the
footprints of their large paws could be seen distinctly
marked on the sand. After ten or eleven o'clock at
night, no native could be seen on the sea-shore without
torches.

During the day the leopard hides himself either in the
hollow of some one of the gigantic trees with which
these forests abound, or sleeps quietly on some branch,
waiting for the approach of night. He seldom goes out
before one o'clock in the morning, unless pressed by
hunger, and about four o'clock he goes back to his lair.

I was now getting accustomed to face danger. Killing
the buffalo that attacked me had given me confidence.

To kill a leopard must be my next exploit.

I selected a spot very near the sands of the sea, where
I remarked the leopards used to come every night, when
the tide was low. I chose a day when the moon began
to rise at midnight, so that it might not be so dark that
I could not take a good aim at the leopard, and see what
was going on.

I then began to build a kind of pen or fortress, and I
can assure you I worked very hard at it. Every day I
went into the forest and cut branches of trees, with which

I made a strong palisade. Every stick was about six feet high, and was put in the ground about a foot deep. These posts were fastened together with strong creepers. My little fortress, for so I must call it, was about five feet square. This would never answer; for the leopard might leap inside and take hold of me. So, with the help of some stout branches all tied strongly together, I built a roof. Then I made loop-holes on all sides for my guns, so that I might fire at the beast whenever he came in sight.

I was glad when I had finished, for I felt very tired. My axe was not sharp, and it had required several days to complete my work.

One clear starlight night, at about nine o'clock, I went and shut myself up in my fortress. I had taken a goat with me, which I tied a few yards from my place of concealment. It was quite dark. After I had tied the goat, I went back and shut myself very securely inside my strong-hold.

I waited and waited, but no leopard came. The goat cried all the time. It was so dark that even if the leopard had come I could not have seen it.

The moon rose by one o'clock. It was in its last quarter; and very strange and fantastic it made every thing look. There were the shadows of the tall trees thrown upon the white sand of the beach, while in the forest the gloom was somewhat greater. The sea came rolling on the beach in gentle waves, which, as they broke, sent up thousands of bright phosphorescent flashes. There was a dead silence every where, except when the goat cried, or some wild beast made the forest resound with its dismal howl. The wind whispered gently, mournfully through the woods.

I could not account for it, but now and then a cold shudder ran through me. I was quite alone, for the negro I had taken with me was fast asleep.

One o'clock. No leopard. I looked in vain all round me; I could see nothing.

Two o'clock. Nothing yet.

Suddenly I spied something a long way off on the beach, so far that I could not make out what it was. It came slowly toward me. What could it be? I asked myself. Soon I recognized a big spotted leopard. The goat, which had seen it, began to cry more loudly. The big beast came nearer and nearer. He began to crouch. Then he lay flat on the ground. How his eyes glittered! They looked like two pieces of bright, burning charcoal.

My heart beat. The first thought that came to me was, Is my house strong enough to resist his attack, in case I should wound him, or if, perchance, he should prefer me to the goat, and make an onslaught upon it?

The savage beast crawled nearer, and again crouched down on the ground. I took my gun, and, just as I was getting ready to fire, he made an immense leap, and bounded upon the goat. I fired. I do not know how, but, in the twinkling of an eye, the goat was seized, and both leopard and goat disappeared in the dark forest. I fired again, but with no better success. In the morning I saw nothing but the traces of the poor goat's blood.

I did not return to the village till morning, for I dared not go outside of my palisade that night. So, the goat being gone, I concluded I had better light a fire, to warm myself, and drive away the musquitoes. I always carried a box of matches with me. I struck one, and soon succeeded in making a blaze with the little firewood I had collected.

Strange enough I must have looked, inside of my cage, while the fire sent its glimmering light around.

Finally, seeing that every thing was well secured, I went to sleep, taking good care to put myself in the middle of the fort, so that if, by any chance, a leopard came, he could not get hold of me with his paw. When I awoke it was broad daylight, and I immediately started for Imonga's village.

FLOCKS OF BIRDS.

CHAPTER V.

THE BAY OF CORISCO.—THE MANGROVE-TREES.—THE WON-
DERFUL FLOCK OF BIRDS.—WHAT I FOUND IN THE POUCH
OF A PELICAN.—HOW AN OLD KING IS BURIED, AND THE
NEW KING CROWNED.

Now that you have followed me in the Benito country, and to Cape St. John, I will take you a little farther
down the coast to the Bay of Corisco. There, two rivers
empty their waters into the sea. One of them is called
the Muni River, and the other the Monda.

I will leave the Muni, for we shall have to come to it
by-and-by, and will speak to you only of the Monda. It
is throughout a low-banked, swampy stream. The banks
are covered with mangrove-trees. Every limb or branch
that grows in the water is covered with oysters—real
oysters, too—so that at low tide you can see, in some

places for a long distance, immense beds of this kind of shell-fish.

The mangroves, on which the oysters grow so curiously, are very extraordinary trees. The main trunk, or parent tree, grows to an immense size. From a single tree a whole forest will grow up in time, for the branches send down shoots into the ground, which in their turn take root and become trees; so that, generally, almost the whole of the mangrove forest may be said to be knitted together.

The inhabitants of the country at the mouth of the river are called Shekiani. They are a very warlike tribe, and many of them are armed with guns, which they obtain from the vessels which come here from time to time to buy barwood, ivory, or India-rubber.

I arrived at the mouth of the river in a small canoe manned by several Mbinga men. The canoe was made of the trunk of a single tree, and had a mat for a sail. At the mouth of the river, high above the swamps that surround its banks, are two hills. On the top of one of these hills a village was situated. There I staid. It was a village of insignificant size.

At low tide, the high, muddy banks of the river are exposed. So many birds as are there I never saw elsewhere: they are to be seen in countless thousands. The shore, the mud islands, and the water were so covered with them that it was really a sight worth seeing. Here and there flocks of pelicans swam majestically along, keeping at a good distance from my canoe. You would probably wish to know what these pelicans are like. I will tell you. They are large birds, and have an enormous bill, under which is a large pouch, capable of containing several pounds of fish. They have webbed feet, and their feathers are white. I wish you could see them looking out for their prey. How slyly they pry in the water for the fish they are in search of, and how quickly they pounce upon them unawares with their powerful beak! In an instant the fish are killed and stored away in the pouch; and when this is full, then Master Pelican begins to eat. The fish are put in the pouch as if it were a store-house.

Now and then a string of flamingoes go stretching along the muddy shore, looking for all the world like a line of fire. Most beautiful are these flamingoes! and very singular they appear when not on the wing, but standing still on their long red legs! They are very wild, however, and difficult of approach.

Wherever the mud peeped out of the water, there were herons, cranes, gulls of various kinds. Scattered everywhere were seen those beautiful white birds (*Egretta flavirostris*). Some of the shore trees were covered with them, looking like snow in the distance.

Of course I wished to kill some of these birds. So I took a tiny little canoe, and covered it with branches of trees, that the birds might think it was a tree coming down the stream, as is often the case. Then I took a Shekiani with me to paddle, and, putting two guns in the canoe, we made for the pelicans. The sly birds seemed to suspect something, and did not give me a chance to approach them for a long time. But, as you know, in order to succeed in any thing, people must have patience and perseverance. So, after chasing many, I finally succeeded in approaching one. He was just in the act of swallowing a big fish when—bang!—I fired, and wounded

him so that he could not fly. His wing had been broken
by my shot. At the noise made by firing my gun, the
birds flew away y thousands. I made for Master Pelican. The chase became exciting; but, at last, we succeeded in coming near him. But how to get hold of
him was now the question. His wing only was broken;
and, with his great beak, he might perhaps be able to
cut one of my fingers right off. I was afraid to spoil his
feathers if I fired again. He became exhausted, and
with one of the paddles I gave him a tremendous blow
on the head, which stunned him. Another blow finished
him, and we lifted him into the canoe.

I can not tell you how pleased I was. His pouch was
full of fish. They were so fresh that I resolved to make
a meal out of them.

I had hardly put the bird at the bottom of the canoe,
when there came flying toward me a flock of at least two
hundred flamingoes. In a moment I had my gun in
readiness. Would they come near enough for me to get
a shot at them? I watched them anxiously. Yes!
Now they are near enough; and—bang! bang!—I fired
the two barrels right into the middle of the flock, and
two beautiful flamingoes fell into the water. Quickly
we paddled toward them. In order to go faster, I took
a paddle also, and worked away as well as I could. They
were dead. Both had received shots in the head.

We made for the shore. When I opened the pouch
of the pelican—just think of it!—I found a dozen large
fishes inside! They were quite fresh, and I am sure
they had not been caught more than half an hour. You
will agree with me that the pelican makes quick work
when he goes a fishing.

In the evening I felt so tired that I went straight to bed; and I slept so soundly, that if the Shekianis had chosen, they could have murdered me without my even opening my eyes.

This village had a new king; and I wondered if his majesty were made king in the same fashion as the sovereign of the Mpongwe tribe—a tribe of negroes among whom I have resided, and I will tell you how their king was made.

Old King Glass died. He had been long ailing, but clung to life with determined tenacity. He was a disagreeable old heathen; but in his last days he became very devout—after his fashion. His idol was always freshly painted and brightly decorated; his fetich, or "monda," was the best-cared-for fetich in Africa; and every few days some great doctors were brought down from the interior, and paid a large fee for advising the old king. He was afraid of witchcraft; he thought every body wanted to put him out of the way by bewitching him. So the business of the doctors was to keep off the witches, and assure his majesty that he would live a long time. This assurance pleased him wonderfully, and he paid his doctors well.

The tribe had got tired of their king. They thought, indeed, that he was himself a most potent and evil-disposed wizard; and, though the matter was not openly talked about, there were very few natives indeed who would pass his house after night, and none who could be tempted inside by any slighter provocation than an irresistible glass of rum. In fact, if he had not been a great king, he would probably have been killed.

When he got sick at last, every body seemed very

sorry; but several of my friends told me, in confidence, that the whole town hoped he would die, and die he did. I was awakened one morning by those mournful cries and wails with which the African oftener covers a sham sorrow than expresses a real grief. All the women of the village seemed to be dissolved in tears. It is a most singular thing to see how readily the women of Africa can supply tears on the slightest occasion, or for no occasion at all. They will cry together at certain times of the day, on mourning occasions, when a few minutes before they were laughing. They need no pain or real grief to excite tneir tears. They can, apparently, weep at will.

The mourning and wailing on this occasion lasted six days. On the second day the old king was secretly buried by a few of the most trusty men of the tribe, very early in the morning, before others were up—or perhaps at night. Some said he had been buried at night, while others said he had been buried in the morning, thus showing that they did not know. This custom arises from a belief that the other tribes would much like to get the head of the king, in order that with his brains they might make a powerful fetich.

During the days of mourning the old men of the village busied themselves in choosing a new king. This, also, is a secret operation, and the result is not communicated to the people generally till the seventh day.

It happened that Njogoni (fowl), a good friend of mine, was elected. I do not know that Njogoni had the slightest suspicion of his elevation. At any rate, he shammed ignorance very well.

While he was walking on the shore on the morning of the seventh day—probably some one had told him to go

—he was suddenly set upon by the entire populace, who proceeded with a ceremony which is preliminary to the crowning. In a dense crowd they surrounded him, and then began to heap upon him every manner of abuse that the worst of mobs could imagine. Some spat in his face. Some beat him with their fists—not very hard, of course. Some kicked him. Others threw dirty things at him. Those unlucky ones who stood on the outside, and could only reach the poor fellow with their voices, assiduously cursed him, and also his father, and especially his mother, as well as his sisters and brothers, and all his ancestors to the remotest generation. A stranger would not have given a farthing for the life of him who was presently to be crowned.

Amid the noise and struggle, I caught the words which explained all to me; for every few minutes some fellow, administering a comparatively severe blow or kick, would shout out, "You are not our king yet; for a little while we will do what we please with you. By-and-by we shall have to do your will."

Njogoni bore himself like a man and a prospective king, and took all this abuse with a smiling face. When it had lasted about half an hour, they took him to the house of the old king. Here he was seated, and became again for a little while the victim of his people's curses and ill usage.

Suddenly all became silent, and the elders of the people rose, and said solemnly (the people repeating after them), "Now we choose you for our king; we engage to listen to you, and to obey you."

Then there was silence; and presently the silk hat, of "stove-pipe" fashion, which is the emblem of royal ty among the Mpongwe and several other tribes was brought in, and placed on Njogoni's head. He was then dressed in a red gown, and received the greatest marks of respect from all those who had just now abused him.

Then followed six days of festival, during which the poor king, who had taken the name of his predecessor, was obliged to receive his subjects in his own house, and was not allowed to stir out. The whole time was occupied in indescribable gorging of food, and drinking of bad rum and palm wine. It was a scene of beastly gluttony, and drunkenness, and uproarious confusion. Every thing to eat and drink was furnished freely, and all comers were welcome.

Old King Glass, for whom during six days no end of tears had been shed, was now forgotten; and *new* king Glass, poor fellow, was sick with exhaustion.

Finally, the rum and palm wine were drunk up, the food was eaten, the allotted days of rejoicing had expired, and the people went back to their homes.

SCENE WITH THE MBOUSHA.

CHAPTER VI.

AN OLD MAN KILLED FOR WITCHCRAFT.—JOURNEY TO THE
COUNTRY OF THE CANNIBALS.—STARTING ON THE ROUTE.

In the year 1856 I was again in the equatorial regions.
I was in the great forest, on my way to the Cannibal
country; yes, the country where the people eat one another. It was a long way off, and how was I to get there
through the dense jungle? How was I to find my way
in that vast African forest? These were the thoughts
that troubled me when I was in the village of Dayoko.

A glance at the map will show you how the village
of Dayoko is situated. It lies not far from the banks of
the Ntambounay River, and is surrounded by beautiful
groves of plantain-trees.

Dayoko is one of the chiefs of the Mbousha tribe, and
a wild and savage set of people they are, I can tell you.

But Dayoko became my friend, and said he would spare me a few men to take me part of the way.

These Mbousha people look very much like the Sheki-ani I have already described. They are superstitious and cruel, and believe in witchcraft. I staid among them only a few days. I will now tell you what I saw there.

In a hut I found a very old man. His wool (hair) was white as snow, his face was wrinkled, and his limbs were shrunken. His hands were tied behind him, and his feet were placed in a rude kind of stocks. Several negroes, armed to the teeth, stood guard over him, and now and then insulted him by angry words and blows, to which he submitted in silence. What do you suppose all this meant?

This old man was to be killed for witchcraft'

A truly horrible delusion this witchcraft is!

I went to Dayoko, the chief, to try to save the old man's life, but I saw it was in vain.

During the whole night I could hear singing all over the town, as well as a great uproar. Evidently they were preparing for the sacrifice of the old man.

Early in the morning the people gathered together with the fetich-man. His bloodshot eyes glared in savage excitement as he went around from man to man. In his hands he held a bundle of herbs, with which he sprinkled, three times, those to whom he spoke. Meantime there was a man on the top of a high tree close by, who shouted from time to time, "Joeou! Jocou!" at the same time shaking the trees.

"*Jocou*" means devil among the Mbousha; and the business of this man was to scare the evil spirit, and keep it away.
4

At last they all declared that the old man was a most potent wizard, that he had killed many people by sorcery, and that he must be killed.

You would like to know, I dare say, what these Africans mean by a wizard or a witch? They believe that people have within themselves the power of killing any one who displeases them. They believe that no one dies unless some one has bewitched him. Have you ever heard of such a horrible superstition? Hence those who are condemned for witchcraft are sometimes subjected to a very painful death; they are burnt by slow fire, and their bodies are given to the Bashikouay ant to be devoured. I shall have something to tell you about ants by-and-by. The poor wretches are cut into pieces; gashes are made over their bodies, and Cayenne pepper is put in the wounds. Indeed, it makes me shudder to think of it, for I have witnessed such dreadful deaths, and seen many of the mutilated corpses.

After I witnessed the ceremony, the people scattered, and I went into my hut, for I was not well. After a while I thought I saw a man pass my door almost like a flash, and after him rushed a horde of silent but infuriated men toward the river. In a little while I heard sharp, piercing cries, as of a man in great agony, and then all became still as death.

I came out, and, going toward the river, was met by the crowd returning, every man armed with axe, spear, knife, or cutlass; and these weapons, as well as their own hands, and arms, and bodies, were sprinkled with blood. They had killed the poor old man they called a wizard, hacked him to pieces, and finished by splitting open his skull, and scattering the brains into the water. Then they returned. At night these blood-thirsty men seemed to be as gentle as lambs, and as cheerful as if nothing had happened.

Ought we not to be thankful that we were born in a civilized country?

Now came the "grand palaver" over my departure. I called Dayoko and all the elders of the village together. When they had all assembled, I told them I must go into the Fan country inhabited by the Cannibals.

Dayoko said I should be murdered by the Cannibals, and eaten up, and tried to dissuade me from going.

Finally I said that go I would.

So it was determined that I should go under Dayoko's protection. Accordingly he gave me two of his sons to accompany me, and ordered several men to carry my chests, guns, powder, bullets, and shot.

They were to take me to one of Dayoko's fathers-in-law, a Mbondemo chief who lived in the mountains.

I was going farther and farther from the sea; if the savages were to leave me and run away in the forest, what would become of me?

We started in canoes, ascended the Muni River, and then paddled up a river called the Ntambounay (you must not mind these hard names—they are not of my choice. I must call things by the names the natives give them).

After paddling all day, toward sunset we all felt very tired, for we had gone a long way up the river, and reached a Shekiani village. I was quite astonished to meet Shekiani here, but so it happened.

I shall always remember this Shekiani village, for I thought I should be murdered and plundered there. Aft·

er we had landed in the village, I was told, at once, that
I could not go any farther, for the road belonged to them.
I must pay a tribute of six shirts similar to those I wore,
three great-coats, beads, etc., etc.   This would have entirely ruined me.

I could not sleep at all.   Through the whole night a
crowd surrounded my hut, talking, shouting, and singing
in the greatest excitement.   My guns and revolvers were
all loaded, and I made up my mind not to be killed without fighting desperately.   If I was to die, I resolved, at
all events, to die like a brave man.   All my party were
in my hut except Dayoko's two sons, who had gone to
talk with the Shekiani chief.   The Shekiani chief was
a friend of Dayoko, and Dayoko's sons told him I was
their father's stranger-friend.

At last things became more quiet, and toward morning the people were still or asleep.

We left the hut.   All was still peaceful.   My men
said that Dayoko's sons had a big fetich to avert war.

I gave a present to the Shekiani chief, and off we
started.   We left our large canoes and took smaller ones,
for we were to go through a very small stream.

As we ascended the beautiful river, we could see the
lofty mountains of the interior.   A great many islands
studded the stream.   From the trees on the banks the
monkeys looked down at us with astonishment.   What
curious creatures they were, with their black faces peeping out through the dark foliage, and looking as if they
were making grimaces at us.   By-and-by we left the
river, and made our way along the creeks or through the
woods toward the Mbondemo village.   Now and then we
walked freely through the wide openings which the ele-

phants had made. The rushing of a herd of elephants effects quite a clearing in the forest. On we went, till finally we came to a place where a great number of large trees had been prostrated. Wherever we looked trees were lying on the ground, many of them of enormous size. As I looked I heard, not far off, a tremendous crash—a most awful noise. I could not conjecture what was the matter. It turned out that a tree had come down; and as it fell, being a huge one, it crushed a dozen others around it, and each, as it broke, gave a great crash, so that the combined effect was awful to hear.

We had to go through these fallen trees; and what tough work it was! I never had seen any thing like it. Now we had to climb on a fallen tree and follow its trunk; then we had to come down, and were entangled in its branches, or in those of other trees. At other times we had to creep under them. I was continually afraid that my gun would be fired off by some creepers or boughs getting hold of the trigger.

At last, when my patience was entirely gone, and my few clothes literally hanging in ribbons about me, my legs sadly wounded, and my face and hands scratched, we arrived at the camp of the Mbondemos, situated almost at the foot of the mountain.

These mountains were covered with an immense forest; and so thick were the trees that no open view could be obtained in any direction. The mountains ended somewhere in the interior, no one knew where, but this they knew, that it was near the home of the Fans, a Cannibal tribe, and that elephants were plentiful, and gorillas were occasionally seen there. This encampment of the Mbondemos was called an olako. There was not a house in the camp, and it was a romantic scene to look at. Scattered under huge trees, on the edge of the woods, were leafy shelters, opening toward the forest. Under these the people lived. A few sticks put close together formed their beds. They contrived to sleep upon them, and I did the same. I assure you that they were hard enough, and reminded me that a mattress was a very good thing. Every family had its fire prepared beside the beds, and around these fires in the evening they clustered, men, women, and children.

The chief of this Mbondemo encampment was called Mbéné, and I liked him very much. He was very kind to me, and always tried to furnish me with food. There was scarcity of provisions, at the time, in the camp of the Mbondemos. There were no plantain and cassada fields near, and often I had to go without breakfast or dinner. The people lived chiefly on the nuts of the forest, and at that season of the year these were very scarce.

Poor Mbéné said they had very little to eat, but would give me what they could. I had carried with me a few little crackers, which I found very precious—more precious than gold, and which I reserved for time of sickness; but one by one they disappeared. I looked at them every time I took one, but I felt so hungry that I could not refrain from eating them.

Have you known what hunger is—real craving hunger? I can assure you it is a dreadful feeling.

During that time of the year, this people had half the time nothing to eat but the nut of a kind of palm. This nut was so bitter I could scarcely eat it. It is shaped like an egg, with rounded ends. To prepare it for eating, it is divested of its husk, and soaked in water for twenty-four hours, when it loses part of its exceedingly bitter taste, and becomes tolerably palatable—that is, to a starving man. Sometimes hunger will make them eat the nut without soaking it. I have done so myself when lost in the forest. It is dreadfully disagreeable.

Now and then the women succeeded in getting a few little fish in the streams, and gave me some. I could bear a good deal, for I had firmly resolved to go into the Cannibal country.

These Mbondemos are continually moving their villages. Mbéné had moved his village three times within a few years. I asked him why he made these frequent changes. He said that he moved the first time because a man had died, and the place was "not good" after that event. The second time he was forced to move because they had cut down all the palm-trees, and would get no more mimbo (palm wine), a beverage of which they are excessively fond. They tap the palm, just as the maple-tree is tapped in America, only they tap the tree at the top. This palm wine has somewhat of a milky color; and, when drunk in great quantity, it intoxicates. The palm-trees are very plentiful all over this part of the country, and it seems easier for them to move than to take care of the trees surrounding their settlements, useful as they are to them; for they furnish not only the wine they love, but the bitter nut I mentioned before, which often keeps them from actual starvation. When the tree is cut down they get what we call the palm cabbage which grows at the top. When cooked this palm cabbage is very good.

A country which has plenty of palm-trees, plenty of game, a good river or rivulet, and plenty of fish, is the country for a Mbondemo settler or squatter.

In these forests there is a vine or creeper which I might call the traveler's vine. If thirsty you may cut it, and within less than a minute a tumblerful of water will come out of it. This vine hangs about in the forest, and seemed to me to grow without leaves. What a capital thing it would be if water were not abundant in this country! The water procured from it has hardly any taste, and is perfectly pure and limpid.

Being unable to endure the continual hunger, I called Mbéné, and told him that his place had no food to give, and he must take me to a country where there was something to eat, and which would be on my way to the Fan country. Good Mbéné said, "Spirit, I will try the best I can to take you where you want to go. I will send some of my people with you."

In the mean time, Dayoko's people had all returned to their village. These forests had no game. I spent hour after hour scouring the forest, but I could see nothing except birds, some of which were extremely pretty. I am afraid that if I had succeeded in killing a snake I should have eaten it, as I felt desperately hungry. I did not like the bitter nuts; so it was agreed that Mbéné's brother Meomo, together with several of his people, should accompany me as far as the country of the Fan tribe. I could hardly believe such good news could be true.

Mbéné's wife always cooked my food. She was a dear good old woman, and I gave her a fine necklace of beads when I left. She was delighted with my present. They were big white porcelain beads of the size of a pigeon's egg. One day Mbéné succeeded in getting a fowl for me. His wife cooked it; she made soup, and put plenty of Cayenne pepper into it. I had also some plantain. How I enjoyed this meal! the more so that it was probably the last I should get for a good many days, unless we were unusually lucky, and should kill some antelopes or elephants on our road to the Fan country.

Elephant meat is execrable, as you would say on tasting it. But, as you may not have the chance, I will tell you by-and-by how it tastes.

As much food as possible was collected for our journey, and at last every thing was ready.

CHAPTER VII.

OUR JOURNEY THROUGH THE WILDERNESS CONTINUED. — A REBELLION IN CAMP.—NOTHING TO EAT.—I SHOOT A FISH AND MISS AN ELEPHANT.—I KILL A BIG SNAKE, AND THE OTHERS EAT HIM.—MY FIRST SIGHT OF GORILLAS.

BEFORE we renewed our journey, the natives had done all they could to gather provisions; but the result was poor enough. By going to distant villages they had succeeded in getting a few bunches of plantain.

Mcomo, Mbéné's brother, backed out. He said he was not going into the Cannibal country to be eaten up. But I must tell you that Mbéné had some friends among the Cannibals. And he sent with me two of his sons, called Miengai and Makinda, together with twelve good hunters, and six women who were the wives of some of the men. The women carried the provisions, etc.

I took seventy pounds of shot and bullets, nineteen pounds of powder, ten pounds of arsenic for preserving the birds and animals I should kill, for I knew I should probably succeed in getting some new specimens.

When all was arranged, when every body had taken leave of all his friends, for this was a very great journey, and they came back half a dozen times to take leave over again, or say something they had forgotten, when all the shouting and quarreling about who should carry the smallest load was over, we at last got away.

KILLING THE SNAKE

We had left the camp of Mbéné behind us at a distance of about five miles when we came to the banks of a little river called the Noonday, a clear and beautiful stream. I was ahead of the party with Miengai, and was waiting for the others to come up before crossing. As we stood on the bank I spied a fish swimming along. Immediately the thought came into my mind, " How nicely that fish would taste if I could get it and boil it in a pot over the fire!" I fired a charge of small shot into it; but no sooner had I pulled the trigger than I heard a tremendous crash on the opposite bank, about six or seven yards off. Small trees were torn down violently, and then we heard the shrill trumpetings of a party of frightened elephants. They were probably sleeping or standing in a dead silence on the opposite bank in the jungle. I was sorry I had fired, for after crossing the stream we might have killed an elephant. Poor Miengai was terribly vexed. " I am sure," said he, " they had big tusks of ivory."

Our party, as soon as they heard the gun, came up in haste, and asked what was the matter. When they heard the story, they began to lament our not killing an elephant, for then we should have had meat enough for the whole journey; and they shouted with one accord, " Elephant meat is so good!"

This exclamation made me wonder how an elephant steak would taste.

On we went, and got fairly into the mountainous country. The hills became steeper as we advanced. How tired I felt; for the diet at Mbéné's camp had not strengthened me. These Mbondemos had a great advantage over me. They used their bare feet almost as deftly as monkeys, and hence got their foothold more easily than I.

Miengai and I were in advance. All at once he made me a sign to keep very still. I thought he had discovered a herd of elephants, or seen the traces of an enormous leopard. He cocked his gun; I cocked mine; the other men did the same; and there we stood, in perfect silence, for at least five minutes. Suddenly Miengai sent a "hurrah" echoing through the forest. It was immediately answered by shouts from many voices not very far off, but whose owners were hidden from us by huge rocks and trees. Miengai replied with the fierce shout of the Mbondemo warriors, and was again answered. Thinking we were going to have a general fight, I looked carefully after my powder-flask and my bullets, and found they were all right.

Going a little farther on we came in sight of the encampment of a large party, who proved to be some of Mbéné's people just returning from a trading expedition to the interior. Two men of this camp offered to go with us. Their names were Ngolai and Yeava. We consented to take them.

What a journey it was! Nothing but thick woods to struggle through, hills to climb, rivers to cross, and nearly all the time it rained; in fact, I was wet from morning to night. How glad I was when, in the evening, we had made our camp, and built great fires! For my part, I had three fires lit about my bed of leaves; and in the evening I always hung up my clothes to dry, so as to have them ready for the next day.

One morning my men came to tell me they were tired, and would not go a step farther unless I gave them more cloth.

They seemed in earnest; and I began to question my-self whether they meant to plunder me or to leave me in these mountains? To be left thus alone would have been almost certain death. To give them what they asked was to show them I was afraid of them. If they knew I was afraid of them I did not know what they might next do. So I determined to put on a bold front. Taking my two revolvers in my hand, I said, "I will not give you any more cloth. I will not let you leave me, because your father Mbéné has given you to me to accompany me to the Fan tribe. You must therefore go with me, or" (here I motioned with my pistols) " there will be war between us. But," said I, " this is a very hard road, and at the end of the journey I will give you something more."

This satisfied them, and we again resumed our journey. Up, and up, and up we struggled, and now we began to meet with immense boulders. Not the scream of a bird, or the shrill cry of a monkey, broke the stillness of the dark solitude. Nothing was heard but the panting breaths of our party as we ascended the hills.

At last we came to an immense mountain torrent, which rushed down the hill side with fearful force, and was white with foam. Its course was full of huge gran-ite boulders, which lay about as though the Titans had been playing at skittles in that country. Against these the angry waters dashed as if they would carry all before them, and, breaking, threw the milky spray up to the very tree-tops. As I looked up the torrent seemed to pour its foaming waters directly down upon us.

This was the head of the Ntabounay River which I had ascended in a canoe, and on the banks of which I came near being murdered in the Shekiani village.

What a change had taken place in it! Here a canoe would be dashed into a hundred pieces against the rocks.

I was so thirsty and tired that I went to the river's bank, and drank a few handfuls of the pure, clean cold water

After resting a little while, we continued our course till we reached the top of a very high mountain, whence I could see all the country round. How wild and desolate it looked! Nothing but forest and mountains stretching away as far as the eye could reach.

I was sitting under a very large tree, when, suddenly looking up, I saw an immense serpent coiled upon the branch of a tree just above me; and I really could not tell whether he was not about to spring upon me and entangle me in his huge folds. You may well believe that I very quickly "stood from under." I rushed out, and, taking good aim with my gun, I shot my black friend in the head. He let go his hold, tumbled down with great force, and after writhing convulsively for a time, he lay before me dead. He measured thirteen feet in length, and his ugly fangs proved that he was venomous.

My men cut off the head of the snake, and divided the body into as many pieces as there were people. Then they lighted a fire, and roasted and ate it on the spot. They offered me a piece; but, though very hungry, I declined. When the snake was eaten I was the only individual of the company that had an empty stomach; I could not help reflecting on the disadvantage it is sometimes to have been born and bred in a civilized country, where snakes are not accounted good eating.

We now began to look about the ruins of the village

near which we sat. A degenerate kind of sugar cane was growing on the very spot where the houses had formerly stood. I made haste to pluck some of this, and chew it for the little sweetness it had. While thus engaged my men perceived what instantly threw us all into the greatest excitement. Here and there the cane was beaten down or torn up by the roots, and lying about were fragments which had evidently been chewed. There were also footprints to be seen, which looked almost like those of human beings. What could this mean? My men looked at each other in silence, and muttered "Nguyla!" (Gorillas!)

It was the first time I had seen the footprints of these wild men of the woods, and I can not tell you how I felt. Here was I now, it seemed, on the point of meeting, face to face, that monster, of whose ferocity, strength, and cunning the natives had told me so much, and which no white man before had hunted. My heart beat till I feared its loud pulsations would alarm the gorilla. I wondered how they looked. I thought of what Hanno the Carthaginian navigator said about the wild hairy men he had met on the West Coast of Africa more than two thousand years ago.

By the tracks it was easy to know that there must have been several gorillas in company. We prepared at once to follow them.

The women were terrified. They thought their end had come; that the gorilla would be soon upon them; so, before starting in search of the monster, we left two or three men to take care of them and reassure them. Then the rest of us looked once more carefully at our guns · for the gorilla gives you no time to reload, and
5

woe to him whom he attacks! We were fortunately armed to the teeth.

My men were remarkably silent, for they were going on an expedition of more than usual risk; for the male gorilla is literally the king of the forest—the king of the equatorial regions. He and the crested lion of Mount Atlas are the two fiercest and strongest beasts of that continent. The lion of South Africa can not be compared with either for strength or courage.

As we left the camp, the men and women left behind crowded together, with fear written on their faces. Miengai, Ngolai, and Makinda set out for the hunt in one party; myself and Yeava formed another. We determined to keep near each other, so that in case of trouble, or in a great emergency, we might be at hand to help one another. For the rest, silence and a sure aim were the only cautions to be given.

As we followed the footprints, we could easily see that there were four or five of them, though none appeared very large. We saw where the gorillas had run along on all fours, which is their usual mode of progression. We could perceive also where, from time to time, they had seated themselves to chew the canes they had borne off. The chase began to be very exciting.

We had agreed to return to the women and their guards, and consult about what was to be done, after we had discovered the probable course of the gorilla, and this was now done. To make sure of not alarming our prey, we moved the whole party forward a little way, to some leafy huts, built by passing traders, and which served us for shelter and concealment. Here we bestowed the women, whose lively fear of the terrible gorilla arises from various stories current among the tribes of women having been carried off into the woods by the fierce animal. Then we prepared once more to set out on our chase, this time hopeful to get a shot.

Looking once more to our guns, we started off. I confess that I was never more excited in my life. For years I had heard of the terrible roar of the gorilla, of its vast strength, of its fierce courage when only wounded. I knew that we were about to pit ourselves against an animal which even the enormously large leopards of the mountains fear, which the elephants let alone, and which perhaps has driven away the lion out of this territory; for the "king of beasts," so numerous elsewhere in Africa, is not met with in the land of the gorilla.

We descended a hill, crossed a stream on a fallen log, crept under the trees, and presently approached some huge boulders of granite. In the stream we had crossed we could see plainly signs that the animals had just crossed it, for the water was still disturbed. Our eyes wandered every where to get a glimpse of our prey. Alongside of the granite blocks lay an immense dead tree, and about this the gorillas were likely to be.

Our approach was very cautious; I wish you could have seen us. We were divided into two parties. Makinda led one, and I the other. We were to surround the granite block, behind which Makinda supposed the gorillas to be hiding. With guns cocked and ready, we advanced through the dense wood, which cast a gloom, even in midday, over the whole scene. I looked at my men, and saw that they were even more excited than myself.

Slowly we pressed on through the dense bush. fearing

almost to breathe, for fear of alarming the beasts. Makinda was to go to the right of the rock, while I took the
left. Unfortunately, he and his party circled it at too
great a distance. The watchful animals saw him. Suddenly I was startled by a strange, discordant, half human, devilish cry, and beheld four young and half-grown
gorillas running toward the deep forest. I was not ready.
We fired, but hit nothing. Then we rushed on in pursuit; but they knew the woods better than we. Once I
caught a glimpse of one of the animals again; but an
intervening tree spoiled my mark, and I did not fire. We
pursued them till we were exhausted, but in vain. The
alert beasts made good their escape. When we could
pursue no more we returned slowly to our camp, where
the women were anxiously expecting us.

I protest I felt almost like a murderer when I saw the
gorilla this first time. As they ran on their hind legs,
with their heads down, their bodies inclined forward,
their whole appearance was that of hairy men running
for their lives. Add to all this their cry, so awful, yet
with something human in its discordance, and you will
cease to wonder that the natives have the wildest superstitions about these " wild men of the woods."

In our absence the women had made large fires, and
prepared the camp. I changed my clothes, which had
become drenched by the frequent torrents and puddles
we ran through in our eager pursuit. Then we sat down
to our supper, which had been cooked in the mean time.
I noticed that all my plantains were gone — eaten up.
What was to become of us in the great forest? I had
only two or three biscuits, which I kept in case of actual
starvation or sickness.

As we lay by the fire in the evening before going to sleep, the adventure of the day was talked over to those who had not gone with us, and, of course, there followed some curious stories of the gorillas. I listened in silence.

One of the men told a story of two Mbondemo women who were walking together through the woods, when suddenly an immense gorilla stepped into the path, and, clutching one of the women, bore her off in spite of the screams and struggles of both. The other woman returned to the village much frightened, and told the story. Of course her companion was given up for lost. Great was the surprise when, a few days afterward, she returned to her home.

"Yes," said one of the men, "that was a gorilla inhabited by a spirit." This explanation was received by a general grunt of approval.

One of the men told how, some years ago, a party of gorillas were found in a cane-field tying up the sugar-cane in regular bundles preparatory to carrying it away. The natives attacked them, but were routed, and several killed, while others were carried off prisoners by the gorillas; but in a few days they returned home, not uninjured indeed, for the nails of their fingers and toes had been torn off by their captors.

Then several people spoke up, and mentioned names of dead men whose spirits were known to be dwelling in gorillas.

Finally came the story that is current among all the tribes who are acquainted with the habits of the gorilla, that this animal will hide himself in the lower branches of a tree, and there lie in wait for people who go to and fro. When one passes sufficiently near, the gorilla grasps the luckless fellow with his powerful feet, which he uses like giants' hands, and, drawing the man up into the tree, he quietly chokes him there.

Hunger and starvation began to tell upon us severely. When we started I did not calculate on meeting with gorillas. I had eaten all my sea-bread. There was not a particle of food among us, and no settlement near us. I began to feel anxious for fear that we should die. Berries were scarce, and nuts were hardly to be found. The forest seemed deserted. There was not even a bird to kill. To make matters worse, we had been misled. We were lost—lost in the great forest!—and we failed to reach a certain settlement where we had expected to arrive.

Traveling on an empty stomach is too exhausting to be very long endured. The third day I awoke feeble, but found that one of the men had killed a monkey. This animal, roughly roasted on the coals, tasted delicious. How I wished we had ten monkeys to eat! but how glad and grateful we were for that single one.

Presently Makinda, looking up, discovered a bee-hive. He smoked the bees out, and I divided the honey. There might have been a fight over this sweet booty had I not interposed and distributed it in equal shares. Serving myself with a portion not bigger than I gave the rest, I at once sat down, and devoured honey, wax, dead bees, worms, dirt, and all, I was so hungry. I was only sorry we had not more.

I had really a hard time getting through the old elephant tracks, which were the best roads through the jungle. The men seemed to have lost their way. We saw no animals, but found several gorillas' tracks.

At last my men began to talk more cheerfully; they knew where they were; and, soon after, I saw the broad leaves of the plantain, the forerunner of an African town. But, alas! as we approached we saw no one coming to meet us; and when we reached the place we found only a deserted village. But even for this how thankful I was! Since I left Dayoko I had experienced nothing but hunger and starvation, and these were the first human habitations we had met.

Presently, however, some Mbicho people made their appearance. They were relatives of Mbéné, and their village was close by. They gave us some plantains, but no fowls. I wished very much to get a fowl. I felt *gouamba* (which means hunger) for meat, and knew that a good warm fowl broth would have done me a great deal of good. We spent the evening in the houses, drying and warming ourselves. It was much better than the forest, even if it was only a deserted town.

I asked if we should ever reach the Cannibal country, and found that, with the exception of the Mbicho village near at hand, we were already surrounded on three sides by Fan villages.

I was too tired to rest. Besides, I was getting deep into the interior of Africa, and was in the neighborhood of the Fans, the most warlike tribe that inhabited the country. So I barricaded my hut, got my ammunition ready, saw that my guns were all right, and then lay awake for a long time before I could go to sleep.

KING ASTONISHED AT A LOOKING-GLASS.

CHAPTER VIII.

I ARRIVE AMONG THE CANNIBALS.—THEIR SPEARS, BOWS
AND BATTLE-AXES. — THEY TAKE ME FOR A SPIRIT. —
THEIR KING SHAKES WHEN HE SEES ME.—I GIVE HIM A
LOOKING-GLASS.—IT ASTONISHES HIM.

WE were, at last, near the Fan country. We had
passed the last Mbichos village, and were on our way to
the villages of the *man-eaters*.

I remember well the first Fan village I approached.
It stood on the summit of a high hill in the mountains
All its inhabitants were very much excited when they
perceived we were coming toward it, through the plantation path; for the trees around the hill had been cut
down. The men were armed to the teeth as we entered
the village, and I knew not whether hundreds of spears

and poisoned arrows might not be thrown at me, and I
be killed on the spot. What dreadful spears those Cannibals had; they were all barbed. Each man had several in his hand; and, besides, had a shield made of elephant's hide, to protect himself with. Others were armed with huge knives, and horrible-looking battle-axes, or '
with bows and poisoned arrows.

Wild shouts of astonishment, which, for all I knew,
were war-shouts, greeted me as I entered the village. I
must own that I felt not quite at my ease. How wild
and fierce these men looked! They were most scantily
dressed. When they shouted they showed their teeth,
which were filed to a point, and colored black. Their
open mouths put me uncomfortably in mind of a tomb;
for how many human creatures each of these men had
eaten!

How ugly the women looked! They were all tattooed, and nearly naked. They fled with their children
into their houses as I passed through the street, in which
I saw, here and there, human bones lying about. Yes,
human bones from bodies that had been devoured by
them! Such are my recollections of my first entrance
into a village of Cannibals.

The village was strongly fenced or palisaded, and on
the poles were several skulls of human beings and of
gorillas. There was but a single street, about two thirds
of a mile long. On each side of this were low huts,
made of the bark of trees.

I had hardly entered the village when I perceived some
bloody remains, which appeared to me to be human.
Presently we passed a woman who was running as fast
as she could toward her hut. She bore in her hand a

piece of a human thigh, just as we would go to market and carry thence a joint or steak.

This was a very large village. At last we arrived at the palaver house. Here I was left alone with Mbéné for a little while. There was great shouting going on at a little distance, at the back of some houses. One of them said they had been busy dividing the body of a dead man, and that there was not enough for all.

They flocked in presently, and soon I was surrounded by an immense crowd. Not far from me was a ferocious-looking fellow. On one arm he supported a very large shield, made of an elephant's hide, and of the thickest part of the skin, while in his other hand he held a prodigious war-knife, which he could have slashed through a man in a jiffy.

Some in the crowd were armed with cross-bows, from which are shot either iron-headed arrows, or the little insignificant-looking, but really most deadly darts, tipped with poison. These are made of slender, harmless reeds, a foot long, whose sharpened ends are dipped in a deadly vegetable poison, which these people know how to make. These poisoned darts are so light that they would blow away if simply laid in the groove of the bow. Hence they use a kind of sticky gum to hold them.

The handle of the bow is ingeniously split, and by a little peg, that acts as a trigger, the bow-string is disengaged. The bow is very stiff and strong, and sends the arrow to a great distance. As you see by the representation of a Fan bowman, they have to sit down and apply both feet to the middle of the bow, while they pull with all their strength on the string to bend it back.

These little poisoned arrows are much dreaded by

them, and are very carefully kept by them in little bags, and which are made of the skin of wild animals.

Some bore on their shoulders the terrible war-axe. One blow of this axe suffices to split a human skull. I saw that some of these axes, as well as their spears and other iron-work, were beautifully ornamented.

The war-knife, which hangs by their side, is a terrible weapon. It is used in hand-to-hand conflict, and is designed to be thrust through the enemy's body. There was also another sort of huge knife used by some of the men in the crowd before me. It was a foot long, about eight inches wide, and is used to cut through the shoulders of an adversary. It must do tremendous execution.

A few of the men had also a very singular pointed axe, which is thrown from a distance. When thrown, it strikes with the point down, and inflicts a terrible wound. They handle it with great dexterity. The object aimed at with this axe is the head. The point penetrates to the brain, and kills the victim immediately.

The spears were six or seven feet long, and are ingeniously adapted to inflict terrible wounds. They are thrown with an accuracy and a force which never ceased to astonish me. The long, slender staff fairly whistles through the air, and woe to the man who is within twenty or thirty yards of their reach.

Most of the knives and axes were ingeniously sheathed in covers made of snake or antelope skins, or of human skin. These sheaths were slung round the shoulder or neck by cords, which permit the weapon to hang at the side, out of the wearer's way.

These Fan warriors had no armor. Their only weapon

of defense is the huge shield of elephant hide of which I spoke to you. It is three and a half feet long, by two and a half feet wide.

Besides their weapons, many of the men wore a small knife, as a table-knife or jack-knife.

From this description of the men by whom I was surrounded, you may judge with what amazement I looked around me, with my guns in my hands. It was a grand sight to see such a number of stalwart, martial, fierce-looking fellows, fully armed and ready for any desperate fray, gathered together.

Finer-looking savages I never saw; and I could easily believe them to be brave; and the completeness of their warlike equipments proved that fighting is a favorite pastime with them. No wonder they are dreaded by all their neighbors!

Here was I, at this time only a lad, alone in the midst of them.

Presently came the king, a ferocious-looking fellow. His body was naked. His skin in front was painted red, and his chest, stomach, and back were tattooed in a rude but effective manner. He was covered with charms, and wore round his neck a necklace made with leopard's teeth. He was fully armed. Most of the Fans wore queues; but the queue of Ndiayai, the king, was the biggest of all, and terminated in two tails, in which were strung brass rings. His beard was plaited in several plaits, which contained white beads. His teeth were filed sharp to a point. He looked like a perfect glutton of human flesh.

I looked around me in a cool, impassive manner. Ndiayai, the king, fairly shook at the sight of me. He had refused to come and see me, at first, from a belief that he would die in three days after setting eyes on me. But Mbéné had persuaded him to come.

Ndiayai was accompanied by the queen, the ugliest woman I ever saw, and very old. She was called Mashumba. She was nearly naked, her only covering being a strip of cloth about four inches wide, made of the soft bark of a tree, and dyed red. Her body was tattooed in the most fanciful manner; her skin, from long exposure, had become rough and knotty. She wore two enormous iron anklets, and had in her ears a pair of copper rings two inches in diameter. I could easily put my little fingers in the holes through which the earrings passed.

The people looked at me, wondered at my hair, but never ceased to look at my feet. They thought my boots were my own feet. "Look at the strange being," said they to each other; "his feet are not of the color of his face, and he has no toes!"

Finally the king said to Mbéné that, when surrounded by his people, he was not afraid of any body.

I could well believe him. When fighting they must look perfect devils.

When night came I entered my house, and looked about to see how I could barricade myself for the night, for I did not fancy putting myself entirely at the mercy of these savage Fans. Their weapons had been sufficient to show me that they were men who were not afraid to fight. I told Mbéné to send for Ndiayai. The king came, and I presented him a large bunch of white beads, a looking-glass, a file, fire-steels, and some gun-flints. His countenance beamed with joy. I never saw such astonishment as he exhibited when I held the looking-glass be-

fore his face. At first he did not know what to make of
it, and did not want to take the glass, till Mbéné told him
that he had one. He put his tongue out, and he saw it
reflected in the looking-glass. Then he shut one eye, and
made faces; then he showed his hands before the looking-glass—one finger—two fingers—three fingers. He
became speechless, and with all I had given him, he went
away as "happy as a king;" and "every inch a (savage)
king" he was.

Shortly afterward, Mashumba, the queen, thinking that
probably I had something for her, also came and brought
me a basketful of plantains. They were cooked. At
once the idea rushed into my mind that perhaps the very
same pot that cooked the plantains had cooked a Fan's
head in the morning, and I began to have a horrible
loathing of the flesh-pots of these people. I would not
have cooked in their pots for the world.

A little after dark, all became silent in the village. I
barred my little bit of a door as well as I could with my
chest, and, lying down on that dreadful Fan bed, I placed
my gun by my side, and tried hard, but in vain, to go to
sleep. I wondered how many times human flesh had entered the hut I was in. I thought of all I had seen during the day, which I have related to you. The faces of
those terrible warriors, and the implements of war, were
before my eyes, though it was pitch dark.

Was I afraid? Certainly not. What feeling was it
that excited me? I can not tell you. It was certainly
not fear; for if any one the next day had offered to take
me back where I came from, I should have declined the
offer. Probably I was agitated by the novel and horrible
sights that had greeted my eyes, and which exceeded all

my previous conceptions of Africa. Now and then I
thought that as these men not only killed people, but ate
them also, they might perhaps be curious to try how I
tasted.

Hour after hour passed, and I could not get to sleep.
I said my bed was a dreadfully bad one.   It was a frame
composed of half a dozen large round bamboos.   I might
as well have tried to sleep on a pile of cannon-balls.
Finally I succeeded in going to sleep, holding my gun
tightly under my arm.

When I got up in the morning, and went out at the
back of the house, I saw a pile of ribs, leg and arm bones,
and skulls piled together.   The Cannibals must have had
a grand fight not long before, and devoured all their
prisoners of war.

In what was I to wash my face?   I resolved at last
not to wash at all.

ENTRAPPING THE ELEPHANT.

CHAPTER IX.

AN ELEPHANT HUNT.

AFTER a few days the Fans began to get accustomed to me and I to them, and we were the best friends in the world.

They are great hunters. One day a woman returning from the plantations brought news that she had seen elephants, and that one of the plantain-fields had been entirely destroyed by them. This was an event of common occurrence in the country; for the elephants are not very particular, and whatever they like they take, not caring a bit how much hunger they may occasion among the poor natives.

When the news arrived a wild shout of joy spread among the villagers. The grim faces of the Fans smiled, and, in doing so, showed their ugly filed teeth. "We are going to kill elephants," they all shouted "We are going to have plenty of meat to eat," shrieked the women.

So, in the evening, a war-dance took place; a war-dance of Cannibals! It was the wildest scene I ever saw. It was pitch-dark, and the torches threw a dim light around us, and showed the fantastic forms of these wild men. Really it was a wild scene. They were all armed as if they were going to war. How they gesticulated. What contortions they made! What a tumult they raised! How their wild shouts echoed from hill to hill, and died away in the far distance! They looked like demons. Their skins were painted of different colors; and, as the dancing went on, their bodies became warm, and shone as if they had been dipped in oil.

Suddenly a deafening shout of the whole assemblage seemed to shake the earth. Their greatest warrior (Leopard) came to dance. Leopard was, it appears, the bravest of them all. He had killed more people in war than any body else. He had given more human food to his fellow-townsmen than many other warriors put together. Hence they all admired and praised him; and a song describing his feats of arms was sung by those who surrounded him. How ferocious he looked! He was armed to the teeth. He had a spear like one of those I have already described. A long knife hung by his side, and the hand that held the shield carried a battle-axe also. In dancing, he acted at times as if he were defending himself against an attack; at other times, as if he were himself attacking somebody. Once or twice I thought he really meant to throw his spear at some one. I could hardly breathe while looking at him. He appeared ac-

6

tually to be a demon. Finally he stopped from sheer exhaustion, and others took his place.

The next day the men furbished up their arms. I myself cleaned my guns, and got ready for the chase, so that, if I should get a chance, I might send a bullet through an elephant.

The war-dish was cooked. It is a mixture of herbs, and is supposed to inspire people with courage. They rubbed their bodies with it, and then we started. There were about five hundred men. After leaving the village we divided into several parties. Each party was well acquainted with the forest, and knew just where to go. The march was conducted in perfect silence, so that we might not alarm the elephants. After preceeding six hours we arrived not far from the hunting-ground where the elephants were supposed to be. The Fans built shelters, and these were hardly finished when it began to rain very hard.

The next day some Fans went out to explore the woods, and I joined the party. The fallen trees, the broken-down limbs, the heavy footprints, and the trampled underbrush, showed plainly that there had been many elephants' about. There were no regular walks, and they had strayed at random in the forest.

When the elephants are pleased with a certain neighborhood, they remain there a few days. When they have eaten all the food they like, and nothing remains, they go on to some other place.

The forest here, as every where else, was full of rough, strong climbing plants, many of which reach to the top of the tallest trees. They are of every size; some bigger than a man's thigh, while many are as large as the ropes of which the rigging of a ship is made. These creepers the natives twist together, and, after working very hard, they succeed in constructing a huge fence, or obstruction. Of course it is not sufficient to hold the elephant; but when he gets entangled in its meshes, it is strong enough to check him in his flight till the hunters can have time to kill him. When an elephant is once caught, they surround the huge beast, and put an end to his struggles by incessant discharges of their spears and guns.

While the others worked, I explored the forest. Seeing that the men were careful in avoiding a certain · place, I looked down on the ground, and saw nothing. Then, looking up, I saw an immense piece of wood suspended by the wild creepers high in the air, and fixed in it at intervals I saw several large, heavy, sharp-pointed pieces of iron pointing downward. The rope that holds up this contrivance is so arranged that the elephant can not help touching it if he passes underneath. Then the *hanou* (such is the name given to the trap) is loosed, and falls with a tremendous force on his back; the iron points pierce his body, and the piece of wood, in falling, generally breaks his spine.

I also saw, in different places, large, deep ditches, intended as pitfalls for the elephant. When he runs away, or roams around at night, he often falls into these pits, and that is the end of him; for, in falling, he generally breaks his legs. Sometimes, when the natives go and visit the pit they have made, they find nothing but the bones of the elephants and his ivory tusks.

The fence that the natives had made must have been several miles long, and in many places was several rows deep; and now there were elephant pits beside, and the *hanous*.

We were, you must remember, in a mountainous country; and I could hardly believe my eyes when I saw plainly the footprints of this animal where I myself had to hold to the creepers to be able to ascend.

When every thing was ready, part of the men went silently and hid themselves upon the limbs or beside the trunks of trees near the barrier or "tangle." Others of us took a circuitous route in an opposite direction from that in which we had come. After we had got miles away from the "tangle," we formed a chain as long in extent as the fence, and moved forward, forming a semi-circle, with the men ten or twenty yards apart from each other.

Presently, all along the line the hunting horns were sounded, wild shouts were sent up, and, making all the noise they could, the Fans advanced in the direction of the "tangle." The elephants were entrapped. Hearing the noise, of course they moved away from us, breaking down every thing before them in their flight. If they tried to go to the right, they heard the same wild shouts; if they tried to go to the left, they heard the same. There was no other way for them to go but straight ahead; and there, though they did not know it, were the tangle, the pits, and the *hanou*. They were going to surer death than if they had tried to break our lines; for then most, if not all of them, would have escaped. We were too far from each other to hinder them.

Onward we pressed, the circle of those giving chase becoming smaller and smaller, and the crashing of the underbrush more distinct, as we approached the elephants in their flight. The men's countenances became excited. They got their spears in readiness; and soon we came in sight of the tangles. What an extraordinary sight lay before me! I could distinguish one elephant, enraged, terrified, tearing at every thing with his trunk and feet, but all in vain! The tough creepers of the barrier in no instance gave way before him. Spear after spear was thrown at him. The Fans were every where, especially up on the trees, where they were out of the reach of the elephant. The huge animal began to look like a gigantic porcupine, he was stuck so full of spears. Poor infuriated beast! I thought he was crazy. Every spear that wounded him made him more furious! But his struggles were in vain. He had just dropped down when I came close to him, and, to end his sufferings, I shot him through the ear. After a few convulsions of limb all became quiet. He was dead.

Some of the elephants had succeeded in going through the tangle, and were beyond reach.

Four elephants had been slain; and I was told that a man had been killed by one of the elephants, which turned round and charged his assailants. This man did not move off in time, and was trampled under foot by the monstrous beast. Fortunately, the elephant got entangled, and, in an instant, he was covered with spears, and terribly wounded. After much loss of blood he dropped down lifeless.

I am sure you will agree with me, after the description I have given of a Fan elephant hunt, that the men of this tribe are gifted with remarkable courage and presence of mind.

They have certain rules for hunting the elephant.

These tell you never to approach an elephant except from behind; he can not turn very fast, and you have, therefore, time to make your escape. He generally rushes blindly forward. Great care must also be taken that the strong creepers, which are so fatal to the elephant, do not also catch and entangle the hunters themselves. A man lying in wait to spear an elephant should always choose a stout tree, in order that the infuriated beast, should he charge at it, may not uproot it.

The next day there was a dance round the elephant, while the fetich-man cut a piece from one of the hind legs. This was intended for their idol. The meat was cooked in presence of the fetich-man, and of those who had speared the elephant. As soon as all the meat had been cooked they danced round it, and a piece was sent into the woods for the spirit to feed upon, if he liked. The next day the meat was all cut up in small pieces, then hung up and smoked.

The cooking and smoking lasted three days, and I can assure you it is the toughest meat I ever tasted. Of course, like the Fans, I had no other food, and for three days I ate nothing but elephant meat. I wish I could give you a notion how it tastes, but really I do not know what to compare it with. Beef, mutton, lamb, pork, venison, make not the slightest approach to a resemblance; and as for poultry, such a comparison would be positively aggravating!

The proboscis being one of the favorite morsels, a large piece of it was given to me. The foot is another part reputed to be a great dainty, and two feet were sent me, together with a large piece of the leg for a roast.

But the meat was so tough that I had to boil it for twelve hours, and then I believe it was as tough as ever; it seemed to be full of gristle. So, the next day, I boiled it again for twelve hours; all my trouble, however, was unavailing, for it was still hopelessly tough! I may say that the more I ate of elephant meat the more I got to dislike it. I do not think I shall ever hanker after elephant steak as long as I live. I wonder if you boys would like it? I wish I had some, and could induce you to taste of it. I am inclined to think you would agree with me, and never desire to renew your acquaintance with it.

How glad I was when I returned to Ndiayai village; and no wonder, for we had rain every day in the woods. As for the poor man who had been killed by the elephant, his body was sent to another clan to be devoured, for the Cannibals do not eat their own people.

FAN BLACKSMITHS AT WORK.

CHAPTER X.

LIFE AMONG THE CANNIBALS. — CURIOUS MUSICAL INSTRU-
MENTS.—COOKING UTENSILS.—A BLACKSMITH'S BELLOWS
AND ANVIL.—CANNIBAL DIET.

AFTER we reached Ndiayai, I went back to my little
hut, and found every thing I had left there. I had hidden my powder and shot in different places, and had dug
holes in which to hide my beads.

The news had spread among the surrounding Cannibal villages that the spirit, as they called me, was still in
the village of Ndiayai, and the people flocked to see me.
Among those who came to see me was a chief of the
name of Oloko. He gave me the long war-knife, of
which you have seen a drawing, and explained to me
how it had several times gone right through a man.

Mbéné went away for a while, and left me entirely

alone with these Cannibals. During his absence I studied the habits of these strange people, and you may be
ure that wherever I went I kept my eyes wide open.

By the way, I see I have omitted to give a description
of the town of King Ndiayai. It was a very large town,
composed of a single street. When I say a large town,
I do not mean, of course, that it could bear any comparison as to size with London, Paris, or New York. I mean
that it was a large town for this part of Africa. It contained five or six hundred men. The houses were quite
small, and were all made of the bark of trees; none of
them had windows. They were nearly all of the same
size.

Strange to say, these Fans seemed to be very fond of
music, and very funny instruments they make use of!
To hear some of their music would make you laugh.
They have not the slightest idea of what we consider
harmony in sound, but they evidently have a great liking
for music after their own notion. It is very much the
same with their dancing. They have not the slightest
idea of the dances in use with us, such as waltzes, galops,
polkas, or quadrilles; and I am sure, if they were to see
us dancing in our fashion, they would laugh quite as
much as you would laugh if you could see them caper-
ing in their uncouth style.

Like all the savage tribes of Africans, they are very
fond of the tom-tom, or drum. These drums are of different sizes, but many are from four to six feet in length,
and about ten inches in diameter at one end, but only six
or seven at the other. The wood is hollowed out quite
thin, and skins of animals are stretched tightly over the
ends. The drummer holds the tom-tom slantingly be-

tween his legs, and with two sticks he beats furiously
upon the larger end of the drum, which is held upper-
most.   Sometimes they beat upon it with their hands.
The people form a circle round the tom-tom, and dance
and sing, keeping time with it.   They often invited me
to hear them.

But now I am going to speak to you of a far more
curious instrument.   It is called by these Cannibals the
handja, and I never saw it except among their tribes.

Ndiayai was very fond of hearing the handja, and I
often went to his shed to hear some one play upon it.
Sometimes, on these occasions, Ndiayai would come out,
surrounded by Queen Mashumba and some of his other
wives, and listen for an hour or two to the music of the
handja.

I give you here a representation of the handja, so that
you will understand it better when I describe it to you.

THE HANDJA.

It consists of a light reed frame, about three feet long
and eighteen inches wide, in which are set, and securely
fastened, a number of hollow gourds.   The handja I saw
contained seven gourds.   These gourds are covered by

strips of a hard red wood found in the forest. These gourds and cylinders, as you see, are of different sizes, so graduated that they form a regular series of notes. Each gourd has a little hole, which is covered with a skin thinner than parchment. And what kind of skin do you think it was? It was the skin of the very large spider which abounds in that country, and from which I should not care to receive a bite, it is so poisonous.

The performer sits down, with the frame across his knees, and strikes the strips lightly with a stick. There are two sticks, one of hard wood, the other of much softer wood. The instrument is played on the same principle as a chime of bells, or an instrument used in France, and which, perhaps, some of you have seen, composed of a series of glasses. The tone of the handja is very clear and good, and, though their tunes were rude, they played them with considerable skill.

The Fans work iron better than any tribe I met with. They are very good blacksmiths. Their warlike habits have made iron a very necessary article to them. It is very plentiful in their mountainous country.

At the head of this chapter is a picture of two Fan blacksmiths. Look at the curious bellows they have. It is made of two short, hollow cylinders of wood, surmounted by skins very well fitted on, and having an appropriate valve for letting in the air. As you see, the bellows-blower is on his knees, moving down these coverings with great rapidity. There are two small wooden pipes, connected with two iron tubes which go into the fire.

The anvil, as you see in the picture, is a solid piece of iron. The sharp end is stuck into the ground; and the blacksmith sits alongside his anvil, and beats his iron with a singular-looking hammer, clumsy in form, and with no handle; in fact, it is merely made of a heavy piece of iron.

The blacksmiths sometimes spend many days in making a battle-axe, knife, or spear. They make, also, their own cooking utensils and water-jugs. They also make their own pipes, for they are great smokers. Some of their pipes are not at all ungraceful in shape.

Besides the water-jug, they frequently use the calabash as a vessel to carry water in; and some of their calabashes are really pretty, and very nicely ornamented. Some of the spoons, with which they eat their human broth, are very beautiful. They are made of various woods, and sometimes of ivory.

It is quite sickening to think what horrible people these Fans are! Such inveterate cannibals are they, that they even eat the poor wretches who die of disease. As I was talking to the king one day, some Fans brought in a dead body, which they had bought, or bartered for, in a neighboring town, and which was to be divided among them. I could see that the man had died of some disease, for the body was very lean. They came round it with their knives; and Ndiayai left me to superintend the distribution. I could not stand this; and when I saw them getting ready, I left the spot and went to my hut. Afterward I could hear them growing noisy over the division of their horrid spoil.

In fact, the Fans seem to be perfect ghouls. Those who live far in the interior practice unblushingly their horrid custom of eating human flesh. It appears they do not eat the dead of their own family, but sell the corpse to some other clan, or make an agreement that when one of their number dies they will return the body in exchange.

Until I saw these things I could not believe a story I had often heard related among the Mpongwe tribe, which is as follows: A party of Fans once came down to the sea-shore to view the ocean. While there, they actually stole a freshly buried body from the cemetery, and cooked and ate it. Another body was taken by them and conveyed into the woods, where they cut it up and smoked the flesh. These acts created a great excitement among the Mpongwes.

But you must not think that the Fans are continually eating human flesh. They eat it when they can get it, but not every day. They kill no one on purpose to be eaten.

One day Ndiayai took me to an Osheba town, the king of which tribe was his friend; and let me tell you that the Oshebas were also great man-eaters, like the Fans, whom they greatly resemble in appearance. The chief of that Osheba village was called Bienbakay.

The Fans are the handsomest and most resolute-looking set of negroes I have ever seen in the interior. Eating human flesh does not seem to disagree with them, though I have since seen other Fan tribes whose men had not the fine appearance of these mountaineers. Here, as every where else, the character of the country doubtless has much to do with the matter of bodily health and growth. These Cannibals were living among the mountains, and had come from still higher mountain regions, and this accounts for their being so robust and hardy.

The strangest thing in connection with the Fans, next to their hideous cannibalism, is their constant encroach-

ments upon the land westward. Year by year they have
been advancing nearer to the sea. Town after town has
been settled by them on the banks of the Gaboon River.
In fact, they seem to be a conquering race, driving every
other tribe before them.

The color of these people is dark brown rather than
black. They feed much upon manioc and the plantain.
They have also two or three kinds of yams, splendid
sugar-cane, and squashes, all of which they cultivate with
considerable success. Manioc seemed to be the favorite
food. Enormous quantities of squashes are raised, chiefly
for the seeds, which, when pounded and prepared in their
fashion, are much prized by them, and I confess I relish
this food myself. At a certain season, when the squash
is ripe, their villages seem covered with the seeds, which
every body spreads out to dry. When dried they are
packed in leaves, and placed over the fire-places in the
smoke, to keep off an insect which also feeds upon them.
They are all suspended by a cord, for, besides being in-
fested by insects, they are subject to the depredations of
mice and rats, both of which are fond of them.

The process of preparation is very tedious. A portion
of the seeds is boiled, and each seed is divested of its
skin; then the mass of pulp is put into a rude wooden
mortar and pounded, a vegetable oil being mixed with it
before it is cooked.

While on the subject of the food of the Cannibals, I
ought to mention that they do not sell the bodies of their
chiefs, kings, or great men; these receive burial, and remain undisturbed. It is probable, also, that they do not
eat the corpses of people who die of special diseases.

NET-HUNTING.

CHAPTER XI.

On my way to the sea-shore from the Cannibal country I had a good deal of trouble. I had taken quite another route to come back; Mbéné and his people left me on the banks of a river called the Noya, at the village of a chief called Wanga. From there I pushed my way toward Yoongoolapay, a village whose chief is called Alapay. But before reaching that place we came one evening to a village called Ezongo. The inhabitants, seeing our heavy loads, turned out with the greatest amount of enthusiasm to receive me. Their ardor cooled somewhat when they learned the contents of my packages, for they were the birds and animals I had collected. The rascally chief, thinking I must place a great value on things I had gone so far to get, determined to detain me till I paid a heavy price to get away, and for a while things looked as if I should have a good deal of trouble. The king, urged on by his people, who seemed to be a greedy set of rascals, insisted on his price, which would have left me empty-handed.

At last my Mbicho guides from the Noya tried to set tle the matter. They were wise enough to get the king to come to me with them alone. I gave the rascal a coat and an old shirt, and I told him what was literally true, that I was very poor, and could not pay what his people wanted. After this palaver, he went out at once and harangued the turbulent extortioners.

So I passed on safely to the village of my old friend, King Alapay, whom I had known before, and who was very glad to see me again. He asked me to stay some days; and, being really worn out with constant exposure, much anxiety, and frequent annoyance, I determined to do so. His village is charmingly situated upon a high hill, which overlooks the surrounding country, and has a beautiful stream skirting its base. Moreover, I found the people very kind, peaceable, and hospitable.

A considerable number of independent Mbicho villages lay within a circuit of a few miles, the inhabitants of which lived in great harmony with one another, having prudently intermarried to such a degree that they really constitute a large family. I was made welcome among them all, and spent some very pleasant days in hunting with these kind-hearted people, and particularly in that kind of sport called by them *osheza*, or net-hunting, a practice very common among the Bakalai, who called it *ashinga*.

This singular sport is very much practiced in this part of Africa; and as it is generally successful, it is a local amusement, and brings out the best traits of the natives. I was always very fond of it.

The ashinga nets are generally made of the fibres of the bark of a kind of tree, which are twisted into stout cords. They are from sixty to eighty feet long, and four to five feet high, and every well-to-do village owns at least one. But, as few villages have enough nets to make a great spread, it generally happens that several unite in a grand hunt, and divide the proceeds, the game caught in any particular net falling to the share of its owners.

The first day we went out, the people of half a dozen villages met together at an appointed place, the men of each bringing their nets. Then we set out for a spot about ten miles off, where they had a clearing in the dense woods, which had been used before, and was one of their hunting-grounds. We moved along in silence, so as not to alarm the animals which might be near our ground. The dogs—for dogs are used in this hunt—were kept still, and close together.

Finally, we arrived on the ground, and the work of spreading the toils began. Each party stretched a single net, tying it up by creepers to the lower branches of trees. As all worked in the same direction, and each took care to join his net to that of his neighbor, in a very short time we had a line of netting running in a wide half circle, and at least half a mile long.

This done, a party went out on each side to guard against the chance of escape, and the rest of us were ready to beat the bush. We started at about a mile

7

from the nets, and, standing about fifty yards from each
other, we advanced gradually, shouting and making all
the noise we could, at the same time keeping our arms
in readiness to shoot or spear down any thing which
might come in our way.

Though this very spot had been frequently used for
net-hunting, and was therefore better cleared than the
neighboring woods, yet we were obliged to proceed almost step by step. Nearly every native carried, besides
his gun, a heavy cutlass or bill, with which it was necessary literally to hew out a way, the vines and creepers
making a network which only the beasts of the forest
could glide through without trouble.

As we advanced, so did the men that guarded the
flanks; and thus our party gradually closed round the
prey. Presently we began to hear shouts, but we could
see nothing; and I could only hold my gun in readiness,
and pray that my neighbors might not shoot me by mistake, for they are fearfully reckless when on a chase.

The dogs had for some time been let loose. At last
we came in sight of the nets. We had caught a gazelle
of very minute size, called *ncheri*. It is a very graceful
little animal, and would make a pretty pet, though I
have never seen one tamed. A large antelope also was
brought to bay, and shot before I came up; and another
antelope, being shot at and missed, rushed forward and
got entangled in the net.

Having drawn this cover, we gathered up the nets and
went off with the dogs, who enjoyed the sport vastly, to
try another place. After walking about three quarters
of an hour we again spread our nets. Here we had better luck, catching a considerable number of antelopes,

gazelles, and some smaller animals. It was pretty busy work for us. Nearly all the animals got very much entangled, and the more they tried to get through the nets the more they became bewildered.

Before breaking up, all the game caught was laid together, that all might see it. And now I had an opportunity to notice the curious little sharp-eared dogs, about a foot high, which had been so useful in driving the animals into our toils. They stood looking at their prizes with eager and hungry eyes. These dogs often go and hunt for themselves; and it is no unusual thing for half a dozen dogs to drive an antelope to the neighborhood of their village, when their barking arouses the hunters, who come out and kill their quarry.

It was almost dark when we returned to the village of Alapay. One antelope was put aside for me, being a peculiar species which I wanted to stuff, and the rest of the meat was immediately divided. The villagers were delighted at our luck. We were all very hungry, and cooking began at once. I could hardly wait for the dinner, which was one worthy of an emperor's palate. It consisted of plantain, cooked in various ways, and venison of the tenderest sort, stewed in lemon-juice, and afterward roasted on charcoal.

I was glad to go to bed early, for I felt very tired. I had traveled during the day very nearly thirty miles.

But I had scarcely got sound asleep when I was fairly turned out of the house by a furious attack of the Bashikouay ants. They were already upon me when I jumped up, and I was bitten by them terribly. I ran out into the street, and called for help and torches. The natives came out, the lights were struck, and presently I was relieved. But now we found that the whole village was attacked. A great army of ants was pouring in on us, attracted doubtless by the meat in the houses, which they had smelt afar off. My unfortunate antelope had probably brought them to my door. All hands had to turn out to defend themselves. We built little cordons of fires, which kept them away from places they had not entered, and in this way protected our persons from their attacks. We scattered hot ashes and boiling water right and left; and toward morning, having eaten every thing they could get at, they left us in peace. As was to be expected, my antelope was literally eaten up—not a morsel was left.

The vast number, the sudden appearance, and the ferocity of these frightful creatures never ceased to astonish me. On this occasion they had come actually in millions. The antelope on which they fed was a vast mass of living ants, which we could not approach; and it was only when many fires were lighted that they were forced from their onward and victorious course, which they generally pursue. Then, however, they retreated in parties with the greatest regularity, vast numbers remaining to complete the work of destruction. Little would I give for the life of a man who should be tied up to a tree when these ants pass that way and attack him; in two or three hours nothing would be left of him but the bare bones.

MANGROVE SWAMP. TUMBLING AND FALLING.

CHAPTER XII.

RETURNING TO THE COAST.—CAVERNS AND WATERFALLS IN
THE HIGHLANDS.—CROSS A RIVER ON MANGROVE ROOTS.
—STIRRING UP A BIG SNAKE.—A MUTUAL SCARE.

I LEFT the good villagers of Yoongoolapay, and pursued my way to the sea-shore. On the route we came to
a high ridge, or plateau. This was the highest land I
had seen between the Moonda and the Muni, and it is
probable that, if it had not been for the trees, I should
have seen the ocean very well. Along this ridge were
strewn some of the most extraordinary boulders I ever
saw. These immense blocks of granite covered the
ground in every direction. Several of them were between twenty and thirty feet high, and about fifty feet
long.

Near the largest of these granite masses a huge rock

rose some forty or fifty feet out of the ground. I saw
an opening in the solid rock leading to a fine large cavern. It had, no doubt, been made by the hands of man;
it was not of natural formation, for the entrance had
evidently been cut out of the solid rock by human beings; and now it was much used by the natives as a
house to stop in overnight when they were traveling to
and fro. Its vast opening admits such a flood of sun-
light and air that it is not likely to be used as a lair for
wild beasts. We saw the remains of several fires inside,
but I am bound to say we also saw the tracks of leopards
and other dangerous beasts on the outside, for which reason I did not care to sleep there.

While exploring the cavern I thought several times I
heard a trickling, which was almost like the noise of rain,
and which I had not noticed before, probably on account
of the great shouting of my men. But when we got out
I was surprised to find not a cloud in the sky. Turning
for an explanation to Alapay, he led me along a path,
and as we went forward the trickling noise gradually
grew into the sound of rushing waters. Presently we
came to the edge of a steep declivity, and here I saw before and around me a most charming landscape, the
centre of which was a most beautiful waterfall. A little
stream, which meandered along the slope of the plateau,
and which had hitherto escaped our view, had here worn
its way through a vast granite block which barred its
course. Rushing through the narrow and almost circu-
lar hole in this block, it fell in one silvery leap perpen-
dicularly forty or fifty feet. The lower level of the
stream ran along between high, steep banks covered with
trees, the right bank being quite abrupt. It was a min-

iature Niagara. Clear, sparkling, and pure as it could be, the water rushed down to its pebbly bed—a sight so charming that I sat down for some time and feasted my eyes upon it.

I then determined to have a view from below. After some difficult climbing we got to the bottom, and there beheld, under the fall, a large hole in the perpendicular face of the rock, which evidently formed the mouth of a cavern. The opening of the cavern was partly hidden by the waterfall, and was cut through solid rock. Between the opening and the waterfall there were a few feet of clear space, so that by going sideways one could make good his entrance into the cavern without receiving a shower-bath.

I determined to enter this cavern ; but, before venturing, I went first and tried to get a peep at the inside. It was so dark that I could see nothing, so it was not very inviting. We lit torches ; I took my revolver and gun, and accompanied by two men, who also were armed with guns, we entered. How dark it was! Once inside, we excited the astonishment of a vast number of huge vampire bats. There were thousands and thousands of them. They came and fluttered around our lights, threatening each moment to leave us in darkness, and the motion of their wings filled the cavern with a dull thunderous or booming roar. It really looked an awful place, and the dim light of our torches gave to every shadow a fantastic form.

The cavern was rather rough inside. When we had advanced about one hundred yards we came to a stream, or puddle of water, extending entirely across the floor, and barring our way. My men, who had gone thus far under protest, now desired to return, and urged me not to go into the water. It might be very deep; it might be full of horrible water snakes; all sorts of wild beasts might be beyond, and land snakes also. At the word snake I hesitated, for I confess to a great dread of serpents in the dark or in a confined place, where a snake is likely to get the advantage of a man. A cold shudder ran through me at the thought that, once in the water, many snakes might come and swim round me, and perhaps twist themselves round me as they do around the branches of trees; so I paused and reflected.

While peering into the darkness beyond I thought I saw two eyes, like bright sparks or coals of fire, gleaming savagely at us. Could it be a leopard, or what? Without thinking of the consequences, I leveled my gun at the shining objects, and fired. The report for a moment deafened us. Then came a redoubled rush of the great hideous bats. It seemed to me that millions of these animals suddenly launched out upon us from all parts of the surrounding gloom. Some of these got caught in my clothes. Our torches were extinguished in an instant, and, panic-stricken, we all made for the cavern's mouth. I had visions of enraged snakes springing after and trying to catch me. We were all glad to reach daylight once more, and nothing could have induced us to try the darkness again. I confess that, though I think it takes a good deal to frighten me, I did not at all relish remaining there in entire darkness.

The scene outside was as charming as that within was hideous. I stood a long time looking at one of the most beautiful landscapes I ever beheld in Africa. It was certainly not grand, but extremely pretty. Before me,

REGRET NOT EXPLORING A CAVERN.

the little stream, whose fall over the cliff filled the forest
with a gentle murmur, resembling very much, as I have
said, when far enough off, the pattering of a shower of
rain, ran along between steep banks, the trees of which
seemed to meet above it. Away down the valley we
could see its course, traced like a silver line over the
plain, till it was lost to our sight in a denser part of the
forest.

I have often thought of these caverns since I saw
them, and I have regretted that I did not pay more attention to them. If I had made my camp in the vicinity, and explored them, and dug in them for days, I think
that I should have been amply rewarded for the trouble.
At that time I did not feel greatly interested in the subject. I had not read the works of M. Boucher de Perthes
and others, or heard that the bones of animals now ex-
tinct had been discovered in caverns in several parts of
Europe, and that implements made of flint, such as axes,
sharp-pointed arrows, etc., etc., had been found in such
places. If I had excavated I might perhaps have found
the remains of charcoal fires, or other things, to prove
that these caverns had been made by men who lived in
Africa long before the negro. I feel certain these caverns must have been human habitations. I do not see
how they could have been made except by the hand of
man.

On my last journey I thought once or twice of going
to them from the Fernand-Vaz, to explore and dig in
them. I thought I might be rewarded for my labor by
discovering the bones of unknown beasts, or of some remains of primitive men.

These caverns are fortunately not far away from the

sea—I should think not more than ten or fifteen miles—
and are situated between the Muni and the Moonda Rivers. Any one desiring to explore them would easily find
the way to them. The cavern under the waterfall would
be extremely interesting to explore.

The valley itself was a pleasant wooded plain, which,
it seemed, the hand of man had not yet disturbed, and
whence the song of birds, the chatter of monkeys, and
the hum of insects came up to us, now and then, in a
confusion of sounds very pleasant to the ear.

But I could not loiter long over this scene, being anxious to reach the sea-shore. After we set off again we
found ourselves continually crossing or following elephant tracks, so we walked very cautiously, expecting
every moment to find ourselves face to face with a herd.

By-and-by the country became quite flat, the elephant
tracks ceased, and presently, as we neared a stream, we
came to a mangrove swamp. It was almost like seeing
an old friend, or, I may say, an old enemy, for the re-
membrances of musquitoes, tedious navigation, and malaria, which the mangrove-tree brought to my mind, were
by no means pleasant. It is not very pleasant to be laid
up with African fever, I assure you.

From a mangrove-tree to a mangrove swamp and forest is but a step. They never stand alone. Presently we
stood once more on the banks of the little stream, whose
clear, pellucid water had so charmed me a little farther
up the country. Now it was only a swamp—a mangrove
swamp. Its bed, no longer narrow, was spread over a flat
of a mile, and the now muddy water meandered slowly
through an immense growth of mangroves, whose roots
extended entirely across, and met in the middle, where

they rose out of the mire and water like the folds of some vast serpent.

It was high tide. There was not a canoe to be had. To sleep on this side, among the mangroves, was to be eaten up by the musquitoes, which bite much harder than those of America, for they can pierce through your trowsers and drawers. This was not a very pleasant anticipation, but there seemed to be no alternative, and I had already made up my mind that I should not be able to go to sleep. But my men were not troubled at all with unpleasant anticipations. We were to cross over, quite easily too, they said, on the roots which projected above the water, and which lay from two to three feet apart, at irregular distances.

It seemed a desperate venture, but they set out jumping like monkeys from place to place, and I followed, expecting every moment to fall in between the roots in the mud, there to be attacked perhaps by some noxious reptile whose rest my fall would disturb. I had to take off my shoes, whose thick soles made me more likely to slip. I gave all my baggage, and guns, and pistols to the men, and then commenced a journey, the like of which I hope never to take again. We were an hour in getting across—an hour of continual jumps and hops, and holding on. In the midst of it all, a man behind me flopped into the mud, calling out "Omemba!" in a frightful voice.

Now *omemba* means snake. The poor fellow had put his hands on an enormous black snake, and, feeling its cold, slimy scales, he let go his hold and fell. All hands immediately began to run faster than before, both on the right and the left. There was a general panic, and every one began to shout and make all kinds of noises to frighten the serpent. The poor animal also got badly scared, and began to crawl away among the branches as fast as he could. Unfortunately, his fright led him directly toward me, and a general panic ensued. Every body ran as fast as he could to get out of danger. Another man fell into the mud below, and added his cries to the general tumult. Two or three times I was on the point of getting a mud bath myself, but I luckily escaped. My feet were badly cut and bruised, but at last we were safe across, and I breathed freely once more, as soon after I saw the deep blue sea.

SLAVE BARRACOONS.   BURIAL-GROUND.

CHAPTER XIII.

CAPE LOPEZ is a long sandy arm of land reaching out
into the sea. As you approach it from the ocean it has
the appearance of overflowed land. It is so low that the
bushes and the trees growing on it seem, from a distance
seaward, to be set in the water.

The bay formed by Cape Lopez is about fourteen miles
long. Among several small streams which empty their
water into it is the Nazareth River, one of whose branches
is the Fetich River. The bay has numerous shallows and
small islands, and abounds in all sorts of delicious fish.
On the cape itself many large turtles from the ocean
come to lay their eggs. I will tell you by-and-by what a
nice time I had fishing at Cape Lopez, but I have many
other things to talk about before I come to that.

I arrived at Cape Lopez one evening when it was almost dark. The next morning I prepared myself for a
visit to King Bango, the king of the country. The royal
palace is set upon a tolerably high hill, and fronts the
sea-shore. Between the foot of this hill and the sea there
is a beautiful prairie, over which are scattered the numerous little villages called Sangatanga. I never tired

of looking at this prairie. I had lived so long in the gloomy forest that it gave me great delight to see once more the green and sunlit verdure of an open meadow. I found the royal palace surrounded by a little village of huts. As I entered the village I was met by the *mafouga*, or officer of the king, who conducted me to the palace. It was an ugly-looking house of two stories, resting on pillars. The lower story consisted of a dark hall, flanked on each side by rows of small dark rooms, which looked like little cells. At the end of the hall was a staircase, steep and dirty, up which the mafouga piloted me. When I had ascended the stairs I found myself in a large room, at the end of which was seated the great King Bango, who claims to be the greatest chief of this part of Africa. He was surrounded by about one hundred of his wives.

King Bango was fat, and seemed not over clean. He wore a shirt and an old pair of pantaloons. On his head was a crown, which had been presented to him by some of his friends, the Portuguese slavers. Over his shoulders he wore a flaming yellow coat, with gilt embroidery, the cast-off garment of some rich man's lackey in Portugal or Brazil. When I speak of a crown you must not think it was a wonderful thing, made of gold and mounted with diamonds. It was shaped like those commonly worn by actors on the stage, and was probably worth, when new, about ten dollars. His majesty had put round it a circlet of pure gold, made with the doubloons he got in exchange for slaves. He sat on a sofa, for he was paralyzed; and in his hand he held a cane, which also answered the purpose of a sceptre.

This King Bango, whom I have described so minutely,

was the greatest slave king of that part of the coast. At that time there were large slave dépôts on his territory. He is a perfect despot, and is much feared by his people He is also very superstitious.

Though very proud, he received me kindly, for I had come recommended by his great friend, Rompochombo, a king of the Mpongwe tribe. He asked me how I liked his wives. I said, Very well. He then said there were a hundred present, and that there were twice as many more, three hundred in all. Fancy three hundred wives! He also claimed to have more than six hundred children. I wonder if all these brothers and sisters could know and recognize each other!

The next night a great ball was given in my honor by the king. The room where I had been received was the ballroom. I arrived there shortly after dark, and I found about one hundred and fifty of the king's wives, and I was told that the best dancers of the country were there.

I wish you could have seen the room. It was ugly enough : there were several torches to light it ; but, not-withstanding these, the room was by no means brilliant-ly illuminated. The king wanted only his wives to dance before me. During the whole of the evening not a sin-gle man took part in the performance; but two of his daughters were ordered to dance, and he wanted me to marry one of them.

Not far from the royal palace were three curious and very small houses, wherein were deposited five idols, which were reputed to have far greater power and knowl-edge than the idols or gods of the surrounding countries. They were thought to be the great protectors of the

8

Oroungon tribe, and particularly of Sangatanga and of the king. So I got a peep inside the first house. There I saw the idol called Pangeo: he was made of wood, and looked very ugly; by his side was his wife Aleka, another wooden idol. Pangeo takes care of the king and of his people, and watches over them at night.

I peeped also into the second little house. There I saw a large idol called Makambi, shaped like a man, and by his side stood a female figure, Abiala his wife. Poor Makambi is a powerless god, his wife having usurped the power. She holds a pistol in her hand, with which, it is supposed, she can kill any one she pleases; hence the natives are much afraid of her; and she receives from them a constant supply of food, and many presents (I wonder who takes the presents away?). When they fall sick they dance around her, and implore her to make them well. For these poor heathen never pray to the true God. They put their trust in wooden images, the work of their own hands.

I looked into the third house, and there I saw an idol called Numba. He had no wife with him, being a bachelor deity. He is the Oroungon Neptune and Mercury in one—Neptune in ruling the waves, and Mercury in keeping off the evils which threaten from beyond the sea.

As I came away after seeing the king, I shot at a bird sitting upon a tree, but missed it, for I had been taking quinine and was nervous. But the negroes standing around at once proclaimed that this was a "fetich bird" —a sacred bird—and therefore I could not shoot it, even if I fired at it a hundred times.

I fired again, but with no better success. Hereupon

they grew triumphant in their declarations; while I, loth to let the devil have so good a witness, loaded again, took careful aim, and, to my own satisfaction and their utter dismay, brought my bird down.

During my stay in the village, as I was one day out shooting birds in a grove not far from my house, I saw a procession of slaves coming from one of the barracoons toward the farther end of my grove. As they came nearer, I saw that two gangs of six slaves each, all chained about the neck, were carrying a burden between them, which I knew presently to be the corpse of another slave. They bore it to the edge of the grove, about three hundred yards from my house, and, throwing it down there on the bare ground, they returned to their prison, accompanied by the overseer, who, with his whip, had marched behind them.

"Here, then, is the burying-ground of the barracoons," I said to myself, sadly, thinking, I confess, of the poor fellow who had been dragged away from his home and friends—who, perhaps, had been sold by his own father or relatives to die here and be thrown out as food for the vultures. Even as I stood wrapped in thought, these carrion birds were assembling, and began to darken the air above my head; ere long they were heard fighting over the corpse.

The grove, which was, in fact, but an African Aceldama, was beautiful to view from my house, and I had often resolved to explore it, or to rest in the shade of its dark-leaved trees. It seemed a ghastly place enough now, as I approached it more closely. The vultures fled when they saw me, but flew only a little way, and then perched upon the lower branches of the surrounding trees, and watched me with eyes askance, as though fearful I should rob them of their prey. As I walked toward the corpse, I felt something crack under my feet. Looking down, I saw that I was already in the midst of a field of skulls and bones. I had inadvertently stepped upon the skeleton of some poor creature who had been lying here long enough for the birds and ants to pick his bones clean, and for the rains to bleach them. I think there must have been the relics of a thousand skeletons within sight. The place had been used for many years; and the mortality in the barracoons is sometimes frightful, in spite of the care they seem to take of their slaves. Here their bodies were thrown, and here the vultures found their daily carrion. The grass had just been burnt, and the white bones scattered every where gave the ground a singular, and, when the cause was known, a frightful appearance. Penetrating farther into the bush, I found several great piles of bones. This was the place, years ago—when Cape Lopez was one of the great slave-markets on the West Coast, and barracoons were more numerous than they are now—where the poor dead were thrown, one upon another, till even the mouldering bones remained in high piles, as monuments of the nefarious traffic. Such was the burial-ground of the poor slaves from the interior of Africa.

EMBARKING SLAVES.

CHAPTER XIV.

THE SLAVE BARRACOONS.—A BIG SNAKE UNDER MY BED.—
A SLAVE-SHIP OFF THE COAST.

ONE day I passed by an immense inclosure protected by a fence of palisades about twelve feet high, and sharp-pointed at the top. Passing through the gate, which was standing open, I found myself in the midst of a large collection of shanties, surrounded by shade-trees, under which were lying, in various positions, a great many negroes. As I walked round, I saw that the men were fastened, six together, by a little stout chain, which passed through a collar secured about the neck of each. Here and there were buckets of water for the men to drink; and, they being chained together, when one of the six wanted to drink, the others had to go with him.

Then I came to a yard full of women and children. These could roam at pleasure through their yard. No men were admitted there. These people could not all understand each other's language; and you may probably wish to know who they were. They were Africans belonging to various tribes, who had been sold, some by their parents or by their families, others by the people of their villages. Some had been sold on account of witchcraft; but there were many other excuses for the traffic. They would find suddenly that a boy or girl was " dull," and so forth, and must be sold. Many of them came from countries far distant.

Some were quite merry; others appeared to be very sad, thinking they were bought to be eaten up. They believed that the white men beyond the seas were great cannibals, and that they were to be fattened first, and then eaten. In the interior, one day, a chief ordered a slave to be killed for my dinner, and I barely succeeded in preventing the poor wretch from being put to death. I could hardly make the chief believe that I did not, in my own country, live on human flesh.

Under some of the trees were huge caldrons, in which beans and rice were cooking for the slaves; and others had dried fish to eat. In the evening they were put into large sheds for the night. One of the sheds was used as a hospital.

In the midst of all this stood the white man's house— yes, the white man's house!—and in it were white men whose only business was to buy these poor creatures from the Oroungou people!

After I had seen every thing I left the barracoon, for that is the name given to such a place as I have just described. I wandered about, and it was dark before I re- turned to the little bamboo house which the king had

given me. I got in, and then, striking a match carefully,
I lighted a torch, so that I might not go to bed in darkness. You may smile when I say bed, for my couch
was far from bearing any resemblance to our beds at
home, with mattress, and pillows, and sheets, and blankets. Travelers in Equatorial Africa are utter strangers
to such luxuries.

After I had lighted the torch, I cast my eyes round to
see if any thing had been disturbed; for a thief, so disposed, could easily break into these houses. I noticed
something glittering and shining under my *akoko*, or
bedstead. The object was so still that I did not pay any
attention to it; in fact, I could not see it well by the dim
light of the torch. But when I approached the bed to
arrange it, I saw that the glitter was produced by the
shining scales of an enormous serpent, which lay quietly
coiled up there within two feet of me. What was I to
do? I had fastened my door with ropes. If the snake
were to uncoil itself and move about, it might, perhaps,
take a spring and wind itself about me, quietly squeeze
me to death, and then swallow me as he would a gazelle.
These were not comforting thoughts. I was afraid to
cry out for fear of disturbing the snake, which appeared
to be asleep. Besides, no one could get in, as I had bar
ricaded the only entrance, so I went quietly and unfast-
ened the door. When every thing was ready for a safe
retreat, I said to myself, "I had better try to kill it."
Then, looking for my guns, I saw, to my utter horror,
that they were set against the wall at the back of the
bed, so that the snake was between me and them. After watching the snake intently, and thinking what to do,
I resolved to get my gun; so, keeping the door in my

rear open, in readiness for a speedy retreat at the first
sign of life in the snake, I approached on tiptoe, and, in
the twinkling of an eye, grasped the gun which was loaded heavily with large shot. How relieved I felt at that
moment! I was no longer the same man. Fortunately,
the snake did not move. With my gun in one hand, I
went again toward the reptile, and fairly placing the
muzzle of the gun against it, I fired, and then ran out of
the house as fast as I could.

At the noise of the gun there was a rush of negroes
from all sides to know what was the matter. They
thought some one had shot a man, and run into my
house to hide himself; so they all rushed into it, helter-
skelter; but I need not tell you they rushed out just
as fast on finding a great snake writhing about on the
floor. Some had trodden upon it, and been frightened
out of their wits. You have no idea how they roared
and shouted; but no one appeared disposed to enter the
house again, so I went in cautiously myself to see how
matters stood, for I did not intend to give undisputed
possession of my hut so easily to Mr. Snake. I entered,
and looked cautiously around. The dim light of the
torch helped me a little, and there I saw the snake on
the ground. Its body had been cut in two by the dis-
charge, and both ends were flapping about the floor. At
first I thought these ends were two snakes, and I did not
know what to make of it; but, as soon as I perceived my
mistake, I gave a heavy blow with a stick on the head
of the horrible creature, and finished it. Then I saw it
disgorge a duck—a whole duck—and such a long duck!
It looked like an enormous long-feathered sausage. After eating the duck, the snake thought my bedroom was

just the place for him to go to sleep in and digest his meal; for snakes, after a hearty meal, always fall into a state of torpor. It was a large python, and it measured —would you believe it?—eighteen feet. Fancy my situation if this fellow had sprung upon me, and coiled round me! It would soon have been all over with me. I wonder how long it would have taken to digest me, had I been swallowed by the monster!

One fine day, while walking on the beach of this inhospitable shore, I spied a vessel. It approached nearer and nearer, and at last ran in and hove-to a few miles from the shore. Immediately I observed a gang of slaves rapidly driven down from one of the barracoons. I stood and watched. The men were still in gangs of six, but they had been washed, and each had a clean cloth on. The canoes were immense boats, with twenty-six paddles, and held about sixty slaves each. The poor slaves seemed much terrified. They had never been on the rough water before, and they did not know what that dancing motion of the sea was. Then they were being taken away, they knew not whither. As they skimmed over the waves, and rolled, now one way, now another, they must have thought their last day had come, and that they were to be consigned to a watery grave.

I was glad that these poor creatures could not see me, for I was hidden from their view by trees and bushes. I felt ashamed of myself—I actually felt ashamed of being a white man! Happily, such scenes are rarely, if ever, witnessed nowadays, and the slave-trade will soon belong to the past.

Two hours afterward, the vessel, with a cargo of six hundred slaves, was on her way to Cuba.

THE GAZELLE.

CHAPTER XV.

GOING INTO THE INTERIOR. — SLEEPING WITH THE KING'S RATS.—THE CHIMPANZEE.—KILL A GAZELLE.—TOO COLD TO SLEEP.—THE GRAY PARTRIDGE.

AFTER this I went again to visit King Bango, and was announced to his majesty by his great mafouga. I had an important object in paying this visit. I wished to ask the king to permit me to go into the interior, and to spare me some people to show me the way.

Bango liked me, though I had declined to marry one of his beautiful daughters. So he granted my request, and gave me twenty-five men, some of whom were reputed great hunters in that country. They had killed many elephants, and brought all the ivory to their king. They were the providers of the royal table, and passed their lives in the hunt and in the forest.

We made great preparations for the chase, for game was said to be plentiful. We were to encamp many days in the forest, and to have a jolly time, and a hard time too, for the hunter's life is not an easy one. I was invited by the king to sleep in his palace, so that the next day I might start early; so I was led to my bedroom by the great mafouga. It was so dirty and gloomy that I wished myself fast asleep under a tree in the forest. I looked around, thinking that perhaps the king wanted to get rid of me, and had invited me there to have me murdered; but, finding nothing suspicious, I concluded that old King Bango had never entertained such ideas, and I felt vexed at myself for having such thoughts on my mind. Then I extinguished the light, and lay down on the royal couch. I had scarcely lain down when I began to hear a strange noise. At first I did not know what it meant. The noise in the room increased. What could it be? I tried to see through the darkness, but could distinguish nothing. Just then I felt something getting under my blanket. Confounded, I jumped up, not knowing what it might be. It was an enormous rat. As soon as I got up, I heard a perfect scrambling of rats going back where they came from, and then all became silent. I lay down on the bed again, and tried to sleep, but in vain, on account of the assaults and gambols of the rats, of which there was a prodigious number. They seemed inclined to dispute possession of my room with me. They were continually on my bed and running over my face. I soon got quite enough of the royal palace. I wished I had never come into it. But it was an excellent place for getting up early. No sooner had the morning twilight made its appearance than I rose, and called my men together; and, though we could hardly see, we set out at once on the march.

I went in advance with Aboko, my head man, and Niamkala, the next best man, at my side. Both these men were great hunters, and had spent the principal part of their lives in the woods. They seemed really like men of the woods, so very wild were their looks. Aboko was a short, somewhat stout man; very black, and extremely muscular; very flat-nosed, and with big thick lips. His eyes were large and cunning, and seemed to wander about; his body bore marks of many scratches from thorny trees and briers; his legs display-ed great strength. Niamkala, on the contrary, was tall and slender, not very dark; he had sharp, piercing eyes, and seemed to be continually looking after something. Both were first-rate elephant hunters.

Aboko, Niamkala, and I became great friends, for we were all three hunters, and loved the woods.

Our way led through some beautiful prairies, each surrounded by dark forests, and seeming like natural gardens planted in this great woody wilderness. The country was really lovely. The surface was mostly roll-ing prairie, with a light sandy soil. The highest hills often broke into abrupt precipices, on which we would come suddenly; and if any of us had tumbled down to the bottom, he would never have been heard of again. The woods are the safe retreat of the elephant. Great herds of buffaloes are found there; also antelopes, which go out into the great grass-fields by night to play and feed. Leopards are also abundant.

I was much pleased to be able to travel in an open space, and not always through the dark forest. The breeze fanned our faces as we went onward. Presently we saw the footprints of huge elephants and of wild buffaloes. Friend Aboko now warned us to look sharp, for we were sure to see game. Sure enough, he had hardly spoken when we saw a bull standing, deer-like, upon the edge of the wood, watching us, I suppose, and no doubt greatly puzzled to make out what kind of animals we were. He stood for some minutes, safe out of range, and then turned into the woods, evidently not liking our appearance. We ran around to intercept him; and I waited at one pass in the woods for Aboko to go clear around and drive the bull toward me.

I was waiting, when suddenly I saw something approaching me out of the deep gloom of the forest. I thought it was Aboko coming toward me, and I waited anxiously for news. I did not say a word for fear of frightening the game that might be near us. The object came nearer and nearer to me, till I thought I could recognize Aboko's dark face distinctly through the foliage. I stood with my gun resting on the ground, when suddenly I heard a shrill scream, and then what I thought to be Aboko turned and ran into the woods, showing a broad, big, hairy body. It was one of the wild men of the woods—the chimpanzee—and a big one it was, I assure you.

How glad I was to have seen this wild man of the woods. For a few minutes I felt so astonished that I did not move. His black face certainly did look very much like that of an African, so much so that, as I have already said, I took the chimpanzee to be Aboko.

By-and-by the real Aboko made his appearance. This time there was no illusion, and we had a good laugh over my mistake. I felt quite vexed that I had not shot the chimpanzee, I should have liked so much to look at the animal closely; but I felt it was almost like shooting a man.

We left the woods and started once more for the interior. We had not been long on our way when I spied a gazelle right in the middle of the prairie. How could one approach it without being seen? for the grass was short. We wanted very much to kill it, for we had not killed any thing yet; and what were we to have for our dinner and supper? No one likes to go without dinner, especially when working hard. Aboko, Niamkala, and I held a council. We lay down flat on the ground for fear of being seen, and finally it was agreed that I should go toward the gazelle with my long-range gun, and shoot it if I could. So I started. I almost crawled, now and then raising my head just to the level of the grass, to see if the animal was still there. When I thought I was near enough, I quietly lay down flat on the ground, and rested my gun on an ant-hill that looked like a mushroom. Taking careful aim at the unsuspicious animal, I fired, and down it tumbled, to my great delight. Aboko and Niamkala, who had been watching afar off, came rushing and shouting, their faces beaming with joy. The prospect of a good dinner cheered them up.

Others of the party soon joined us. The gazelle was cut up on the spot, and we continued our journey till we came to a beautiful little stream, which was too deep to be forded. A huge tree had been felled, and we crossed to the other side on it, though it was hard work.

I assure you I thought once or twice I should have tumbled into the water.

At sunset we stopped, quite tired out. We made our camp in the midst of the prairie in order to have the nice grass to lie upon. It was the dry season, and we were not afraid of getting wet. The people went into the nearest forest and collected an immense quantity of firewood; not a difficult task, as so many dead limbs were lying on the ground.

We lighted a great many large fires, which blazed up fiercely, for the wind blew hard. The country around was illuminated, and the glare of our fires must have been seen a long way off. We took our dinner and supper at the same time. I roasted my own share of the gazelle myself; I put a piece of stick through the flesh, and laid the skewer across two forked sticks, which I fixed in the ground on each side of the fire. I longed for some lard to baste the roasting meat; but I was thankful for the good dinner I had, and I enjoyed it thoroughly. I had a little bit of salt to eat with it, and also some nice Cayenne pepper.

My men also seemed to enjoy their meal very much, for they had meat to their heart's content; and these negroes are very gluttonous generally. It was laughable to see how lazily we lay around on the grass by our fires; some were smoking, others tried to sleep, while others told stories, but we all tried to warm ourselves, and kept continually adding fuel to the already bright fires.

The night was clear and almost frosty. The stars shone brilliantly above our heads, and it was bright moonlight. It became so windy and cold that we regretted we had not encamped by the forest, where we should have been sheltered from the wind. It was too cold to sleep, even with my blanket; and my poor men, who had no blankets, were shivering around the fires.

So at two o'clock in the morning I ordered the men to get up. A couple of hours' sharp walking brought us to a thick wood, and there we were sheltered. We quickly made up one very large fire, enough for all of us, and stretched ourselves pell-mell around it for a short nap. We were so tired that we soon fell asleep, not caring for leopards or any thing else. We were awakened by the cry of the gray partridge (*Francolinus squamatus*), called *quani* by the natives.

I will now say a word about these partridges. Unlike our partridges, they perch on trees. When evening comes, the old cock perches himself first, and calls the flock together. They all settle near each other. In the morning, before daylight, they begin to cluck; and it was this noise that we heard. They do not sleep on the ground, like our partridges, because there are too many snakes crawling about, and too many carnivorous animals.

AFTER DINNER.

CHAPTER XVI.

THE HIPPOPOTAMUS.—A SPECK OF WAR.—REACH NGOLA.—
A SUNDAY TALK. — THE BLACK MAN'S GOD AND THE
WHITE MAN'S GOD.—HOW KING NJAMBAI PUNISHED HIS
WIFE.—WE BUILD AN OLAKO IN THE WOODS.

SUNRISE found us under way again; and before us lay a fine stretch of prairie, on the farther borders of which were quietly grazing several herds of buffaloes, which, as we approached them, quickly ran into the woods. While they remained in sight they gave the country a civilized appearance; it looked like a large grazing farm in June, with cattle, and hay almost ready for harvest; a fine, quiet, Old-country picture here in the wilds of Africa, that reminded me so much of home scenes that I felt happy and elated.

We pushed on rapidly in order to travel as far as pos-

9

sible before the heat of the day should set in. We came
to a large pool or lakelet, and, while looking at the water, I suddenly saw something strange coming out from
under its surface. It was a hippopotamus — the first I
had seen. I thought it was a log of wood; then I fancied it was the head of a horse; for certainly, from a
distance, the head of a hippopotamus looks like that of
a horse. Then I heard a great grunt, and down went
the head under water. Suddenly a number of the animals made their appearance; there were at least a dozen
of them. They began sporting in the water, now popping their huge heads out and snorting, and then diving
to the bottom, and remaining there for some time.

I watched them for a while, and then I took my gun,
intending to send a bullet into the head of one and haul
him ashore, but Aboko said they would sink to the bottom. Not wishing to kill one of these creature for nothing, I took Aboko's advice, and we went away.

We had not met a single human being since we left
Sangatanga till now. As we journeyed, I saw in the
distance what I at first took to be a herd of buffaloes,
but soon perceived it was a caravan of natives coming in
our direction. Immediately we looked at our guns; for
in this country there is no law, and every man's hand is
against his brother. We saw that they, too, prepared
for an encounter; that most of them hid in the grass,
watching. Four fellows came toward us to reconnoitre,
and to ask if it was peace or war; when suddenly they
got a glimpse of me, and I do not know how, but they
at once saw, from the fact of my being there, that there
would be no war. They shouted to their companions to
come and see the Otangani.

They were Shekianis, who, as I have said, are a very warlike people, and·this part of the country, I was told, was thickly inhabited by them. We left them in the midst of their wonders, and traveled as fast as we could, for we wanted to reach a village of their tribe, named Ngola, whose chief was a friend of King Bango, and was his vassal, having married one of his daughters.

At last, after much traveling, we reached the village of Ngola. As we approached, and as soon as the women caught sight of me, they ran screaming into the houses. Njambai, the chief, received us very kindly, and gave me a house to live in.

Ngola was a very pretty village, and the house I lived in belonged to Shinshooko, the brother of the chief. You will agree with me that Shinshooko had a funny name. He was a worthy fellow, and tolerably honest too, for he gave me the key of one of his doors—(I wonder where he got the old padlock that was on it)—and he recommended me to shut my door every time I went away, as the people might steal something.

Sunday came ; I remained in the village. They all understood the Oroungou language, so I could speak to them. I told them there was no such thing as witchcraft, and that it was very wrong to accuse people of it, and kill them; that there was only one God, who made both the whites and the blacks, and we should all love him. This elicited only grunts of surprise and incredulity. They all shouted that there were two Gods—the God of the *Ntangani* (white men), and the God of the *Alombai* (black men). The God of the black men had never given them any thing, while the God of the white men had sent them guns, powder, and many other fine things. Then Shinshooko remarked, "You have rivers of *alongon* (rum) flowing through your land. When I go to Sangatanga I taste it 'at King Bango's; how much I should like to live on the banks of such rivers!" They would not believe that we had only rivers of water like theirs, and that we ourselves made our powder, and guns, and rum also.

I staid for a few days in the village of Ngola, where the people were very kind to me. One day I heard a woman crying out as if she were in great pain. Asking what was the matter, a man told me the king was punishing one of his wives; and others said that, if I did not go to her help, she might be killed. I hurried to the king's house, and there, in front of the veranda, a spectacle met my eyes which froze my blood with horror. A woman was tied by the middle to a stout stake driven into the ground. Her legs were stretched out and fastened to other smaller stakes, and stout cords were bound round her neck, waist, ankles, and wrists. These cords were being twisted with sticks; and, when I arrived, the skin was bursting from the terrible compression. The poor woman looked at me. The king was in a perfect rage; he himself was the chief executioner. His eyes were bloodshot, and his lips were white with foam. I had to be careful in expostulating with the king, for fear that he might kill her at once in a fit of rage. I walked up, and, taking him by the arm, asked him, for my sake, to release the poor woman, and not to kill her. He seemed to hesitate; he did not answer, and went into his house. I threatened to leave if he did not release her. Finally he consented, and said, "Let her loose yourself; I give her to you."

How glad I was! I rushed out immediately, and began to untie the savage cords, and to cut them away with my knife. The poor creature was covered with blood. I sent her to my house, and took care of her. I learned that she had stolen some of her husband's beads.

After this I left the Shekiani village of Ngola, and went on my journey with my friends Aboko and Niam-kala. We traveled on, till, on reaching a place in the midst of a forest, not far from a little lake, we determined to build an olako, for I liked the country so much that I did not want to leave it. There were a great many wild animals in the neighborhood, and we thought the place was likely to afford us good sport, especially as the lake would draw beasts down to its banks to drink. We were not only near water, but we had a wide stretch of forest and prairie-land about us. We worked very hard that day, building and arranging our encampment, in such a way as to make every thing comfortable and secure. Of course we selected the prettiest part of the forest, and where there were many tall and shady trees. We first cut the underbrush from under the trees, and also many of the vines or creepers, which looked very singular as they hung down over our heads. Then we collected a great number of large leaves, which are called by some tribes *shayshayray*, and *guaygayra*, to roof our sheds with. After this we proceeded to cut a number of small sticks, seven or eight feet long, and began to construct our habitations. Then we cut branches of trees to shield us from the wind, and collected a great quantity of firewood, for we had made up our minds to keep ourselves warm. After we had arranged and lighted the fires, our camp looked quite like a little village. It

was very romantic and beautiful. I had arranged my
own shelter very nicely; and it was first in the row. To
be sure, my bed was rather hard, being composed of sticks
and leafy branches; while for a pillow I had merely a
piece of wood.

In the midst of our work, ten slaves of Njambai came,
laden with provisions, which the good fellow had sent
after me. After doing a hard day's work, I think we
deserved to rest comfortably in the evening. We began
cooking our dinner, and a right good dinner it was. My
men had monkey and buffalo meat, but I had a nice fat
fowl which my friend Njambai had sent me.

Before dinner I warned my men to be honest, and
keep their fingers at home. They were good fellows, but
I found that all savages will steal. So I threatened to
kill the first man I caught meddling with my property,
and told them I would shoot without mercy; " and then,"
said I, with great sternness, " when I have blown your
brains out, I will settle the matter with your king." To
which Aboko coolly replied that the settlement was not
likely to do them any particular good.

Of course they all protested that they were honest, but
I knew them better than they knew themselves. I knew
the effect of temptation on them, poor fellows! and had
more confidence in their faith that I would kill the thief,
than I had in their good resolutions.

When this little matter was settled, they drew round
the blazing fire. By this time, the buffalo-meat, suspended in a huge kettle over the fire, was cooked and ready
to be eaten; the monkeys had been roasted on charcoal;
my fowl had been cooked; and before us was a great
pile of roasted plantain. We enjoyed a hearty meal to-

gether; I eating off a plate, and using a fork, while the black fellows took fresh leaves for plates, and used the "black man's fork," as they call their five fingers. After dinner they drunk a large calabash-full of palm wine, that had been brought from Ngola; and then, to crown their feast with the greatest delight of all, I went to one of my boxes, and lifting the lid, while the shining black faces peered at me with saucer-eyes of expectation, I took out a huge plug of Kentucky tobacco. There was a wild hurrah of joy from them all. They shouted that I was their friend; they loved only me; they would go with nobody else; I was their good spirit; I was like one of themselves. I distributed the tobacco among them, and in a few minutes all were lying about the fire, or seated round it, with their pipes in their mouths.

After making the fire burn brightly, I, being tired, went and lay down, as you see me in the picture. My blanket was the only article of bedding I had; I wrapped this around me, and rested my head on the wooden pillow, which I assure you was not of the softest kind. I felt pleased to see my men so contented. Their wild stories of hunting adventures, of witchcraft, and evil spirits, well fitted the rude, picturesque surroundings; and they lay there talking away, till, at last, I was obliged to remind them that it was one o'clock, and time to go to sleep, especially as some of us were to get up very early and go hunting. Then all became silent, and soon we all fell asleep, except the men appointed to keep the fires bright on account of the leopards, and also to watch that we might not be surprised by some enemy.

A LEOPARD AND HER YOUNG ONE.

CHAPTER XVII.

AN UNSUCCESSFUL HUNT FOR ELEPHANTS.—I TAKE AIM AT
A BUFFALO.—A LEOPARD IN THE GRASS NEAR US.—WE
SHOOT THE LEOPARD AND HER KITTEN.—GREAT REJOIC-
ING IN CAMP.—WHO SHALL HAVE THE TAIL?—A QUAR-
REL OVER THE BRAINS.—THE GUINEA-HENS.—THE MON-
KEYS.

EARLY the next morning Aboko and I got up. Aboko
covered himself with his war fetiches, and also with the
fetiches that were to bring him good luck and give him
a steady hand. On the middle of his forehead was a
yellow spot made with clay. When he had finished these
preparations we started.

Our desire was to kill elephants. We saw plenty of
tracks, and we hunted all day long. In many places, to
judge by the tracks, the elephants had been only an hour

or two before ourselves. But we did not see a single elephant, and I killed only a few monkeys for my men's dinner, as well as a few birds.

We were returning to the camp rather downhearted, when I heard the cry of the gray male partridge, of which I have already spoken, calling for his mates to come and perch on the tree he had chosen. We turned back to get a shot if possible, for they are fine eating. We were just on the edge of the forest; and, as I pushed out into the prairie, suddenly I saw several buffaloes, one of which I made sure of, as he stood a little in advance of the rest, where the grass was high enough for a stealthy approach. I immediately put a ball into the barrel that had only shot, so that I might have my two barrels loaded with bullets. Then Aboko and I advanced slowly toward the unconscious bull, which stood a fair mark, and I was about to raise my gun, when Aboko made a quick sign to hold still and listen. Aboko, at the same time, breathed as if he were smelling something.

I did not know why it was that Aboko had stopped me, but I knew there must be better game at hand, or some other good reason for his doing so. Perhaps he had heard the footsteps of an elephant. I looked at his face, and saw that it appeared anxious.

As we stood perfectly motionless, I heard, at apparently a little distance before us, a low purring sound, which might have been taken, by a careless ear, for the sound of the wind passing through the grass. But to Aboko's quick ear it betokened something else. His face grew very earnest, and he whispered to me " njego" (leopard).

What were we to do? The noise continued. We cocked our guns, and moved, slowly and cautiously, a

few steps ahead, to get a position where we thought we
might see over the grass. The leopard might pounce
upon us at any moment. What would prevent him from
doing so if he chose? Certainly not our guns, for we did
not know exactly where the beast was. To tell you the
truth, I did not feel comfortable at all; I had a slight ob-
jection to being carried away in the jaws of a leopard,
and devoured in the woods.

Our situation was far from being a pleasant one. The
leopard comes out generally by night only, and nothing
but extreme hunger will bring him out of his lair in open
day. When he is hungry, he is also unusually savage,
and very quick in his motions.

We knew the animal was near, but we could not succeed in getting a sight of him. As the wind blew from
him toward us, I perceived plainly a strong peculiar odor
which this animal gives out, and this fact proved still
more decidedly that the leopard could not be far off.
The thought passed through my mind, Is he watching us?
Is he coming toward us — crouching like a cat on the
ground, and ready to spring upon us when near enough?
Do his eyes penetrate the grass which we can not see
through? If so, is he ready to spring?

Meantime our buffalo bull stood stupidly before his
herd, not twenty yards from us, utterly innocent of the
presence of so many of his formidable enemies — the
leopard, Aboko, and myself.

Just then we moved a little to one side, and, peering
through an opening in the grass, I beheld an immense
leopard, a female, with a tiny young leopard by her side.
The beast saw us at the same moment, having turned her
head quickly at some slight noise we made. She had

been watching the buffalo so intently as not to notice our approach. It seemed to me as if a curious look of indecision passed over her face. She, too, had more game than she had looked for, and was puzzled which to attack first. Her long tail swished from side to side, and her eyes glared as she hesitated for a moment to decide which of the three—the bull, Aboko, or me—to pounce upon and make her victim.

But I saved her the trouble of making up her mind; for, in far less time than it takes me to tell you what took place, I had put a ball into her head, which, luckily for us, relieved her of farther care for prey. She dropped down dead. At the same moment Aboko fired into the little leopard and killed it. At the noise of the guns, the buffalo bull and the herd decamped in the opposite direction at a tremendous pace, the bull little knowing the circumstances to which he owed his life.

I felt much relieved, for I had never before been in quite so ticklish a situation, and I felt no particular desire ever to be in a similar plight again.

When we returned to the camp there was a great excitement as soon as they heard the news that two leopards had been killed. Aboko carried in the young leopard on his back; but mine was too heavy, and had to be left in the field. Guns were fired in rejoicing, and the big leopard was fetched in. When the people returned with it to the camp, all shouted, "What an enormous beast! what an enormous beast! We heard gun firing," etc., etc.

In the midst of this noise Niamkala made his appearance with some of our party, bringing in some wild boars, and a pretty little gazelle which the natives called *ncheri*.

Of course the wild boars had been cut up into several pieces, for they were too heavy to carry whole.

Niamkala and his party were received with great cheers. The prospect of a good supper brightened all their faces, and mine also; and I shouted, " Well done, Niamkala and boys !"

Every thing was brought to my feet. There was so much to eat that there was no use in dividing the meat into equal shares, so I let every one take as much as he liked.

After supper the leopards were hung on a pole resting on two forked sticks, and then the negroes danced round them. They sang songs of victory, and exulted over and abused the deceased leopard (the mother). They addressed to her comical compliments upon her beauty (and the leopard is really a most beautiful animal). They said, " What a fine coat you have ! (meaning her skin). We will take that coat off from you." They shouted, " Now you will kill no more people ! Now you will eat no more hunters ! Now you can not leap on your prey ! What has become of the wild bull you were looking after so keenly ? Would you not have liked to make a meal of Aboko or of Chaillie ?" (for they called me Chaillie).

Thus they sung and danced round till toward morning, when I made them go to sleep.

Next morning there was great quarreling among my men. What could be the matter ? I found that Niamkala was declaring his determination to have the end of my leopard's tail, while the rest of the hunters asserted their equal right to it. Aboko said he did not care, as he would have the tail of the one he had killed.

I skinned the two leopards in the most careful manner, and gave the end of the tail to Niamkala, and I
promised Fasiko to give him the tail of the next one I
should kill. They all shouted, " I hope you will kill leopards enough to give to each of us a tail!"

Poor Fasiko looked very downhearted. When I in-
quired why, he said, " Don't you know that when a man
has the end of a leopard's tail in his possession, he is sure
to be fortunate in winning the heart of the girl he wants
to marry ?"

I said, " Fasiko, you have one wife, what do you care
for a leopard's tail?"

He replied, " I want a good many wives."

The palaver about the tail was hardly over when another quarrel broke out. This time it was about the
brains. Aboko, Niamkala, and Fasiko each wanted the
whole brain of the animal. The others said they must
have some too; that there was only one end to each tail,
but that the brains could be divided among them all.
For a few minutes a fight seemed imminent over the
head of the leopard.

I said " You may quarrel, but no fighting. If you do,
you will see me in the fight, and I will hit every body,
and hit hard too." At the same time I pointed out to
them a large stick lying by my bedside. This immediately stopped them.

They all wanted the brain, they said, because, when
mixed with some other charms, it makes a powerful
monda (fetiche), which gives its possessors dauntless
courage and great fortune in the hunt. Happily I was
able to persuade my three best hunters that they wanted
no such means to bolster up their courage.

The dispute over the brains being settled, Aboko, in the presence of all the men, laid the liver before me. As this had no value or interest for me, since I was certainly not going to eat the liver of the leopard for my dinner, I was about to kick it aside, when they stopped me, and entreated me to take off the gall and destroy it, in order to save the party from future trouble. These negroes believe the gall of the leopard to be deadly poison, and my men feared to be suspected, by their friends or enemies at Sangatanga, of having concealed some of this poison. So I took off the gall, put it under my feet and destroyed it, and then taking the earth in which it had been spilled, I threw it in every direction, for I did not want any of these poor fellows to be accused of a crime, and lose their lives by it. I intended to inform the king, on my return, that we had destroyed the liver. But I told my men that their belief was all nonsense, and a mere superstition. They said it was not. As I could not prove their notion to be false, I stopped the discussion by saying I did not believe it.

Having plenty of game, we carried the leopard meat a long way off, and threw it away.

We did not go hunting for two days, but spent our time in smoking the meat we had on hand. It was just the sort of weather for hunting, and for living in the woods. The air was cool and refreshing, for it was June, and the dry season; but the sky was often clouded, which prevented the sun from being oppressive. To add to our pleasure, the forest trees were in bloom, and many of them were fragrant. The nights were very cold indeed for this country, the thermometer going down to sixty-eight degrees Fahrenheit. The wind blew hard, but against that we managed to protect ourselves. The dews were not nearly so heavy as they are in the rainy season. The grass was in great part burned off the prairies.

Every day we succeeded in shooting more or less game, among which were antelopes, gazelles, wild boars, monkeys without number, and Guinea-fowls. These Guinea-fowls were of a beautiful species. In this country you have never seen any like them.

My joy was great when I killed this hitherto unknown species of Guinea-fowl (*Numida plumifera*). It is one of the handsomest of all the Guinea-fowls yet discovered. Its head is naked, the skin being of a deep bluish-black tinge, and is crowned with a beautiful crest of straight, erect, narrow, downy feathers, standing in a bunch close together. The plumage of the body is of a fine bluish-black ground, variegated with numerous *eyes* of white, slightly tinged with blue. The bill and legs are colored a blue-black, similar to the skin of the head.

This bird is not found near the sea-shore. It is very shy, but marches in large flocks through the woods. At night they perch on trees, where they are protected from the numerous animals which prowl about.

I killed several beautiful monkeys, called by the natives *mondi*. What curious-looking monkeys they were! Only the stuffed specimen of a young one had been received in England before this time. The mondi is entirely black, and is covered with long shaggy hair. It has a very large body, and a funny little head, quite out of proportion to the size of the animal. It is a very beautiful monkey; the hair is of a glossy jet black, and it has a very long tail. In Africa no monkeys have prehensile tails; I mean by that, tails which they can twist round the branch of a tree, and so hang themselves with the head downward.   That kind of monkey is only found in South America.

The mondi has a dismal cry, which sounds very strangely in the silent woods, and always enabled me to tell where these monkeys were.

ZBORO KILLS A ROGUE ELEPHANT.

CHAPTER XVIII.

ONE fine day I remained in the camp, for I had been
hunting so much that I wanted a day of rest. All the
others had gone to hunt. I was left alone, and I enjoyed the solitude, every thing around me was so beautiful and quiet. Nature seemed to smile on all sides. I
placed myself at the foot of a large tree, and wrote in
my journals; and then I thought of the dear friends I
had at home, and wondered if they sometimes thought
of me. Then I called to mind all I had seen in the
wonderful country which I had explored. I could hardly believe it myself; it seemed like a dream. What extraordinary people and what curious beasts had I not
met! How many wonderful dangers I had escaped!
How kind God had been in protecting me! How He
had watched over the poor lonely traveler, and taken
care of him during sickness! Thus my heart went up
in gratitude, and I silently implored that the protection
of God might still be granted me.

Toward sunset Aboko and Niamkala made their appearance, and brought a fine young boar with them. As
usual, without saying a word, they came right to me, and

put the dead animal at my feet. Then, seating themselves and clapping their hands, Aboko began to tell me
what had happened from the time they started in the
morning until the time they returned. They forgot
nothing, even mentioning the tracks of the animals they
had seen. They reported they had found fresh elephant
tracks, and thought the elephants had made their head-
quarters there for a few days. After hearing this, we
immediately resolved that we would all turn out after
elephants on the following day.

Accordingly, in the evening, we cleaned and prepared
our guns, and every body went to sleep early.

The next morning we started about daybreak, each of
us carrying some provisions. We were to fire no guns
in the forest for fear of frightening the elephants, who
are very shy in this region. We had taken pains to load
our guns in the most careful manner.

We hunted all day, but in vain; no elephants were to
be seen. Wo slept out in the woods, for we were too
far from the camp to return. We felt so tired that we
had only sufficient strength left to enable us to fetch
fire-wood, and to cut a few branches of trees, and lie
down upon them. I had lost or forgotten the matches,
so I had to light the fire with a piece of steel and a gun-
flint. This took a little longer.

Very soundly we all slept, as you may easily suppose.
When I awoke in the midst of the night our fires were
almost out; at least they did not blaze up enough to
frighten the wild beasts. Aboko, Niamkala, and Fasiko
were snoring tremendously. One was lying flat on his
back, the other had his legs up, while Fasiko had his
arm extended at full length. By the side of each was

his gun, which touched him in some way, so that it could not be taken without awaking him. I believe it was their snoring that had roused me. They were so tired, and seemed to sleep so soundly, that I did not want to wake them, so I went and added fuel to the fire, which soon began to blaze up again.

The next day found us again exploring the woods in every direction. Elephants certainly were not plentiful; besides, they traveled much in search of their favorite food — a kind of fern, which was not very abundant. Again I got very tired; but at last, in the afternoon, we came across our quarry.

Emerging from a thick part of the forest into a prai-rie which bordered it, we saw to our left, just upon the edge of the wood, a solitary bull elephant. There we stood still. I wonder what he was thinking about! I had seen the great beast in menageries, and also among the Fans, and I have described to you an elephant hunt in their country, but then there was great confusion.

Here the huge animal stood quietly by a tree, innocent of our presence; and now, for the first time in my life, I was struck with the vast size of this giant of the forests. Large trees seemed like small saplings when compared with the bulk of this immense beast which was standing placidly near them.

What were we to do but to kill him? Though 1 felt a sense of pity at trying to destroy so noble an animal, yet I was very anxious to get the first shot myself; for it was a "rogue elephant"— that is, an elephant unattached.* It was an old one, as we could see by the great

---

* Sir Emerson Tennent ("Ceylon," vol. ii., p. 304) speaks of "the class of solitary elephants which are known by the term of *Goondapo* in India,

size of its tusks. I remembered that rogue elephants are said to be very ferocious. So much the better, I thought. I had killed a good deal of game, and I had ceased to be afraid of any of them, though I felt that hunting was no child's play.

You must not think that we were standing up all this time in sight of the elephant. As soon as we had seen him, we lay down and hid ourselves in the forest in such a manner as not to lose sight of him. Then we held a grand council, and talked over what must be done to bag the beast.

The grass was burnt in every direction to the leeward of him, and we dared not risk approaching him from the windward for fear he should smell us. What was to be done? The eyes of my men were fixed upon me with a keenly inquisitive look. They expected me to tell them what I thought best to do about the matter.

I looked at the country, and saw that the grass was very short; and, after taking account of all the chances of approach, I was compelled to admit that I could not manage to get near the beast myself with any certainty. I could not crawl on the ground; my clothes were sure to be seen by the elephant; therefore, as a sensible hunter, I was reluctantly compelled to resign in favor of Aboko, who, I thought, was the best man for the difficult undertaking. His eyes glistened with pleasure as he thought that now he could show his skill. Besides, among hunters there is something pleasant and exciting in knowing that you are about to rush into danger.

After cocking his musket, Aboko dropped down in the

and from their vicious propensities and predatory habits are called Hora, or Rogues, in Ceylon."

short grass, and began to creep up to the elephant slowly on his belly. The rest of us remained where we had held our council, and watched Aboko as he glided through the grass for all the world like a huge boa constrictor; for, from the slight glimpses we caught, his back, as he moved farther and farther away from us, resembled nothing so much as the folds of a great serpent winding his way along. Finally we could no longer distinguish any motion. Then all was silence. I could hear the beating of my heart distinctly, I was so excited.

The elephant was standing still, when suddenly the sharp report of a gun rang through the woods and over the plain, and elicited screams of surprise from sundry scared monkeys who were on the branches of a tree close by us. I saw the huge beast helplessly tottering, till he finally threw up his trunk, and fell in a dead mass at the foot of a tree. Then the black body of Aboko rose: the snake-like creature had become a man again. A wild hurrah of joy escaped from us; I waved my old hat, and threw it into the air, and we all made a run for the elephant. When we arrived, there stood Aboko by the side of the huge beast, calm as if nothing had happened, except that his body was shining with sweat. He did not say a word, but looked at me, and then at the beast, and then at me again, as if to say, "You see, Chaillu, you did right to send me. Have I not killed the elephant?"

The men began to shout with excitement at such a good shot. "Aboko is a man," said they, as we looked again at the beast, whose flesh was still quivering with the death-agony. Aboko's bullet had entered his head a little below the ear, and, striking the brain, was at once fatal.

Aboko began to make fetich marks on the ground around the body. After this was done, we took an axe, which Fasiko had carried with him, and broke the skull, in order to get out the two tusks, and very large tusks they were.

Of course we could not carry off the elephant, so Aboko and I slept that night near our prize on the grass and under the tree. Niamkala and Fasiko had started for the camp to tell the men the news, and the next morning all the men hurried out. While quietly resting under the shade of a tree close to the elephant, I spied them coming. As soon as they recognized us they shouted, and, when near enough, they made a spring at Aboko and then at the elephant. All the cutlasses, all the axes and knives that were in the camp, had been sharpened and brought out. Then the cutting up of the elephant took place. He was not very fat. What a huge beast he was! What a huge liver he had! What an enormous heart, too!

The trunk, being considered a choice morsel, was cut into small pieces. The meat was to be smoked immediately, and then carried to Sangatanga, to be sold and given away. Great bargains were looming before the men's eyes; they were all to get rich by selling the elephant's meat.

I never saw men more happy than these poor fellows were. The negroes believe in eating. Mine ate nothing but meat, and they ate such quantities of it that several of them got sick, and I was obliged to give them laudanum in brandy to cure them. They almost finished my little stock of brandy.

The camp was full of meat, and as we had no salt, the odor that came from it was not particularly agreeable

Indeed, I had to have a separate shanty built on one side, and to the windward of the camp. I could not stand the stench.

At night the negroes lay around the fires, the jolliest of mortals, drinking palm wine, which they made regularly from the neighboring palm-trees, and smoking tobacco when I was generous enough to give them some. In fact, they were as honest a set of negroes as I had met with any where—really good fellows.

As time passed on, you must not think that I did nothing but kill animals. I rambled through the forest, and studied every thing I saw. Sometimes, when too far away from the camp, and after a day of hard hunting, I slept soundly under a tree by the side of a big fire, with my gun by my side. I thought I would go hunting one day for wild animals; on another, for birds; and, when too tired to travel, I would remain in the camp, sleeping sweetly on my primitive conch, which consisted of a couple of mats spread on the bare and soft earth, with a thick blanket for cover, the foliage of a tree, and the blue starlit sky being my canopy and roof. I had given up sleeping upon bare sticks, finding it too hard.

As fresh boar-tracks had been seen near the camp, I could not resist the temptation of having another hunt after that savage beast. However tired I might be, I could hardly keep still whenever news came that game was near us. I was always in the hope of finding some new animal, or something curious to stuff and bring home, to show what I had done.

We had not gone far when we heard, to the right of us, the grunting of some wild boars. As they are very wild, we jumped hastily behind a fallen tree to hide our selves. In our haste to do this, I heedlessly stepped upon something in my path, and, looking down, found I was running upon an immense serpent—a huge python, which lay snugly coiled up beside the tree. Happily he was in a state of stupefaction, consequent, probably, on having eaten too heavy a dinner. He scarcely moved, and did not raise his head. I ran to Niamkala, and borrowed a kind of heavy cutlass which he carried with him, and with a blow of this I cut the python in two pieces, which instantly began to squirm about in a very snaky and horrible way. During his death-struggle the monster disgorged the body of a young gazelle, which was in a half-digested condition. This python was not quite twenty feet long—a pretty good-sized one, you may judge.

The noise we made in killing the snake of course frightened the wild pigs. We pursued them, and succeeded, by good management, and after a hard chase of an hour, in coming up with the herd. They were ten in number, and we managed to bag two. They were not very large. Besides these pigs, my hunters carried the two halves of the serpent to the camp. We were received there with demonstrations of joy. They made a kind of soup with the boa, and seemed to relish it very much. I did not taste it, and can therefore say nothing against it.

I never saw a country like this for game. There was so much prairie land that it reminded me of Southern Africa. The contrast with the great forest, where I had traveled for days without seeing any thing, was very great.

For a few days I remained quiet in the camp. The men had in the mean time been hunting and exploring in various directions. As they reported that great herds of buffalo frequented every night a prairie situated about ten miles from our camp, I determined to have a hunt for them. I was very fond of buffaloes, at least of their meat.

We set out, and left our camp just before sunset. Our route was through the midst of prairie land, and by eight o'clock in the evening we reached the forest beyond. There we hoped to find our game, and, securing for ourselves safe hiding-places in the woods on the edge of the plain, we lay down and waited.

Now waiting is generally tedious, but waiting in a cold night, from eight to two o'clock, every moment expecting that which does not come, is apt to try one's patience severely. Mine was entirely gone, and I wished myself comfortably under my blanket in camp, when suddenly the buffaloes came. Aboko heard them coming, and presently a herd of about twenty-five animals emerged from the woods, and scattered quietly about the grassy plain.

The moon was going down, and we could see from our hiding-places the long shadows of the buffaloes silently gliding one way or another, but never near enough to us for a shot. Soon they felt quite at ease, and began feeding, ever and anon gamboling sportively with one another. Seeing them engaged, we crawled toward them slowly and with great care. We had almost got within safe range, when a sudden change of wind discovered us to them. They snuffed up the air suspiciously, and, instantly gathering together, they disappeared in the woods.

There was ill luck! My hunters cursed in Shekiani, and I grumbled in several languages. But there was still hope. Silently we crawled back to our lair, and waited patiently for two mortal hours; when at last two—a bull and a cow—stalked leisurely into the fields and began to crop the grass. It was now dark. The moon had gone down, leaving us only the uncertain light of the stars. We watched the motion of the buffaloes until we thought we could venture, and then silently crawled toward them again. This time we got within range. I chose the bull for my shot, and Niamkala took the cow, while Aboko was ready to second me with his gun in case I should not kill my animal. We fired both at once, and by good luck, for the light was not enough to afford a chance for a fair shot, both the animals fell down dead.

Daylight soon appeared, and we resolved to return to the camp and send men to bring in the meat, thinking that no wild beasts would trouble our prizes at such unseasonable hours. Aboko and Niamkala first cut off the bushy tails of black glossy hair, and then we made for the camp, where they showed to our companions these trophies of our chase. The men made haste, and reached the place early, but not before the cow was half eaten by a hungry leopard. The poor leopard who ventured out so early in the morning must have been nearly famished. I did not grudge him his meal, though I should have liked to watch for him and shoot him, had I thought of his coming, for I had plenty of friends to whom I could have given his skin on my return.

A few days afterward we broke up our camp, and loaded ourselves with the birds and beasts I had killed and prepared, and also with the meat which my men had smoked; and all the time they were boasting of how much tobacco and other dainties they would get for this.

They seemed very jolly, though groaning under their burdens; and I was pleased to see them so happy. The specimens of the *Bos brachicheros* were an inconvenient load, and I was obliged to be very careful with them.

When I reached Sangatanga, I found that the king was in worse health than he was when I had left. He was alarmed, fearing he would die. He remarked that it was singular he had been taken worse immediately after my departure; and that, in fact, he grew sick on the very night when I slept in his house.

FISHING.

CHAPTER XIX.

NOT long after we returned from our hunting expedition I prepared to go to Fetich Point on a fishing excursion. For this purpose it was necessary to have canoes. I had called on King Bango since I returned, but, remembering the rats, had respectfully declined the hospitality of his palace. Nevertheless, he remained my friend, and gave me all the men I wanted.

I not only wanted to fish, but I also wished to see the burial-ground of the Oroungous, which is not far from Fetich Point. There were also some enormous turtles on Fetich Point, I was told, and I wished to catch some of them.

My old hunting friend, Fasiko, had got together a

party of forty men. Besides Fetich Point, I was to visit the Fetich River and the end of Cape Lopez. There being no houses whatever there, the women had prepared for us a great quantity of powdered manioc, baskets of ground-nuts, sweet potatoes, and bunches of plantain. We had a very large outfit. Fasiko got together a lot of mats to sleep upon, and kettles to cook in, and a great quantity of salt, with which to salt the fish we hoped to catch. We had several fish-nets made of the fibre of a vine. We also had fish-hooks; and I took an enormous hook to catch sharks. I always had a hatred of sharks, they are such savage and voracious monsters.

We had a great number of baskets. The women carried these to put the fish in. We did not forget guns; for leopards lurk in the jungle, on the south side of the cape, and the boa hangs from the trees, waiting for his prey. If you got up early there, as every body at a watering-place should, you could see huge elephants trotting down along the beach, and cooling their tender toes in the surf.

It was a very jolly party, for Cape Lopez is the Cape May, or Nahant of Sangatanga. The dry season there answers to our July, when "every body that is any body" is supposed to be "out of town and down by the seaside."

Niamkala and Aboko were of the party, for we were great friends, and wherever I went they wanted to go. They were slaves of King Bango; but we had shared the same dangers, we had shared the same pleasures.

At last every thing was ready. I embarked in the biggest canoe, which was manned by sixteen oarsmen. As usual, there was a good deal of shouting and bustle before we got off. The sails, made with matting, were unfurled, and we set out across the bay. We had an exciting race to see which canoe was the fastest. There was a stiff breeze; but, unfortunately, the wind was nearly in our faces, so that our sails were of little use. The men worked lustily at their paddles, and, as they paddled, they sang their wild canoe songs. The morning was clear and bright, but in the afternoon the sky became clouded. We reached Fetich Point a little before sunset, and the men, who seemed as lively and jolly as could be, at once cast their net, in a way not materially different from our mode of using the hand-net, and made a great haul of fish, the principal part of which were mullets. How beautiful they looked! They seemed like silver fish.

The men went immediately in search of firewood. We lighted our fires, and, having cooked and eaten our fish, which were delicious, we prepared for a night's rest by spreading mats upon the sand. It was terribly cold, for we were not sheltered from the wind, which went right through my blanket.

Not far from Fetich Point is the River Tetica, one of the tributaries of the Nazareth River. The Nazareth falls into the bay through a tangled, dreary, and poisonous tract of back country, consisting of mangrove swamps, like those I have described on the Monda River, and where, I dare say, no animals except serpents are to be found. There are no human habitations there.

In the morning I wished to see the Oroungou burial-ground before starting for Cape Lopez itself. It lay about a mile from our camp, toward Sangatanga, from which it is distant about half a day's pull in a canoe.

It was only by the promise of a large reward that I persuaded Niamkala to accompany me. The negroes visit the place only on funeral errands, and hold it in the greatest awe, conceiving that here the spirits of their ancestors wander about, and that they are not lightly to be disturbed.

Niamkala and I left the camp, and, following the sea shore, soon reached the place. It is in a grove of noble trees, many of them of magnificent size and shape. As I have said, the natives hold the place in great reverence.

The grove is by the sea. It is entirely cleared of underbrush; and, as the wind sighs through the dense foliage of the trees, and whispers in their darkened, somewhat gloomy recesses, there is something awful about the place. I thought how many lives had been sacrificed on these graves.

Niamkala stood in silence by the strand, while I entered the domain of the Oroungou dead.

The corpses are not put below the surface. They lie about beneath the trees, in huge wooden coffins, many of which were made of trees. By far the greater number were crumbling away. Some new ones betokened recent arrivals. The corpses of some had only been surrounded with a mat. Here was a coffin falling to pieces, and disclosing a grinning skeleton within. On the other side were skeletons, already without their covers, which lay in the dirt beside them. Every where were bleached bones and mouldering remains. It was curious to see the brass anklets and bracelets, in which some Oroungou maiden or wife had been buried, still surrounding her whitened bones, and to note the remains of articles which had been laid in the coffin or put by the side of some

11

wealthy fellow now crumbling to dust. What do you think these articles were? Umbrellas, guns, spears, knives, bracelets, bottles, cooking-pots, swords, plates, jugs, glasses, etc.

In some places there remained only little heaps of shapeless dust, from which some copper, or iron, or ivory ornaments, or broken pieces of the articles I have just mentioned, gleamed out, to prove that here, too, once lay a corpse, and exemplifying the saying of the Bible, " Dust to dust thou shalt return." I could not help saying to myself, " Man, what art thou?"

Suddenly I came to a corpse that must have been put there only the day before. The man looked asleep, for death does not show its pallor in the face of the negro as it does in that of the white man. This corpse had been dressed in a coat, and wore a necklace of beads. By his side stood a jar, a cooking-pot, and a few other articles, which his friend, or his heir, had put by his side.

Passing on into a yet more sombre gloom, I came at last to the grave of old King Pass-all, the brother of the present king. Niamkala had pointed out to me the place where I should find it. The huge coffin lay on the ground, and was surrounded on every side with great chests, which contained some of the property of his deceased majesty. Many of them were tumbling down, and the property destroyed. The wood, as well as the goods, had been eaten up by the white ants. Among some of these chests, and on the top of them, were piled huge earthenware jugs, glasses, mugs, plates, iron pots, and brass kettles. Iron and copper rings, and beads, were scattered around, with other precious things which Pass-all had determined to carry to the grave with him. There lay also the ghastly skeletons of the poor slaves, who, to the number of one hundred, were killed when the king died, that he might not pass into the other world without due attendance.

It was a grim sight, and one which filled me with a sadder feeling than ever the disgusting slave barracoons had given me.

The land breeze was blowing when I returned, and we started for the sandy point of the cape. It is a curious beach, very low, and covered with a short scrub, which hides a part of the view, while the sand ahead is undistinguishable at a distance from the water, above which it barely rises. I was repeatedly disappointed, thinking we had come to the end, when, in fact, we had before us a long narrow sand-spit. Finally we reached the extreme end, and landed in smooth water on the inside of the spit.

The point gains continually upon the sea. Every year a little more sand appears above the water, while the line of short shrubs, which acts as a kind of dam or breakwater, is also extended, and holds the new land firm against the encroachments of old Neptune.

Among these shrubs we built our camp, and here for some days we had a very pleasant and lively time. The weather was delightful; we had no rain, it being the dry season, and we were not afraid of the awful tornadoes.

TURNING TURTLES JUST BEFORE SUNRISE.

CHAPTER XX.

OUR CAMP AT POINT FETICH. — AN AFRICAN WATERING PLACE. — FISHING, BUT NOT BATHING. — THE SHARKS. — CURING MULLETS, ETC.—TURNING TURTLES.—BIRD-SHOOT. ING.—A LEOPARD SPRINGS UPON US.

OUR camp presented a very picturesque appearance, and was very unlike the one described a little while ago, and of which I gave you a picture. Here each man had built for himself a cosy shade with mats, which, by the way, are very beautiful. These mats are about five or six feet in length and three feet wide. We made our walls of them, so that we were sheltered from the wind. Our houses looked very much like large boxes.

As usual, the first day was occupied in making every thing comfortable and in collecting fire-wood, which it was not so easy a matter to find, for the shrubs did not furnish much, and we had to go far to get it; afterward it was made the business of the children to gather brush-wood for the fires, and the poor children had hard work too.

We built large *oralas*, or frames, on which to dry the fish when salted, or to smoke it by lighting a fire be-neath, in which case the oralas were built higher.

Some had brought with them large copper dishes, call-ed Neptunes, which look like gigantic plates, in which they were to boil down salt water to get supplies of salt for salting the fish, and to take home with them. Some of the women were all day making salt; when made, it was packed securely in baskets, and placed near the fire to keep it dry.

Every day we had some new kind of fish to eat or to salt down.

As for myself, as I have said, I had brought along an immense shark-hook and a stout rope. The hook was attached to a strong chain two feet long, so that the teeth of the sharks could not cut the line if they should swal-low the piece of meat or the large fish put on the hook for a bait.

There were so many sharks swarming in the waters about the cape that they were often almost washed upon the beach by the waves. I never saw such an immense number. The Chinese, who eat sharks' fins, would find enough here to glut the Canton market. In truth, I sometimes trembled when in a canoe at the idea that it might upset, for if that had happened, in a short time I should have been seized by a dozen hungry sharks, been dragged to the bottom of the sea, and there been devoured. These sharks are certainly the lions and tigers of the water: they show no mercy. The very sight of them is horrible, for you can not help thinking and saying to yourself, " I wonder how many people this shark has eaten!" There is a superstition among sailors that whenever there is a sick person aboard the sharks will follow the ship, watching for the corpse to be thrown overboard.

I confess I felt a hatred for sharks, and while at Cape Lopez I killed as many of them as I could. Almost every day you could have seen me in a canoe near the shore, throwing my shark-hook into the sea, and after a while making for the beach, and calling all the men together to pull with all our might, and draw in my victim. One day I took a blue-skin shark. He was a tremendous fellow. I thought we should never be able to haul him ashore, or that the line would part. It took us an hour before we saw him safely on the beach. Now and then I thought he would get the better of us, and that we should have to let the line go, or be pulled into the water. At last he came right up on the beach, and a great shout of victory welcomed him. Aboko was ready for him, and with a powerful axe he gave him a tremendous blow that cut off his tail. Then we smashed his head, and cut his body into several pieces, which quivered to and fro for some time. In his stomach we found a great number of fish. If I remember correctly, he had six or seven rows of teeth, and such ugly teeth! I pity the poor man whose leg should unfortunately get caught between them.

Hardly a day passed that I did not catch some sharks, and then for a bait I used to put on my hook a piece of

their own flesh, which, like the Cannibals, they ate apparently without any remorse.

There is another species of shark, of a gray, leaden
color, which is shorter and thicker than the blue-skin
shark; it has a broader head, and a much wider mouth,
and is far more voracious. This species is the most common. It will attack a man in shallow water. I remember a poor boy who was going to his canoe, where the
water was not up to his knees, when suddenly, just as he
was going to get in, he was seized by his leg and dragged
into the water by one of these terrible sharks, which had
probably been for some time swimming along the beach
watching for prey. In that country it is dangerous to
bathe in the sea, and I did not attempt to do so. So
much for the sharks.

Every day, on the muddy banks near the mouth of
the Fetich River, we hauled in with our nets a great
quantity of mullets and other fish. These were split
open, cleaned, salted, dried, and smoked, and then packed
away in baskets.

Sometimes, early in the morning, we went out to turn
turtles. To do this we had to start before daylight.
They come on the beach to lay their eggs in the sand,
which the sea does not reach. There the heat of the sun
hatches them out. I have sometimes spied these turtles
early in the morning coming out of the water and as-
cending the beach in a clumsy way, until they reached
the dry spot where they wished to lay their eggs. After
laying them, they manage to cover them with sand. I
should have liked very much to see the young ones come
out of their eggs. How funny the little wee turtles
must look! But I have never been so fortunate.

One day we caught a turtle which had only three legs; the fourth had been bitten off, no doubt by a hungry shark. The wound had got well, and must have been made long before we caught the turtle.

Would you like to know how we captured turtles?

As soon as they see people coming toward them they generally make for the water. Then we rush with all speed upon the unwieldy turtle, and with one jerk roll it over on its back, where it lies, vainly struggling to recover its legs. Then we kill it.

Hundreds of eggs were sometimes found in one turtle. I was very fond of them when found in the body, otherwise I did not like them. They made splendid omelettes.

The turtles look very curious when they lie fast asleep on the water. At such times I am told that, with great care, they may be approached and captured.

Besides fishing, we had hunting also. South of the cape was a dense forest, in which might be found most of the animals that live in African woods. Several times we saw elephants on the beach, but we shot none. I killed a great number of sea-fowls, which fly about there in such flocks as almost to darken the air. They collect in this way in order to feed on the fish which are so plentiful.

One evening, as Aboko, Niamkala, and I were returning from a fruitless hunt in the woods, we fell in with larger game. Passing along the edge of the forest, we were suddenly startled by a deep growl. Looking quickly about, we perceived an immense male leopard just crouching for a spring upon our party. Fortunately our guns were loaded with ball. No doubt we had come upon the animal unawares. In a flash we all three fired into the beast, for there was no time to be lost. He was already upon the spring, and our shot met him as he rose. He fell dead and quivering almost within a foot of Aboko, who may be said to have had a very narrow escape, for the leopard had singled him out as his prey. He was an immense animal, and his skin, which I preserved as a trophy, is most beautifully shaded and spotted; in fact, there is scarcely a more beautiful animal than the African leopard.

At the mouth of the Nazareth the savage sawfish is found. It is, no doubt, one of the most formidable, and the most terrible of the animals that live in the water.

I was quietly paddling in a little canoe when my attention was drawn to a great splashing of water a little way off. I saw at once it was a deadly combat between two animals. All round the water was white with foam. The cause of this could not be two hippopotami fighting, for in that case I should have seen them.

I approached cautiously, having first made my two rifles ready in case of an emergency. At last I came near enough to see an enormous sawfish attacking a large shark. It was a fearful combat; both fought with desperation. But what could the shark do against the powerful saw of his antagonist?

At last they came too near my canoe. I moved off lest they might attack my canoe, for they would have made short work of my small frail boat, and a single blow of the sawfish would have disabled me. Each tooth of the saw must have been two inches long, and there were, I should say, forty on each side; the saw was about five feet long. In the end, the sawfish, more active than the shark, gave him a terrible blow, making his teeth go right through the flesh of the shark. Several such blows were quickly delivered, and all became still, the foam ceased, and the water resumed its accustomed stillness. I paddled toward the scene, when suddenly I saw at the bottom of the river what I recognized to be a great shark· it was dead, and lay on its back, showing its belly. The body was frightfully lacerated.

The sawfish had killed its antagonist, and left the field of battle, and only the blood of the shark stained the water.

In the Bay of Cape Lopez, in the month of July, I could see whales playing about in every direction, and sending water high into the air.

They come at that time of the year with their young; and the water of the bay being very quiet, they enjoy there the sea, and the young whales get strong before they go into the broad ocean. Very pretty it looks to see them swimming by the side of their big mothers.

Year after year the whales came, always in July; but one year the whalers found them out, and made war upon them; and now, when July comes, they are no more to be seen, for the whale is very intelligent, and knows well the places where he is not safe; so they look out for some other unfrequented bay wherein to play and train their young.

Besides the whale, all the year round can be seen what the sailor commonly calls the *bottle-nose*, an enormous fish, not so big as a whale, but nevertheless of great size. It is of the whale family.

SCHOONER CAUGHT IN A TORNADO.

CHAPTER XXI.

BOUND FOR THE INTERIOR.—A SEA VOYAGE.—A TORNADO.
—WE REACH THE FERNAND-VAZ.—SANGALA WISHES TO
DETAIN ME.—A NIGHT ALARM.—PROSPECT OF A WAR.
—ARRAYED FOR BATTLE.—A COMPROMISE.—MY COMMI
FRIENDS.

I HAVE been a great wanderer. On the 5th of February, 1857, I was on board of a little schooner of forty-
five tons burden, bound for the mouth of a river called
Fernand-Vaz. From there I expected to penetrate into
the interior. I was on my way to a wild and unexplored
region.

The name of the schooner was the Caroline. She was

full of provisions and goods for the long journey I had
to undertake, for I intended to make a very long exploration before my return to America.   The captain was
a Portuguese negro, Cornillo by name.   The crew, seven
in number, were Mpongwes, Mbingos, and Croomen, not
more than two of whom could understand each other,
and not a soul could properly understand the captain.   A
fine prospect for the voyage !

I got aboard at daylight, and should have been glad to
go immediately on shore again ; but, by dint of steady
shouting, and a great deal of standing idle, with a little
work now and then, we got the anchor up just at dusk.
The captain did not like to leave port on Friday.   I told
him I would take the responsibility.   He asked what
good that would do him if he went to the bottom.   It
appears that the Portuguese have the same absurd superstitions as many of the sailors of other nations.

No sooner had we got into the swell than our two black
women, and every man on board (except the captain), got
sea-sick.   The cook was unable to get the breakfast next
morning ; and the men were lying about, looking like dying fish.

We set sail from the Gaboon River, and hoped to get
down to the Commi country in five days ; but for four
days after starting we had light wind and a contrary
current, and on the fifth day we were caught in such a
storm at sea as I hope never to experience again.

The steering went on so badly when Captain Cornillo
was below that I was forced to stand watch myself.   I
had been steering for four hours, and had been perhaps
one hour in my berth, when I was awakened from a
sound sleep by the captain's voice giving orders to take

down the mainsail. I sprang on deck immediately, knowing there must be at least a heavy squall coming. But
no sooner did I cast my eyes to the leeward than I saw
how imminent the danger was. A tornado was coming
down upon us. The black clouds which had gathered
about the horizon were becoming lurid white with start-
ling quickness. It seemed almost as if they were lit up
by lightning. The tornado was sweeping along, and in
a moment would be upon us. As yet all was still—still
as death. There was not a breath of wind.

I turned to see if the mainsail was down, but found
that nothing had been done. The captain was shouting
from the wheel; the men were also shouting and running about, half scared to death; and, in the pitchy darkness (for I could not see my hands when held close before my eyes), no one could find the halliards. In the
midst of our trouble the wind came roaring down upon
us. I seized a knife, determined to cut every thing away;
but just then somebody let go the halliards, and, in the
nick of time, the mainsail came halfway down. The tornado was upon us. The jibs flew away in rags in a moment. The vessel was thrown upon her beam-ends. The
water rushed over her deck, and the men sang out that
they were drowning, as, in fact, we should have been in
a very few minutes. Happily, the wind shifted a little,
and by the light of some very vivid lightning we seized
on the mainsail like men that felt it was their last hope,
and pulled it down, holding it so that the wind should
not catch it again. The vessel righted, and in less than
twenty minutes the squall died away, and was succeeded
by a driving rain, which poured down in such torrents
that in a very short time I was drenched to the skin

The lightning and thunder were something terrific. I was afraid of the lightning striking us, as the Caroline had no lightning-rod, and we had 'powder enough on board to blow us all to atoms. The deck was so leaky that even below I could not get protection from the rain.

The next morning we had no jibs, and our other sails were severely damaged. To add to our difficulties, no one on board, not even the captain, knew where we were. At that time I knew not how to make astronomical observations. The captain was in the habit of bringing up, every day, an old quadrant, but about the use of it he knew as much as a cow does about a musket.

At last we made the land. A canoe came on board, and we asked where we were. We found that we must be somewhere near Cape St. Catharine, and therefore a good many miles south of the mouth of the Fernand-Vaz, the place where I was bound; so we turned about to retrace our path. Sailing close in shore, when I passed the village of Aniambia, or Big Camma, the natives came with a message from their king, offering me two slaves if I would stay with him.

I was immovable, for I had set my heart on going to the Fernand-Vaz River, of which I heard a good deal from my friend Aboko while in the Cape Lopez regions. As we approached that river, the vast column of water, pushing seaward, forced its separate way through the ocean for at least four or five miles, and the water there was almost fresh, and seemed a separate current in the sea.

At last we came to the mouth of the Fernand-Vaz, and our fame had gone before us. Some of the Commi people, the inhabitants of the Fernand-Vaz, had seen me be fore at Cape Lopez. The news had spread that I wanted to settle at the village of a chief called Rampano; so, as we passed his sea-shore village, a canoe came off to ask me to land; but, as the breakers were rather formidable, I begged to be excused.

Rampano's men wanted much to hug me, and were so extravagant in their joy that I had to order them to keep their hands off, their shining and oily bodies having quite soiled my clothes. They went back to the king to tell him the good news. I kept one of these men on board for a pilot, being now anxious to get across the intricate bar, and fairly into the river, before dark.

As we sailed along up the river, canoes belonging to different villages shot out to meet us, and presently I had a crowd alongside anxious to come on board, and sufficient almost to sink us. They took me for a slaver at first, and their joy was unbounded, for there is nothing the African loves so much as to sell his fellow-men. They immediately called out their names in Portuguese: one was Don Miguel, another Don Pedro, another Don Francisco. They began to jabber away in Portuguese. Where they had learned this language I could not tell, unless it were in Sangatanga. I could not understand them, so I sent my captain to talk with them. He had some difficulty to persuade them that I came on no such errand as slave-trading. They insisted that I had, and that the vessel looked exactly like a slaver. They said we must buy some of their slaves; they had plenty of them.

They insisted that I should not go to Rampano. I should put up a factory in their place. They belonged to Elindé, a town just at the mouth of the Fernand-Vaz, whose king is named Sangala. They praised the power and greatness of Sangala, and derided poor Ranpano, until I had to order all hands ashore for the night, being anxious to get a good quiet sleep to prepare for the morrow.

During the night, the men on watch said they heard the paddling of a canoe coming toward us. What could it be? Let us be ready. These men might be coming to board us and make war. At length the canoe came within hailing distance; we shouted to them. (I may say that the Commi speak the same language as the Oroungou people — the inhabitants of Cape Lopez.) They came, they said, with a message from King Sangala. I recognized the voice of the head man in the canoe to be that of Nchouga. He was brother of King Bango, of Cape Lopez. Bango had accused Nchouga of bewitching him, whereupon the latter, to save his life, fled from the country, and, having married one of the daughters of Sangala, he came to his father-in-law for protection.

Nchouga was a very cunning fellow; fortunately I knew him well, and he could not fool me so easily as he thought. He came to tell me that Sangala was the master of all the river; that he was a very great king; that he would not let me go to Ranpano, who was only a vassal of the great Sangala; therefore he advised me as a friend—an old friend—to go ashore at Elindé.

I could read the cunning rogue. He had been one of the greatest rascals of Cape Lopez, and his slave-dealings had not improved him. So I sent Nchouga off: I wanted to go to sleep. He had come out to test me; they thought I was a green hand at slave-trading.

Early next morning Sangala sent off a boat for me. On my arrival at Elindé, which village was about two miles from the river's mouth, I was conducted to the best house. Hither presently came King Sangala, who, in order to nerve himself for the occasion, had got drunk, and came attended by a great crowd of eager subjects. He grew very angry when I stated my intention of pass- ing up the river and going to Ranpano, and also into the interior. He declared that I should not go; he was the big king there and everywhere all over the world, and I must settle in his town.

I declared that I should go on. Sometimes I wonder that they did not at once make me a prisoner.

We had some sharp words, and I explained to his majesty that I was an old African traveler, and saw through all his lies; that he was not the big king of the country, as he said. Then he said I might go wherever I liked provided I would have a factory built in his vil- lage; but I offered to " dash" him (give him some pres- ents).

He refused this offer; and now Ranpano, having just come, assured me that I should be backed· up. I told Sangala I should force my way up. Sangala and all his people shouted with all their might that there should be war; Sangala, as he got up to say so, reeled and tumbled down, he was so drunk.

So I left Sangala. By that time it rained so hard that no one followed us. It is wonderful how a crowd is dis persed by a shower of rain.

A great palaver was looming up; the excitement had spread over the country. In the mean time I had suc- ceeded in going to Ranpano's village, situated up the

12

river, five or six miles above Elindé. Ranpano gave me as much land as I wanted. My goods must come to his village; but it seemed that they could not be brought there without great trouble. Our canoes would be attacked by Sangala's people. Men would be killed; and we might be routed, unless we had a powerful force.

One morning the war drums beat. All Ranpano's friends had gathered to help fight Sangala. Canoe after canoe came in loaded with armed men, with drums beating, and all hands shouting, and waving their swords, guns, and spears. All were prepared to assist Ranpano's white man; all were anxious to burn and plunder Elindé, ready even to die in the undertaking. There was King Ritimbo, with two canoes and fifty men; King Mombon, from Sanguibiuri, also had two canoes; altogether we had no less than twenty big canoes, and could muster about three hundred men, most of whom were drunk on *mimbo* (palm wine), and as noisy and as ready for fight as drunkenness will make an African. The drums were beaten, war-songs were sung, and guns fired as we paddled down the river. All hands had their faces painted white, which is a sign of war; and were covered with fetiches and other amulets. The white chalk or ochre was a sovereign protection against danger, and their war fetiches would prevent them from being killed. I could not recognize old Ranpano, his body was so daubed with paint.

One would have supposed these terrible fellows were bent upon the most bloody of raids. I wondered if all this uproar would end in smoke; I thought it would; nor was I disappointed. As these terrible warriors approached the village of Elindé they became less demonstrative.

When they came in sight of Sangala's town, they pushed over to the other shore, out of the way, and took care to keep the Caroline between the enemy and themselves. The sight of Sangala's warriors had wrought a wonderful change in their warlike feelings. They really began to think that there might be some fighting.

We found that Sangala had also gathered his friends, and had about one hundred and fifty men ready for the fight, who probably felt about as courageous as my men did. These fellows were painted more outrageously than mine, having red as well as white applied in broad stripes. They looked like so many devils, shouting and firing guns, each side knowing their mutual lack of courage, and thinking it prudent to scare the other in advance.

My men fired guns, sung, and danced war-dances. I went on board my schooner. One small canoe on Sangala's side, with two men, who were unarmed, started from the shore toward us. This, of course, meant a palaver; they came on board of the Caroline where I was. I sent word to Sangala, pointing to two little guns we had on deck, that if he stopped me I would blow his canoes out of the water with grape-shot, and would then go and bring a man-of-war to finish him up. I loaded my guns and pistols before them. I made my men put good charges into their pieces, and showed Sangala's men the bag of bullets I loaded them with, and then sent them back, and awaited the event.

I spied them with a glass. As soon as they landed the people surrounded them; there was a grand palaver.

Presently, from Sangala, came a small canoe to ask me ashore. Sangala sent his konde (chief wife) to be hostage for my safety. I determined to go ashore, and, to show these negroes that I had no fear of them, I took the woman along with me, to her great joy. Ranpano and his brother kings protested against my rashness, as they thought it. "Why not keep Sangala's woman on board?" said they. But I told them it was not the fashion of white people to fear any thing. They looked at me as if to say, " If you are not afraid, we are." All this had its effect upon them, and Ranpano and his brother kings were evidently impressed, and so also was old Sangala when he saw me come with his wife by my side.

We met on neutral ground outside his town. His army was drawn up in battle array, and made a fine savage display, many of the men wearing beautiful leopard-skins about their waists. They came up to us at full trot when we were seated, and made as though they would spear us all ; and, if Sangala had not been close to me, I should have thought it was to be the end of us all. Ranpano kept whispering in my ears, "Why did you not keep Sangala's wife on board?"

But this advance upon us was only a kind of military salute. Sangala this time had become more gentle; he was not drunk, and, thinking that perhaps there might really be a fight, he had become very quiet. He did not wish to push matters to extremity.

Presently Sangala said he would let me pass if I would give him a barrel of rum—a big one. I refused; I said I had none. He insisted that they must rejoice and get drunk. He wanted to get drunk for several days, and drink rum to his heart's content. At last the palaver was settled, and I gave him many presents, and thereafter King Sangala became one of my best friends.

Ranpano was delighted; he hugged Sangala; he swore

eternal friendship, and said that he loved him with all his heart. Sangala returned these compliments. We made a sign, agreed upon to our men, that every thing was settled. Immediately they fired guns, embarked in their canoes, and came over to Sangala's village. They made a fine display, as all their canoes came in a line, and they were singing their war-songs. They were met by Sangala's warriors; and they made a rush toward each other as if they were to have a real fight, and then all was over, and they laughed over the palaver, and swore they would not hurt each other for the world.

I need not say how glad I was that every thing had ended so well. Captain Cornillo, when every thing looked black, swore that he never would come again to this wild country; and the crew said I wanted them all to be murdered.

I found these Commi very good people. I took ashore canoe after canoe loaded with goods which might well tempt these poor negroes sorely. Many of the things were brought loose to Ranpano's, and yet not a single thing was stolen, not even the value of a penny. They were proud that I had come to settle among them. I was the first white man who had done so.

I love these Commi people dearly, and I am sure they all love me also, they took such great care of me. Ranpano was a very good king, and he always tried to please me, and so did his people. Now and then they did wrong, but these poor people knew no better, and they were sorry afterward. Not one would have tried to do me an injury, and I could sleep with my doors wide open.

CHAPTER XXII.

I IMMEDIATELY began building a substantial settlement, not an *olako*. I collected from a kind of palm-
tree a great many leaves, with which to cover the roofs
of the building I had to construct. I gathered also a
great quantity of branches from the same palm-trees,
and sticks, and poles, and all that was necessary to make
a house; and finally I succeeded in building quite a village, which I called Washington. My own house had
five rooms; it was forty-five feet long by twenty-five
feet wide, and cost me about fifty dollars. My kitchen,
which stood by itself, cost four dollars. I had a fowl-
house, containing a hundred chickens (and such nice little tiny chickens they are in that country), and a dozen
ducks. My goat-house contained eighteen goats, and
funny goats they were. You had to milk a dozen of
them to get a pint of milk. I built a powder-house
separate, for I do not like to sleep every day in a place
where there is powder. I had a dozen huts for my men.

AFRICAN BALL. KING OLENGA-YOMBI DANCING.

This was Washington in Africa, a very different place from Washington in America.

At the back of my village was a wide extent of prairie. In front was the river Npoulounai winding along; and I could see miles out on the way which I was soon to explore. The river banks were lined with the mangrove-trees; and, looking up stream, I could at almost any time see schools of hippopotami tossing and tumbling on the flats or mud banks.

I was now ready to explore the country, and go to Aniambia, where the big king of the country lived. I bought a splendid canoe, made of large trees, which I hoped would be serviceable to me in my up-river explorations. I was now anxious to be off.

Before starting I called Ranpano and all his people together, and said that I had perfect confidence in them; that I was their white man, and had come to them through much difficulty and many dangers. (Cheers.) That Sangala's people wanted me, but I was determined to live with the honest folks of Biagano (Ranpano's village). (Tremendous applause.) That I was going away for a few days, and hoped to find my goods all safe when I came back.

At this there were great shoutings of "You can go! Do not fear! We love you! You are our white man! We will take care of you!" and so on; amid which my sixteen men seized their paddles and shoved off.

At nine in the evening the moon rose, and we pulled along through what seemed a charming scene. The placid stream was shaded by the immense trees which overhung its banks, and the silence was broken now and then by the screech of some night-prowling beast, or, more frequently, by the sudden plunge of a playful herd of hippopotami, some of which came very dangerously near us, and might have upset our canoe.

Toward midnight my men became very tired, and we went ashore at a little village which was nearly deserted. We could find only three old women, who were fast asleep, and were not particularly anxious to make us welcome. I was too sleepy to stand upon ceremonies, and stowed myself away under a rough shed without walls. I had scarcely lain down when there came up suddenly one of those fierce tornadoes which pass over these countries in the rainy season. Fortunately, it was a dry tornado. In my half-sleepy state I did not care to move. As the tornado had unroofed every other shed as well as mine, nothing would have been gained by moving, even if it had rained.

The next morning we paid for our lodging, not in hard cash, but with some leaves of tobacco, and up the river we paddled until we reached a village called Igala Mandé, which is situated on the banks of the river. In a two-hours' walk through grass-fields we found numerous birds. One, in particular, was new to me, the *Mycteria senegalensis.* It had such long legs that it fairly outwalked me. I tried to catch it; but, though it would not take to its wings, it kept so far ahead that I did not even get a fair shot at it. This *Mycteria senegalensis* is a beautiful bird, and wanders here through the grass of the prairie.

There were also great flocks of a beautiful bird, whose dark golden body-plumage, and long, snow-white downy neck make a very fine and marked contrast with the green grass. Next to these, in point of number, was the snow-white *egretta*, which is found in vast flocks all along this coast.

At last we came to Aniambia. Olenga-Yombi, the king, came in from his plantation when he heard the joyful news that a white man had arrived. I paid him a state visit. He was a drunken old wretch, surrounded by a crowd of the chief men of the town. His majesty had on a thick overcoat, but no trowsers; and, early as it was, he had already taken a goodly quantity of palm wine, and was quite drunk. I was invited to sit at his right hand.

King Olenga-Yombi was one of the ugliest fellows I ever met with. He always carried with him a long stick, and when drunk he struck at his people right and left, and shouted, "I am a big king!" Happily, they manage to keep out of his way.

At nightfall I got a guide, and went out to see if I could get a shot at something larger than a bird. We had gone but a little way when my guide pointed out to me a couple of bright glowing spots visible through a piece of thick brush. The fellow trembled as he whispered "Leopard!" But I saw at once that it was only the light of a couple of fireflies which had got in proper position to make a tolerable resemblance to the glowing eyes of the dreaded leopard.

I did not think much of the bravery of my guide. What a difference between him and Aboko, Niamkala, or Fasiko! I wished that I had them with me.

At two o'clock in the morning we at last heard a grunting, which announced the approach of a herd of wild hogs. I lay in wait for them, and was fortunate enough to kill the big boar of the pack. The rest of the herd made off without showing a desire for fight.

The next day King Olenga-Yombi held a grand dance in my honor. All the king's wives, to the number of forty, and all the women in the town and neighborhood, were present.

Fortunately, the dance was held out in the street, and not in a room, as at Cape Lopez. The women were ranged on one side, the men opposite. At the end of the line sat the drummers, beating their huge tom-toms, which make an infernal din, enough to make one deaf; and, as if for this occasion the tom-toms were not entirely adequate, there was a series of old brass kettles, which also were furiously beaten. In addition, as if the noise was not yet enough, a number of boys sat near the drummers, and beat on hollow pieces of wood. What beauty they found in such music I can not tell. There was, of course, singing and shouting; and the more loudly and energetically the horrid drums were beaten, and the worse the noise on the brass kettles, the wilder were the jumps of the male Africans, and the more disgusting the contortions of the women.

As may be imagined, to beat the tom-tom is not a labor of love; the stoutest negro is worn out in an hour, and for such a night's entertainment as this a series of drummers was required.

The people enjoyed it vastly; their only regret was that they had not a barrel of rum in the midst of the street with which to refresh themselves in the pauses of the dance; but they managed to get just as drunk on palm wine, of which a great quantity was served out.

The excitement became the greatest when the king danced. His majesty was pretty drunk, and his jumps were very highly applauded. His wives bowed down to his feet while he capered about, and showed toward him the deepest veneration. The drums and kettles were belabored more furiously than ever, and the singing, or rather the shouting, became stentorian.

Of course I did not think his majesty's party pleasant enough to detain me all night. I retired, but could not sleep.

Now I think I have given you a sufficient account of a ball at Aniambia, and of how his majesty Olenga-Yombi danced.

There are two very curious fetich-houses in Aniambia, which enjoy the protection of two spirits of great power —Abambou and Mbuiri. The former is an evil spirit, a kind of devil; the latter, as far as I have been able to ascertain, is beneficent.

The little houses where these spirits sometimes condescended to come and sleep for the night were about six feet square. In the house of Abambou I saw a fire which I was told was never permitted to go out. I saw no idol, but only a large chest, on the top of which were some white and red chalk and some red parrot feathers. The chalk was used to mark the bodies of the devout.

Abambou is the devil of the Commi people. He is a wicked and mischievous fellow, who often lives near graves and burial-grounds, and is most comfortably lodged among the skeletons of the dead. He takes occasional walks through the country, and, if he gets angry at any one, he has the power to cause sickness and death. The Commi people cook food for him, which is deposited in lonely places in the woods, and there they address him in a flattering manner, and ask him to be good to them, and, in consideration of their gifts, and of the great

eare they take of him, to let them alone. I was present
once at a meeting where Abambou was being addressed
in public. They cried continually, "Now we are well!
Now we are satisfied! Now be our friend, Abambou,
and do not hurt us!"

The offerings of plantain, bananas, sugar-cane, ground-
nuts, etc., etc., are wrapped in leaves by the freemen, but
the slaves lay them on the bare ground. Sometimes
Abambou is entreated to kill the enemies of him who
is making the offering. A bed is made in Abambou's
house, and there he is believed to rest himself sometimes when he is tired going up and down the coast in
the forest.

Mbiuri, whose house I next visited, is lodged and kept
much in the same way as his rival. He is a good spirit,
but his powers are like those of Abambou, as far as I
could make out. Not being wicked, he is less zealously
worshiped.

These Commi people are full of superstition. They
believe in a third and much-dreaded spirit called Ovengua. This is the terrible catcher and *eater* of men. He
is not worshiped, and has no power over disease ; but he
wanders unceasingly through the forests, and catches and
destroys luckless travelers who cross his path. By day
he lives in dark caverns, but at night he roams freely,
and even sometimes gets into the body of a man, and
beats and kills all who come out in the dark. Sometimes, they relate, such a spirit is met and resisted by a
body of men, who wound him with spears, and even kill
him. In this case the body must be burned, and not even
the smallest bone left, lest a new Ovengua should arise
from it. There are many places where no object in the

world would induce a Commi negro to go by night, for fear of this dreadful monster.

They have a singular belief that when a person dies who has been bewitched, the bones of his body leave the grave one by one, and form in a single line united to each other, which line of bones gradually becomes an Ovengua.

It is not an easy matter to get at the religious notions of these people. They themselves have no well-defined ideas of them, and on many points they are not very communicative.

I suppose they think that sometimes the Ovengua is in a man; hence they kill him, and burn his body.

Of course the Commi people, like all other negroes, are firm believers in witchcraft.

Not very far from Aniambia there is a place in the forest which is supposed to be haunted by the spirit of a crazy woman, who, some hundreds of years ago, left her home. They believe that she cultivates her plantation in some hidden recess of the forest, and that she often lies in wait for travelers, whom she beats and kills out of pure malice.

While at Aniambia I had a great adventure with a *bos brachicheros*, which might have ended in a terrible way. I started out early one day to try and get a shot at some buffaloes which were said to be in the prairie at the back of the town. I had been an hour on the plains with Ifouta, a hunter, when we came upon a bull feeding in the midst of a little prairie surrounded by woods, which made an approach easy. I remember well how beautiful the animal looked. Ifouta walked round through the jungle opposite to where I lay in wait; for, if the

animal should take fright at him, it might fly toward
me. When he reached the right position, Ifouta began
to crawl, in the hunter's fashion, through the grass toward his prey. All went well till he came near enough
for a shot. Just then, unluckily, the bull saw him. Ifouta immediately fired. It was a long shot, and he only
wounded the beast, which, quite infuriated, immediately
rushed upon him. It was now that poor Ifouta lost his
presence of mind. In such cases, which are continually
happening to those who hunt the *bos brachicheros*, the
proper course for the hunter is to remain perfectly quiet
till the beast is within a jump of him, then to step nimbly to one side, and let him rush past. But Ifouta got
up and ran.

The bull ran faster than he, and in a moment had
him on his horns. He tossed him high into the air,
once, twice, thrice, before I could come up; for, as soon
as I saw what had happened, I ran as fast as I could to
the rescue, and my shouts drew the bull's fury upon myself. He left Ifouta, and came rushing at me, thinking
that he would serve me as he had just served Ifouta.
Master Bull was sadly mistaken. I took a good aim,
and down came the bull, to rise no more.

Ifouta proved to be considerably bruised; but, on the
whole, he was more scared than hurt. It was fortunate
for him that the horns of these buffaloes slant backward
a good deal, and are curved.

CAPTURING A YOUNG GORILLA.

CHAPTER XXIII.

CAPTURE OF A YOUNG GORILLA.—I CALL HIM "FIGHTING
JOE."—HIS STRENGTH AND BAD TEMPER.—HE PROVES
UNTAMABLE.—JOE ESCAPES.—RECAPTURED.—ESCAPES
AGAIN.—UNPLEASANT TO HANDLE.—DEATH OF FIGHTING
JOE.

I REMEMBER well the day when I first possessed a live
gorilla. Yes, a gorilla that could roar; a young gorilla
alive! He was captured not far from Cape St. Catharine, and dragged into Washington.

My hunters were five in number, and were walking
very silently through the forest, when suddenly the silence was broken by the cry of a young gorilla for its
mother. Every thing was still. It was about noon, and
they immediately determined to follow the cry.

Soon they heard the cry again. Gun in hand, the

13

brave fellows crept noiselessly toward a clump of wood, where the baby gorilla evidently was. They knew the mother would be near; and there was a likelihood that they might encounter the male also, which they dread more than they do the mother. But they determined to risk every thing, and, if possible, to take the young one alive, knowing how pleased I should be, for I had been long trying to capture a young gorilla.

Presently they perceived the bush moving; and crawling a little farther on, in dead silence, scarcely breathing with excitement, they beheld what had seldom been seen even by negroes. A young gorilla was seated on the ground, as the picture shows you, eating some berries, which grew close to the earth. A few feet farther on sat the mother, also eating some of the fruit.

Instantly they made ready to fire; and none too soon, for the old female saw them as they raised their guns, and they had to pull triggers without delay. Happily, they wounded her mortally.

She fell on her face, the blood gushing from the wounds. The young one, hearing the noise of the guns, ran to his mother and clung to her, hiding his face and embracing her body. The hunters immediately rushed toward the two, hallooing with joy. How much I wished that I had been with them, and been so fortunate as to assist in the capture of a live gorilla!

Their shouts roused the little one, who, by this time, was covered with blood coming from his mother's wounds. He instantly let go of his mother and ran to a small tree, which he climbed with great agility. There he sat, and roared at them savagely. They were now perplexed how to get at him. What was to be done? No one cared to run the chance of being bitten by this savage little beast. They did not want to shoot him, for they knew I should never forgive them for doing so. He would not come down the tree, and they did not care to climb it after him. At last they cut down the tree, and, as it fell, they dexterously threw a cloth over the head of the young monster, and thus gained time to secure it while it was blinded. With all these precautions, one of the men received a severe bite on the hand, and another had a piece taken out of his leg.

The little brute, though very diminutive, and the merest baby in age, was astonishingly strong, and by no means good tempered. They found they could not lead him. He constantly rushed at them, showing fight, and manifesting a strong desire to take a piece, or several pieces, out of every one of their legs, which were his special objects of attack. So they were obliged to get a forked stick, in which his neck was inserted in such a way that he could not escape, and yet could be kept at a safe distance. It must have been very uncomfortable for him, but it was the only way of securing themselves against his nails and teeth, and thus he was brought to Washington.

The excitement in the village was intense as the animal was lifted out of the canoe in which he had come down the river. He roared and bellowed, and looked around wildly, with his wicked little eyes, giving fair warning that if he could get at any of us he would take his revenge. Of course, no one came in his way.

I saw that the stick hurt his neck, and immediately set about having a cage made for him. In two hours we had built a strong bamboo house, with the slats securely tied at such a distance apart that we could see the gorilla, and it could see out. We made it as strong as we could, and I was very careful to provide against every chance of his escaping. In this cage he was immediately deposited; and now, for the first time, I had a fair chance to look at my prize.

As I approached the cage he darted at me; but I could afford to have a good laugh over him, for I knew he could not get near enough to bite me. He looked at me with very savage eyes.

I named the gorilla Joe—"Fighting Joe." He was evidently not three years old, but fully able to walk alone, and possessed, for his age, very extraordinary strength. His height was about three feet and six inches. His hands and face were very black, his eyes were sunken. The hair on his head was of a reddish-brown color. It began just at the eyebrows, and came down the sides of the face to the lower jaw, just as our beards grow. The whiskers, if we may call them so, were of a blackish color. The face was smooth, and intensely black. The upper lip was covered with short coarse hair; I wondered if it was the beginning of a mustache. I found afterward that gorillas had no mustaches. The lower lip had longer hair; and I wondered also if in time an imperial would grow there. There were eyelashes too, though these were slight and thin. The eyebrows were straight.

Excepting the face, and the palms of his hands and feet, his whole body was covered with hair. On the back the hair was of an iron-gray, becoming quite dark near the arms. On the arms the hair was longer than any where else on the body, as you may see by the picture.

After I had looked carefully at the little fellow, and

knew well that he was safely locked in his cage, I ventured to approach him to say a few encouraging words. He stood in the farthest corner; but, as I approached, he bellowed, and made a precipitate rush at me. Though I retreated as quickly as I could, he succeeded in catching my trowsers' legs with the toes of one of his feet, and then retreated immediately to the farthest corner. This taught me caution ; I must not approach too near.

Shall I be able to tame him? I thought I should; but I was disappointed.

He sat in his corner, looking wickedly out of his gray eyes; and I never saw a more morose or ill-tempered face than this little beast had. I do not believe that gorillas ever smile.

Of course I had to attend to the wants of my captive. My first business in the morning was to attend on Joe. I sent for some of the forest berries which these animals are known to prefer, and placed these and a cup of water within his reach. He was exceedingly shy, and would neither eat nor drink till I had removed to a considerable distance.

The second day I found Joe fiercer than the first. He rushed savagely at any one who stood even for a moment near his cage, and seemed ready to tear us to pieces. A fine specimen of man-monkey, thought I ; a tiger under the disguise of a gorilla. I wondered what kind of a cage a full-grown gorilla would require. I should certainly not care to be his keeper.

I threw Joe pieces of pine-apple leaves, and I noticed that he ate only the white part. There seemed to be no difficulty about his food as long as it was gathered from his native woods, but he refused all other kinds

of food.   He was very fond of bananas and ripe plantains.

The third day Joe was still more morose and savage,
bellowing when any person approached, or retiring to a
distant corner to make a rush upon them.

On the fourth day, while no one was near, the little
rascal succeeded in forcing apart two of the bamboo
sticks which composed his cage, and made his escape.   I
came up just as his flight was discovered, and immediately got all the negroes together for pursuit.   Where had
he gone?   I was determined to surround the wood and
recapture him.   Running into my house to get one of
my guns, I was startled by an angry growl issuing from
under my low bedstead.   It was Master Joe; there was
no mistake about it; I knew his growl but too well.
Master Joe lay there hid, but anxiously watching my
movements.   I cleared out faster than I came in.   I instantly shut the windows, and called to my people to
guard the door.   When Joe saw the crowd of black faces
he became furious; and with his eyes glaring, and every
sign of rage in his little face and body, he got out from
beneath the bed.   He was about to make a rush at all
of us.   He was not afraid.   A stampede of my men took
place.   I shut the door quickly, and left Joe master of
the premises.   I preferred devising some plans for his
easy capture to exposing myself and men to his terrible
teeth; for the little rascal could bite very hard, and I did
not care to have a piece taken out of one of my legs.

How to take him was now a puzzling question.   He
had shown such strength and such rage already that I
did not care, and none of my men seemed to care, to run
the chance of getting badly beaten in a hand-to-hand

struggle, in which we were pretty sure to come off the worse. Meantime, peeping through the keyhole, I saw Master Joe standing still in the middle of the room, looking about for his enemies, and examining, with some surprise, the furniture. He seemed to think that he had never seen such things before. I watched with fear, lest the ticking of my clock should attract his attention, and perhaps lead him to an assault upon that precious article. Indeed, I should have left Joe in possession but for a fear that he would destroy the many little articles of value or curiosity I had hung about the walls, and which reminded me so much of America.

Finally, seeing Joe to be quiet, I dispatched some fellows for a net; and, opening the door quickly, I threw this over his head. Fortunately, we succeeded at the first throw in effectually entangling the young monster, who roared frightfully, and struck and kicked in every direction under the net. So fearfully was he excited that I thought he would die in a fit of rage. I took hold of the back of his neck; two men seized his arms, and another the legs; and, thus held by four men, we could hardly manage Joe.

We carried him as quickly as we could to the cage, which had been repaired, and then once more locked him in. I never saw such a furious beast in my life as he was. He darted at every one. He bit the bamboos of his cage. He glared at us with venomous and sullen eyes, and in every motion showed a temper thoroughly wicked and malicious.

After this Joe got worse than ever; and as good treatment only made him more morose and savage, I tried what starvation would do toward breaking his spirit.

Besides, it began to be troublesome to procure his food from the woods, and I wanted him to become accustomed to civilized food, which was placed before him. But he would touch nothing of the kind. How was I to bring him to America? I could not put an African forest on board. As for his temper, after starving him for twenty-four hours, all I gained was, that he came slowly up and took some berries from the forest out of my hand, and then immediately retreated to his corner to eat them. Daily attentions from me, for a fortnight more, did not bring me any farther confidence from him than this. He always snarled at me, and only when very hungry would he take even his choicest food from my hand.

At the end of this fortnight I came one day to feed him, and found that he had gnawed a bamboo to pieces slyly, and again made his escape. Luckily, he had just gone, for, as I looked around, I caught a sight of him making off on all-fours, and with great speed, across the prairie for a clump of trees.

I at once gave the alarm. I called the men up, and we gave chase, taking with us all the fishing-nets. He saw us, and, before we could head him off, made for another clump, which was thicker and larger. This we surrounded. He did not ascend a tree, but stood defiantly at the border of the wood. About one hundred and fifty of us surrounded him. As we moved up he began to yell, and made a sudden dash upon a poor fellow who was in advance. The fellow ran, and tumbled down in affright. By his fall he escaped the tender mercies of Joe's teeth, but he also detained the little rascal long enough for the nets to be thrown over him.

Four of us bore him again struggling into the village. This time I would not trust him to the cage, but fastened a small chain round his neck. This operation he resisted with all his might, and it took us quite an hour to securely chain the little fellow, whose strength was something marvelous.

Ten days after he was thus chained he died quite suddenly. He had been in good health, and ate plentifully of his natural food, which was brought every day from the forest for him. He did not seem to sicken until two days before his death. He died in some pain. To the last he continued utterly untamable, and after his chain was put on he added treachery to his other vices. He would come sometimes quite readily to eat out of my hand, but while I stood by him would suddenly—looking me all the time in the face to keep my attention—put out his foot and grasp at my leg. Several times he tore my pantaloons in this manner. A quick retreat on my part saved my legs from farther injury, but I had to be very careful in my approaches. The negroes could not come near him at all without setting him in a rage. He seemed always to remember that they captured him, and to think he had experienced rather too hard treatment at their hands; but he evidently always cherished toward me also a feeling of revenge.

After he was chained I filled a half barrel with hay and set it near him for his bed. He recognized its use at once, and it was pretty to see him shake up the hay and creep into this nest when he was tired. At night he always shook it up, and then took some hay in his hands, with which he would cover himself when he was snug in his barrel.   He often moaned, for his mother perhaps, at night.

After Joe died I stuffed his body, and brought his skin and skeleton to New York, where many saw it.   Around his neck, where the chain had been, the hair was worn off.

Poor Joe!   I wish he had lived and become tame, so that I could have brought him home with me to show to the children.

Now Poor Joe can be seen stuffed in the British Museum.

HIPPOPOTAMI AT HOME.

CHAPTER XXIV.

THE HIPPOPOTAMUS.—A DUEL.—SHOOTING ON THE RIVER.
—NEARLY UPSET.—A NIGHT-HUNT ON LAND.—MY COM-
PANION FIRES AND RUNS.—APPEARANCE AND HABITS OF
THE HIPPOPOTAMUS.

WHAT have we yonder in the water? A flock of hippopotami! Their bodies look for all the world like so
many old weather-beaten logs stranded on a mud-bank
or a sand-bar.

Every thing was still. The sun was very hot, and all
nature seemed to repose. I was concealed on the banks
of the river under a very shady tree, watching them.
Suddenly, not far from me, two huge beasts rose as by
enchantment to the surface of the water, and rushed toward each other. Their vast and hideous mouths were
opened to their utmost capacity, showing their huge

crooked tusks, which gave their mouths a savage appearance. Their eyes were flaming with rage, and each of
them put forth all his power to annihilate the other.
They seized each other with their jaws; they stabbed
and punched with their strong tusks, lacerating each other in a frightful manner; they advanced and retreated;
now they were at the top of the water, and now they
sank down to the bottom. Their blood discolored the
river, and their groans or grunts of rage were hideous to
listen to. They showed little power of strategy, but rather a piggish obstinacy in maintaining their ground, and
a frightful savageness of demeanor. The combat lasted
an hour. It was a grand sight. The water around them
was sometimes white with foam. At last one turned
about and made off, leaving the other victorious and master of the field. A few days after I killed a hippopotamus, and its thick hide was lacerated terribly. Doubtless it was one of the beasts I had seen fighting.

The hippopotamus is found in most of the rivers of
Africa which empty themselves into the Atlantic or In-
dian Ocean, but in none but the Nile of those which
empty themselves into the Mediterranean; and in the
Nile it is only met far up the river. Many as there were
of them on the Fernand-Vaz, they were more numerous
on the Ogobai.

How much sport I have had with them! How often
have I studied their habits! And now I must give you
some account of my encounters with them.

About five miles above my little settlement at Washington there was a place in the river shallow enough for
them to stand and play around, and where they remained
all day playing in the deep water, sometimes diving, but

for the most part standing on the shallows, with only their ugly noses or heads lifted out of the water.

One fine morning I went toward them. We approach. ed slowly and with caution to within thirty yards of them without seeming to attract the slightest attention from the sluggish animals. One might have asked himself, " Are they hippopotami or not?" Stopping there, I fired five shots, and, so far as I could see, I killed three hippopotami. The ear is one of the most vulnerable spots, and this was my mark every time.

The first shot was received with very little attention by the herd; but the struggles of the dying animal I had hit, which turned over several times and finally sank to the bottom, seemed to rouse the others, who began to plunge about and dive down into deep water. The blood of my victims discolored the water all around, and we could not see whether those who escaped were not swimming for us.

Presently the canoe received a violent jar, and, looking overboard, we perceived that we were in the midst of the herd. " The hippopotami are coming upon us!" shouted the men; " they are going to attack us!" We pulled out of the way as fast as we could, none of us being anxious to be capsized. It would have been a comical sight to see us swimming in the midst of a flock of hippopotami, and some of us, perhaps, raised up on the back of one as he came to the surface, or lifted, maybe, with his two crooked tusks in our body.

We were soon out of the way, and, looking back to see where were the animals I had killed, I saw nothing. They had sunk to the bottom, and of the three only one was recovered. It was found two days afterward on a

little island near the river's mouth. Seeing this, I resolved never to shoot hippopotami while they are in the
water, for I did not want to kill these animals for nothing; I wanted their skins and their skeletons to enrich
our museums.

Some time after Joe had died, I determined to go on
a night hunt after hippopotami. These animals come
ashore by night to feed.

The Fernand-Vaz runs for many miles parallel with
the sea-shore, separated from the sea by a strip of sandy
prairie. On this prairie the hippopotamus feeds. He is
sometimes called the sea-horse, for when his head is out
of the water it looks from a distance exactly like the
head of a horse. The " walk" of a herd is easily discern-
ible. It looks very much like a regular beaten road, only
their immense footprints showing who are its makers. In
their track no grass grows. They always return by the
same path they go out on. This gives the hunter a great
advantage.

I chose a moonlight night, and paddled up to the vicinity of one of these " walks." There Igala, my hunter,
and I set out by ourselves. I had painted my face with
a mixture of oil and soot, which is a prudent measure for
a white hunter in Africa. The beasts there seem to have
a singularly quick eye for any thing white. I made myself look exactly like Igala. We both had black faces
and black hands. I was dressed in the usual dark suit
of clothes for the night; people there must not go hunting in light-colored garments. We chose the windward
side of the track, for the hippopotamus has a very keen
scent, and is easily alarmed at night, feeling, probably,
that on land his sluggish movements, huge bulk, and short
legs have their disadvantages.

We lay down under shelter of a bush and watched. As yet, none of the animals had come out of the water. We could hear them in the distance splashing about in the water, their subdued snort-like roars breaking in upon the stillness of the night in a very odd way. It was the only noise we heard—no, I can not say the only noise, for the musquitoes were busily buzzing around and feeding upon us, taking advantage apparently of our anxiety to keep perfectly quiet.

The moon was nearly down, and the watch was getting tedious, when I was startled by a sudden groan. Peering into the distance, I saw dimly a huge animal looking doubly monstrous in the uncertain light. It was quietly eating grass, which it seemed to nibble off quite close to the ground.

There was another bush between us and our prey, and we crawled up to this in dead silence. Arrived there, we were but about eight yards from the great beast. How terrible he looked! The negroes who hunt the hippopotami are sometimes killed; I thought that one of us might be killed also. The animal, if only wounded, turns savagely upon his assailants, and experience has taught the negro hunters that the only safe way to approach him is from behind. He can not turn quickly, and thus the hunter has a chance to make good his escape. This time we could not get into a very favorable position; but I dtermined to have my shot nevertheless, eight yards being a safe killing distance, even with so poor a light as we had at this time.

We watched the hippopotamus intently, looking at each other as if to say, "Are you ready?" We then raised our guns slowly. Igala and I both took aim

He fired, and, without waiting to see the result, ran away as swiftly as a good pair of legs could carry him. I was not quite ready, but fired the moment after him, and before I could get ready for running (in which I had not Igala's practice) I saw there was no need for it. The beast tottered for a moment, and fell over with a booming sound dead.

This closed our night sport, as none of the herd would come this way while their companion lay there. So we returned home. Poor Igala remonstrated with me for not running as he did. It appears that running was considered one of the chief accomplishments of the hippopotamus hunter. Our good luck created great joy in the village where meat was scarce. The men went out at daylight and brought the flesh home. Basket after basket came in, and as each one arrived all shouted except those who did not eat the hippopotamus. It is *roonda* for them. Some of their ancestry had a long time ago given birth to a hippopotamus, and if they were to eat any, more births of hippopotami would come to them, or they would die. These shouted, "I wish he had killed a bullock instead of a hippopotamus."

The meat does not taste unlike beef, but was not so red. It is rather coarse-grained, and in the case of this animal it was not fat. It makes a welcome and wholesome dish. I tried to have some steaks; I must say they were rather tough, and did not go down easily. The broth was better, and I enjoyed it very much. There was something novel in having hippopotamus soup.

I have killed a good many hippopotami. It is a very clumsily built, unwieldy animal, remarkable chiefly for its enormous head, whose upper jaw seemed to be movable, like the crocodile's, and for its disproportionately short legs. The male is much larger than the female; indeed, a full-grown male sometimes attains the bulk, though not the height, of the elephant. In the larger specimens the belly almost sweeps the ground as they walk.

The feet are curiously constructed to facilitate walk ing among the reeds and mud of the river bottom, and swimming with ease. The hoof is divided into four short, apparently clumsy and unconnected toes; and they are able, by this breadth of foot, to walk rapidly even through the mud. I have seen them make quick progress, when alarmed, in water so deep that their backs were just at the surface.

The color of the skin is a clayey yellow, assuming a roseate hue under the belly. In the grown animal the color is a little darker. The skin of an adult hippopotamus is from one and a half to two inches thick on the middle of the back. It is devoid of hair, with the exception of a few short bristly hairs in the tail, and a few scattered tufts, of four or five hairs each, near the muzzle.

All along the Fernand-Vaz there were scattered herds of hippopotami, and I used to watch them from my house. I could see them at any time during the day. After they have chosen a spot, they like to remain there day after day, and month after month, unless they are disturbed, or their food becomes scarce. These animals consort together in herds of from two to thirty. They choose shallows in the rivers, where the depth of the water allows them to have their whole body submerged when standing. There they remain all day, swimming

14

off into the deep places, diving for their grassy food, or gamboling in the waves. From time to time they throw up a stream of water two or three feet high. This is done with a noise like blowing, and it is doubtless an effort to get breath. It is pleasant to watch a herd peacefully enjoying themselves, particularly when they have two or three young ones among them. Some of the little fellows look very small, and are comically awkward. They chase each other about the shoals or play about their dams; and I have often seen them seated on the back of their mother in the water. How careful their mothers seemed to be when they were swimming about, and carrying their young in the way I have described. It is a sight worth seeing; sometimes the whole herd of hippopotami will disappear for a long time under the water.

They prefer parts of the rivers where the current is not very swift, and are therefore to be found in all the lakes of the interior. They prefer to be near grass-fields. They are very fond of a particular kind of coarse grass which grows on these prairies, and will travel considerable distances to find it. They always return, however, before daylight. Their path overland is very direct. Neither rocks, nor swamps, nor bushes can prove formidable obstacles to a water beast of such bulk. I have seen their path lie through the thickest woods. Unless much pursued and harassed, they are not much afraid of man. If troubled by hunters they move their encampment, or go into countries where they can be more quiet.

Some of their favorite grass was growing on a little plain at the back of my house, and several times I found hippopotami tracks not more than fifty yards from the house. They had not feared to come as neai as this; though probably, if the wind had been blowing toward them, they would have avoided the place.

They always choose a convenient landing-place, where the bank has a long and easy incline. This landing-place they use till they have eaten up all the provender which can be found in that vicinity. Before going ashore, they watch for an hour, and sometimes for two hours, near the landing, remaining very quiet themselves, and listening for danger. The slightest token of the hunter's presence, or any other suspicious appearances on such occasions, will send them away for that night. If no danger appears they begin to wander ashore in twos or threes. I never saw more than three of a herd grazing together; and, during their stay ashore, they place more dependence on their ears than on their eyes. I have watched them closely in many hunts, and I am sure that the beast walks along with his eyes nearly shut.

When playing in the water, this animal makes a noise very much resembling the grunt of a pig. This grunt it utters also when alarmed by the approach of man. When enraged, or suddenly disturbed, it utters a kind of groan—a hoarse sound—which can be heard at a considerable distance. They are quite combative among themselves, as you have seen in the case of the fight I have described.

CHAPTER XXV.

One fine day, as I was quietly seated in my bamboo house, reading over, for the fiftieth time, the letters of the dear friends who had not forgotten me, and were so kind as to remember me in my wandering life in Africa, my attention was suddenly drawn away by the singing of numerous voices coming down the river. Soon afterward there stood before me, accompanied by Ranpano, a tall, venerable-looking, and slender negro of noble but savage bearing; he was evidently, I thought, a chief; there was something commanding about his countenance. He was not very dark. The people who came with him showed him great respect. This tall negro was Quengueza, the great king of the Rembo, and the sovereign of the whole up-river country of the Rembo and Ovenga, the head waters of the Fernand-Vaz.

He came down in considerable state in three canoes, with three of his favorite wives, and about one hundred and thirty men.

My little black boy, Maeondai, brought him a chair, and after he had seated himself I saluted him, according to the usual custom, by saying "Mbolo." After a few

MARABOUS, STORK, AND PELICANS.

seeonds he said " Ai." Then he paused a little while, and said ' Mbolo," to which I replied " Ai." This is the usual mode of salutation in the Commi country, the host beginning first.

He looked at me and seemed very much astonished. He said he expected to see a tall and stout man. He had heard of me as a great hunter. He was now convinced, he said, that I must have a brave heart to hunt as I did.

Fortunately, Quengueza and I could talk together, the Commi being his native language.

He told me there were plenty of gorillas and *nshiegos* in his country, and that, if I would come, I should have liberty and protection to hunt and do what I pleased. No one would hurt my people, or Ranpano's people, or myself, or any body, added he, with emphasis, that should come with me.

I liked the old king at first sight, but I little guessed then that he would afterward become so fond of me, and that I should love him so much. Yes, I shall remember my good friend Quengueza as long as I live. Though he is a poor heathen, his heart was full of love for me, and he possessed many manly and noble qualities.

I was so much pleased with King Quengueza's visit that I sent the kind-hearted old fellow off with his canoes full of presents of iron bars, brass rods, chests, etc.; and I gave him goods on trust with which to buy me ebony. He promised me great sport, and an introduction to some tribes of whom these Commi men of the sea-shore knew nothing.

To do him greater honor, my people fired a salute as he started off, with which he was highly delighted, as an

African is sure to be with noise. He did not go before making me promise to come and see him as soon as the rainy season arrived.

The dry season was now setting in. It was the first I had spent in the Commi country, and I devoted the whole month of July to exploring the country along the sea-shore, between the Fernand-Vaz and the sea.

There was quite a change. The birds, which were so abundant during the rainy season, had taken their leave; and other birds, in immense numbers, flocked in to feed on the fish, which now leave the sea-shore and the bars of the river's mouth, and ascend the river to spawn. Fish, particularly mullet, were so abundant in the river that two or three times when I took my evening airing on the water in a flat upper-river canoe, enough mullet would leap into the boat to furnish me a breakfast the next day. The quantity of fish in the shallow water was prodigious.

The breakers on the shore, never very light, were now frightful to see. The coast was rendered inaccessible by them even to the natives, and the surf increased to such a degree, even at the mouth of the river, that it was difficult, and often impossible, to enter with a canoe. Strong winds from the south prevailed, and, though the sky was constantly overcast, not a drop of rain fell. The thermometer fell sometimes early in the morning to 64° of Fahrenheit, and I suffered from cold, as did also the poor natives. The grass on the prairie was dried up or burnt over; the ponds were dried up; only the woods kept their resplendent green.

I was often left alone in that great prairie with my cook and my little boy Macondai, and a dear little boy he was. I felt perfectly safe among the good Commi. I always had tried to do right with them, and I had reaped my reward. They loved me, and any one who should have tried to injure me would have no doubt been put to death or exiled from the country. I shall always remember my little village of Washington and the good Commi people. When perchance I got a chill, the whole village was in distress. No one was allowed to talk loud, and every one would call during the day, and sit by me with a sad face for hours without saying a word, and, when they went away, they all expressed their sorrow to see me ill. The kind women would bring me wild fruits, or cold water from the spring, in which to bathe my burning and aching head; and sometimes tears would drop from their eyes and run down their kind black faces.

At this season the negroes leave their villages and work on their plantations. The women gathered the crop of ground-nuts which had been planted the preceding rainy season, while the men cut down the trees for the plantations of the coming year, or built canoes, or idled about, or went fishing. Some of their farms are necessarily at some distance off. The sandy prairie is not fit to cultivate, being, in fact, only a deposit of the sea, which must have taken an incalculable period of time to form.

Birds flocked in immense numbers on the prairies, whither they come to hatch their young; especially later in the season, when the ugly marabouts, from whose tails our ladies get the splendid feathers for their bonnets, were there in thousands; and I can assure you they were not very easy to approach. I believe the marabout is the ugliest bird I ever saw, and one would never dream that their beautiful feathers are found only under the tail, and can hardly be seen when the bird is alive.

Pelicans waded on the river banks all day in prodigious swarms, and gulped down the luckless fish which came in their way. I loved to see them swimming about in grave silence, and every now and then grabbing up a poor fish with their enormous long and powerful bills. If not hungry, they left the fish in their huge pouches, till sometimes three or four pounds of reserved food awaited the coming of their appetite. This pouch, you see, performed the office of a pocket, where boys, when not hungry, keep their apples in reserve.

On the sandy islands were seen now and then flocks of the *Ibis religiosa*, the sacred Ibis of the Egyptians. They looked exactly like those that are found mummified, and which have been preserved several thousand years. They are very curious-looking birds; the head and neck have no feathers. I have tried to find their nests, but never succeeded.

Ducks of various kinds built their nests in every creek and on every new islet that appeared with the receding waters. Some of them were of beautiful plumage.

Cranes, too, and numerous other water-fowls flocked in, and every day brought with it new birds. They came, by some strange instinct, from far-distant lands, to feed upon the vast shoals of fish which literally filled the river. I wondered if many of these birds had come from the Nile, the Niger, the Zambesi—from the interi r of Africa where no one had ever penetrated, and from the vast plains of South Africa. What great travelers some of these birds must be! I envied them, and often wished

I could fly away, supported by their wings. What countries I should have seen!—what curious people I should
have looked at!—and how many novel things I should
have found to recount to you.

Along the trees bordering the river, sometimes perched
on their highest branches, sometimes hidden in the midst
of them, I could see that most beautiful eagle, the *Gy-
pohierax angolensis*, called *coungou* by the natives.
This eagle is of a white and black color. He often
watches over the water. How quickly his keen eyes can
see through it! and with what rapidity he darts at his
prey! Then, seizing it in his powerful talons, which sink
deep into it, he rises into the air, and goes where he can
devour it undisturbed. These eagles attack large fish.
They generally make them blind, and then gradually succeed in getting them ashore, though it is hard work for
them. They have a luxurious time on the Fernand-Vaz
River during the dry season, and are very numerous.
They build their nests on the tops of the highest trees,
and come back to them every year. These nests are exactly like those you have seen, only larger. They keep
very busy when their young begin to eat. The male and
female are then continually fishing. Strange to say,
they are very fond of the palm-oil nuts. In the season
when these are ripe, they are continually seen among the
palm-trees.

No wonder these eagles grab fish so easily, they have
such claws! One day, as one passed over my head, I
shot him, and, thinking that he was quite dead, I took him
up, when suddenly, in the last struggle for life, his talons
got into my hands. I could have dropped down from
pain. Nothing could have taken the claws away; one

of them went clear through my hand, and I shall probably keep the mark of it all my life.

On the sea-shore I sometimes caught a bird called the
Sula capensis, which had been driven ashore by the
treacherous waves to which it had trusted itself, and
could not, for some mysterious reason, get away again.

Finally, every sand-bar was covered with gulls, whose
shrill screams were heard from morning till night, as
they flew about greedily after their finny prey.

It was a splendid opportunity for sportsmen, and I
thought of some of my friends. As for myself, I took
more delight in studying the habits of the birds than in
killing them, and I assure you I had a very delightful
time. I love dearly the dry season in Africa. I am sure
you would have enjoyed it quite as much as I did, if you
had been there with me.

THE KING RECEIVES ME.

CHAPTER XXVI.

ANOTHER EXPEDITION TO LAKE ANENGUE.—DIFFICULT PAS-
SAGE UP THE RIVER. — THE CROCODILES. — KING DAMA-
GONDAI AND HIS TROUBLES.—I BUY AN MBUITI, OR IDOL.

ONE fine morning there was a great bustle on the banks
of the river at Washington, where two canoes were load-
ing. I was about to start on another expedition. I called
King Rampano and his people together, and gave them
charge of my property; I declared that if any thing
was stolen during my absence I should surely punish the
thief.

They all protested that I need not even lock the doors
of my house; and I believed them. The Biaganc people
loved me, and did not steal from me.

Then I counted my ten goats in their presence, and
said that I wanted no leopard stories told me when I

came back. At this they shouted and laughed. They declared that neither they nor the leopards should touch my goats.

I counted the fowls, and told them I wanted no snake stories about them. Another hearty laugh, and they all shouted that no snakes should gobble up my fowls. These matters having been satisfactorily arranged, I started with my canoes and a well-armed crew.

I was bound again for Lake Anengue, where I had been a few months before. It was now the dry season. We had armed ourselves well, for fear we might be interrupted, as some people came up this way to make plantations during the dry season, and might dispute our advance; I determined to let no man bar the road to me.

The dry season was at its height, and I found the Npoulounay shallower than before. There was about fifteen feet less depth of water in the Ogobai during the dry season than there was in the rainy season. At this time the river was covered with muddy or sandy islands, many of which were left dry. The muddy islands were covered with reeds, among which sported the flamingo, a bird not seen here in the rainy season.

We pulled hard all day, and slept the first night on a sandy island of the Ogobai River, under our musquito-nets, of which I had laid in a store. These nets, which the natives also use, are made of grass cloth, which comes from the far interior, and does very well outdoors, where it keeps out the dew as well as the musquitoes, and protects the sleeper against the cold winds which prevail.

The next morning when I awoke, I saw, for the first time, a fog in this part of Africa; it was very thick, but the sun drove it off. I sent out my fishing-net, and in a few minutes the men caught fish enough for supper and breakfast.

After our breakfast of fish and plantain, we paddled on up the stream. Though we had seen a few villages, we had not met a single canoe on the water, and nothing human except a corpse that came down the river, and ran against our canoe. It was probably the body of some poor wretch who had been drowned on account of witch-craft. The hands and feet were tied, so that when they threw him into the water he could not swim.

Finally we entered the Anengue; but this river, we found, was entirely changed since May. Then it was a deep, swift stream. Now its surface was dotted with numberless black mud islands, on which swarmed in-credible numbers of crocodiles. We actually saw many hundreds of these disgusting monsters sunning them-selves on the black mud, and slipping off into the water to feed. I never saw such a horrible sight. Many were at least twenty feet long; and when they opened their frightful mouths they seemed capable of swallowing our little canoes without trouble. I wondered what would become of us all if, perchance, our canoe should capsize.

I determined to have a shot at these crocodiles, which seemed nowise frightened at our approach. Making my men paddle the boat quite near to them, I singled out the biggest, and lodged a ball in his body, aiming at the joints of his fore legs, where the thick armor is defective. He tumbled over, and after struggling in the water for a mo-ment, sank into the mud. His companions turned their hideous snaky eyes down at him in momentary surprise, but did not know what to make of it, and dropped back to their sluggish comfort. I shot another, but he sank also, and as my men did not like to venture into the black mud after them, we got neither.

As we ascended the stream it branched off in several places, and became gradually narrower. Crocodiles were seen every where. At length we found ourselves pushing laboriously along through a deep crooked ditch, not more than two yards wide, and overhung with tall reeds, on which a great number of birds balanced themselves, as though enjoying our dilemma. We found this time, to my surprise, a tremendous current running. In May, the water of the lake had overflowed its shores, and its regular outlets had therefore no great pressure upon them. Now this outlet was choked with water, which rushed through at such a rate that, at some of the turns in the crooked channel, we were actually swept back several times before we could make our way ahead. At one point, where the true outlets joined, we could not pass till I made the men smoke their *condouquai*, a long reed pipe, which seems to give them new vigor; I also gave them a sup of my brandy. This done, they gave a great shout, and pushed through, and in an hour after we emerged into the lake, but not without tremendous exertions.

We now lay on our paddles and gazed about us. On one side the lake is bounded by hills which come close down to the shore; on the other side the hills recede, and between them and the water lies a dreary extent of low marsh, covered with reeds. Several towns were in sight, all located on the summits of hills.

The lake, alas! had changed with the season too. It was still a beautiful sheet of water, but all over its placid face the dry season had brought out an eruption of those black mud islands which we had noticed before, and on these reposed I fear to say what number of crocodiles. Wherever the eye was turned, these disgusting creatures, with their dull leering eyes and huge savage jaws, appeared in prodigious numbers. The water was alive with fish, on which I supposed the crocodiles had fat living; but pelicans and herons, ducks and other water-birds also abounded, drawn hither by the abundance of their prey.

Paddling carefully past great numbers of crocodiles, into whose ready jaws I was by no means anxious to fall, and past several villages, whose people looked at us witn mute amazement, we reached at last the town of Dama-gondai. A great crowd was assembled to receive us, headed by the king himself, who stood on the shore. Quarters were provided for me by his majesty, who, a short time after my arrival, presented me with a goat. He was dressed in the usual middle-cloth of the natives, and a tarnished,scarlet soldier's coat, but was innocent of trowsers. His welcome, however, was not the less hearty because the pantaloons were absent.

His town, which contains about fifty huts, lies on some high ground, at a little distance from the water. I distributed presents among the graybeards, and beads among the women, and thus put them all in good-humor.

Damagondai, the king, then insisted that I must get married to at least two or three women. He was amazed when I declined this flattering proposal, and insisted upon it that my bachelor life must be very lonely and disagreeable.

The king was a tall, rather slim negro, over six feet high, and well shaped. In war or in the chase he had the usual amount of courage, but at home he was exceed-

15

ingly superstitious. As night came on he seemed to get
a dread of death, and at last began to groan that some of
the people wanted to bewitch him, in order to get his
property and his authority. Finally he would get excited, and begin to curse all witches and sorcerers. He
would say that no one should have his wives and slaves,
and that the people who wanted to kill him had better
beware; the *mboundou* was ready.

Certainly poor Damagondai must have slept on the
wrong side, as I told him afterward, for the old fellow
began to lecture his wives, telling them to love him and
feed him well, for he had given a great deal of goods and
slaves to their parents for them, and they were a constant
expense to him. To all this the poor women listened
with respect.

Damagondai and I were very good friends. I really
don't know why, but, wherever I went, these negroes
seem to take a liking to me.

In the village of Damagondai there was an *mbuiti*,
"an idol," representing a female figure with copper eyes,
and a tongue made of a sharp, sword-shaped piece of
iron. This explained her chief attribute; she cuts to
pieces those with whom she is displeased. She was
dressed in the Shekiani cloth, covering her from the
neck down. She is said to speak, to walk, to foretell
events, and to take vengeance on her enemies. Her
house is the most prominent one in the whole village.
She comes to people by night, and tells them in their
sleep what is going to happen. In this way, they asserted, my coming had been foretold. They worship her by
dancing around her and singing her praises, and their re-
quests. Sometimes a single woman or man comes alone

to prefer a request; and one evening I saw the whole village engaged in this rite, all dancing and singing around her. They offer her sugar-cane and other food, which they believe she eats.

I tried to buy this goddess, but, ugly as she was, Dama-gondai said that no amount of money would purchase her. He insinuated, however, in a very slight way, that for a proper price I might obtain the mbuiti of the slaves. Then a great council took place with the gray-beards of the village. The slaves were on the planta-tions. They agreed to tell them on their return that they had seen their mbuiti walk off in the woods, and that she had not returned. I could hear them laugh over what they thought to be their clever plot.

I paid them a good price for it. I packed the mbuiti up, and took her off with me, and her portrait, an exact likeness, taken in New York from the idol itself, is found in my book called "Equatorial Africa."

I have often thought since how much I should have enjoyed seeing the return of the slaves to the village. I should like to know if they really believed that their mbuiti had left them; if so, there must have been great wailing and mourning for fear that the wrath of the mbuiti would come upon them.

A CROCODILE HUNT.

CHAPTER XXVII.

A VISIT TO KING SHIMBOUVENEGANI.—HIS ROYAL COSTUME.
—HUNTING CROCODILES.—HOW THEY SEIZE THEIR PREY.
—THE NKAGO.—THE OGATA.

I RESOLVED to embark again on the waters of the Anengue Lake, and make a little journey of exploration. Damagondai went in the canoe with me. He was to take me to another king, a friend of his.

We reached the residence of King Shimbouvenegani, a king with a long name and a small village. We had to paddle through very shallow water before reaching this place.

When we arrived, the king with the long name was not at his village. We were told he was at his *olako*—a place temporarily erected in the woods when villagers go out to hunt, or fish, or pursue agriculture.

They had chosen a charming spot in the woods, just upon the shores of the lake, which here had abrupt banks. The musquito nets were hung up under the trees; every family had a fire built, and from the pots came the fragrant smell of plantain and fish cooking. The savor was very pleasant to me, for I was hungry.

Presently Shimbouvenegani came up. He was re-joiced to see me, and thanked his friend Damagondai for bringing his white man to visit him.

The appearance of Shimbouvenegani was comical. He was between sixty and seventy years of age, and was quite lean. His only garment was a very dirty swallow-tailed coat, which certainly must have belonged to the time of my grandfather. The buttons were all gone. On his head he wore a broad beaver hat, which dated nearly as far back as the coat itself. The fur was en-tirely worn off, and the hat had a very seedy appearance. But the king seemed very proud when he made his ap-pearance. He thought his costume was just the thing, and he looked around, as if to say, "Am I not a fine-looking fellow?" And truly, though his dress did not amount to much according to our notions, I doubt not it had cost him several slaves.

He asked me how I liked his costume, at the same time taking one of the smaller tails in his hand and shaking it.

Presently some large pots of palm wine were brought, with which all hands proceeded to celebrate my arrival. Damagondai and Shimbouvenegani soon got drunk, and swore to each other eternal friendship, and Shimbouven-egani promised to give one of his daughters in mar-riage to Damagondai.

Meantime Damagondai had presented me to his eldest son, Okabi, who resided in the village of Shimbouvene‧gani. Okabi arranged a nice little place for me, with branches of trees, and made a kind of bed for me. He then gave me his two wives to take care of me, and to cook for me.

I had a very agreeable time in hunting while I was with Shimbouvenegani. It was during my stay there that I discovered the *nshieyo mbouvé*, of which I will speak by-and-by.

We also had a great crocodile hunt, which pleased the people very much, as they are extravagantly fond of the meat. Now and then, during my travels, for lack of something better, I have been obliged to eat crocodiles. I have tried it in all sorts of ways—steaks, stews, boiled, and broth, but I must say I was never fond of it.

They killed more or fewer crocodiles every day at this village, but the negroes were so lazy that they were glad to have me go and save them the trouble. Moreover, the crocodile has not much meat on him; so that, though some were killed every day, the village was never sufficiently supplied.

We went in canoes. These canoes on the Anengue are of very singular construction. They are quite flat-bottomed and of very light draught; many of them are about fifty feet long, with a breadth of not more than two feet, and a depth of ten or twelve inches. They are made of a single tree. They are ticklish craft. The oarsmen stand up, and use paddles seven feet long, with which they can propel one of these canoes at a very good rate. They are, of course, easily capsized, the gunwale being but a very few inches above the water; but they do not often tip over. What surprised me most was the way in which the negro paddlers stood up at their work all day without tiring.

The negroes on the Anengue hunt the crocodile both with guns and with a kind of harpoon. The vulnerable part of the animal is near the joints of his fore legs, and there they endeavor to wound it. Though so many are killed they do not decrease in numbers, nor, strange to say, do they seem to grow more wary. They were to be seen every where during the dry season; when the rainy season comes they disappear.

As we started out, we saw them swimming in all directions, and lying on the mud banks sunning themselves. They took no notice of our canoe at all. As we were to shoot them we were obliged to look for our prizes on the shore, for if killed in the water they sink and are lost. Presently we saw one immense fellow extended on the bank among some reeds. We approached cautiously. I took good aim and knocked him over. He struggled hard to get to the water, but his strength gave out ere he could reach it, and, to our great joy, he expired. We could not think of taking his body into our canoe, for he was nearly twenty feet long.

We killed another which measured eighteen feet. I never saw more savage-looking jaws; they were armed with most formidable rows of teeth, and looked as though a man would scarcely be a mouthful for them.

We had brought another canoe along, and, capsizing this upon the shore, we rolled the dead monsters into it, and paddled off for the village. Then we returned to the olako.

During the heat of the day these animals retire to the

reeds, where they lie sheltered. In the morning, and late in the afternoon, they come forth to seek their prey. They swim very silently, and scarcely make even a ripple on the water, though they move along quite rapidly. The motion of their paws in swimming is like those of a dog, over and over. They can remain quite still on the top of the water, where they may be seen watching for prey with their dull, wicked-looking eyes. When they are swimming the head is the only part of the body visible; and when they are still, it looks exactly like an old piece of wood which has remained long in the water, and is tossing to and fro. They sleep among the reeds. Their eggs they lay in the sand on the island, and cover them over with a layer of sand. It is the great abundance of fish in the lake which makes them multiply so fast as they do. The negroes seemed rather indifferent to their presence.

On my journey back to Damagondai's I saw an example of the manner in which the crocodile seizes upon his prey. As we were paddling along I perceived in the distance ahead a beautiful gazelle, looking meditatively into the waters of the lagoon, of which from time to time it took a drink. I stood up to get a shot, and we approached with the utmost silence, but just as I raised my gun to fire a crocodile leaped out of the water, and, like a flash, dived back again, with the struggling animal in its powerful jaws. So quickly did the beast take its prey that, though I fired at him, I was too late. I do not think my bullet hit him.

After hunting on the water I thought I would have a few rambles in the forest near the olako. I killed a beautiful monkey, which the natives call nkago, whose head is crowned with a cap of bright red, or rather brown hair. The nkagos are very numerous in these woods.

While walking in the forest I found, near the water, the hole or burrow of an ogata. This is a species of cayman, which lives near the pools, and makes a long hole in the ground, with two entrances. In this hole it sleeps and watches for its prey. The ogata is very unlike the crocodile in its habits. It is a night-roving animal, and solitary in its ways. It scrapes out its hole with its paws with considerable labor. It lives near a pool, for the double reason, I imagine, that it may bathe, and because thither come gazelles and other animals, for whom it lies in wait. The negroes told me that they rush out with great speed upon any wandering animal, and drag it into the hole to eat it. When the negroes discover one of these holes they come with their guns, which are generally loaded with iron spikes, and watch at one end, while a fire is built at the other entrance. When it becomes too hot, the ogata rushes out and is shot. I killed one, which proved to be seven feet in length. It had great strength in its jaws, and its teeth were very formidable. Like the crocodile, its upper jaw is articulated, and is raised when the mouth is opened.

Sometimes fire is put at both ends of the hole, and the animal is smoked to death. At other times a trap is made at the end where there is no fire, and when the ogata rushes out it is ensnared.

THE NSHIEGO MBOUVÉ.

CHAPTER XXVIII.

As I was trudging along one day in the woods, rather
tired of the sport, and on the point of going back to the
camp, I happened to look up at a high tree which we
were passing, and saw a most singular shelter or home
built in its branches. I immediately stopped and asked
Okabi why the hunters slept in that way in the woods.
Okabi laughed, after looking at me quizzically, and then
he told me that no man had ever built that shelter. He

said that it was made by a kind of man of the woods, called ushiego mbouvé, an animal which had no hair on the top of its head. I really thought Okabi was joking. An animal—a man-monkey—with no hair on the top of his head?—a bald-headed ape? It was now my turn to laugh, for I did not believe Okabi's story about the bald-headed animal, though I believed what he said about the shelter in the tree.

I saw at once that I was on the trail of an animal which no civilized man had ever seen before. I no longer felt tired, but pushed on through the woods with renewed ardor and with increased caution, so as not to alarm our prey. The shelter we had seen was an old one, which had been abandoned, but we had a hope of finding another which should be still occupied.

We were not disappointed. We soon found two more shelters. They were about twenty feet from the ground, and were on two trees which stood a little apart from the others, and which had no limbs below the one on which the nests were placed. This location for its house is probably chosen by the animals to secure them at night from beasts and serpents, and from the falling limbs of surrounding trees. They build only in the loneliest part of the forest. They are very shy, and are seldom seen, even by the negroes.

Okabi, who was an old and intelligent hunter, told me that the male and female together select the material for their nest or shelter. It is constructed in part of the branches of the tree itself, which they twist in with the boughs of other trees collected by them for the purpose. The shelters I saw had the shape of an umbrella.

We concealed ourselves by lying flat on the ground

amid the bushes near by, and keeping perfectly still. My patience was sorely tried. Musquitoes and flies were continually biting me. Ants now and then were creeping upon me, and some of them managed to get under my clothes. Besides, I had some fear of the Bashikouay, or of the white ants, coming to disturb me, or of snakes creeping upon me. So, as you may imagine, I was not comfortable, neither had I pleasant thoughts.

At length, just at dusk, we heard the loud peculiar "hew, hew, hew," which is the call of the male to his mate. I was glad to know I had not waited in vain; and, looking up, I saw a nshiego mbouvé sitting under his nest. His feet rested on the lower branch; his head reached quite into the little dome of a roof; and his arm was clasped firmly about the tree trunk. This, I suppose, is the position in which they sleep. Soon after his mate came and ascended the tree.

After gazing till I was tired, I saw that one of the animals showed signs of being alarmed. Had they smelt us? had we made a noise that excited their suspicions? Anyhow, we raised our guns and fired through the gloom at the one that seemed asleep. I almost felt sorry for the unfortunate beast, which fell with a tremendous crash, and died without a struggle. The other uttered an awful shriek, and came down the tree with the utmost rapidity. I fired, but missed the animal, and in less time than I take to write it the poor creature had disappeared in the woods.

I was very hungry, for I had eaten nothing since breakfast. We built a fire at once, and made our camp. Then we built several more fires, to prevent an attack of the Bashikouay ants, in case they should come that way.

The poor ape was hung up to a limb out of reach. During the night I could hear, now and then, in the distance, the piercing shriek of its mate, which no doubt was calling for the absent one. At last I fell asleep on my bed of leaves and grass, as pleased a man, perhaps, as any in the world.

The next morning I examined the nshiego mbouvé. Okabi, pointing to the head, triumphantly exclaimed, "See, Chaillie, is not the animal bald-headed? Did I not tell you the truth?" So it was. The nshiego was quite bald; not a hair could be seen on the top of his head. He was a full-grown specimen, and measured three feet and eleven inches in height. His color was intensely black, and the body was covered with short, rather blackish hair. On the legs the hair was of a dirty gray, mixed with black. On the shoulders and back the hair grew two or three inches long. This animal was old, and his hair was a little mixed with gray. The arms also, down to the wrists, were covered with long black hair. The hair is much thinner than on the gorilla, and is blacker, longer, and glossier. The nose, also, is not so prominent. Though only three feet and eleven inches in height, the animal had an extremely broad chest, though not so powerful as that of the gorilla. The fingers, also, were much longer, and not large; and the hand was longer than the foot; while the gorilla, like man, has the foot longer than the hand.

Some of the teeth were decayed; so the poor fellow must have had the toothache badly; and I suppose there were no dentists among the nshiego mbouvés. I have killed several of these animals. One of them was a very old one, he had silvery hair; nearly all his teeth were decayed, and some were missing, which had dropped out with age. He was getting so infirm that he had not strength enough to pick berries or break nuts; and, when killed, he had only leaves in his stomach.

After enjoying myself thoroughly at the olako of Shimbouvenegani, we returned to the village of Damagondai. Shimbouvenegani dressed himself again in state, that is to say, he put on his swallow-tailed coat and his beaver hat. In this regal costume he accompanied us to our canoes, and there bid us good-by.

THE BREAKING UP OF MOURNING.

CHAPTER XXIX.

WAR THREATENED.—OSHORIA ARMS HIS MEN.—WE BLUFF
THEM OFF, AND FALL SICK WITH FEVER.—THE MBOLA
IVOGA, OR END OF MOURNING TIME.—A DEATH AND
BURIAL.—FINDING OUT THE SORCERER.—THE VILLAGE
DESERTED.—I BECOME VICEROY AT WASHINGTON.

NEWS came that Oshoria, the chief of Gualmirri, a village situated at the junction of the Ogobai and Anengue
Rivers, intended to stop me on my way back to Washington. It was reported that he had assembled all his
fighting men, and was bent upon war.

Poor Damagondai was much troubled. He wanted
no war. He sent his brother down with a plate, a mug,
and a brass pan, to propitiate Oshoria. These were great
presents. A plate, a mug, and a pan are thought to be
very valuable in the regions of the Anengue.

I was very angry. I had done no harm to the people of Guabuirri. I had passed their village in peace.
Oshoria wanted to exact tribute for my passage; but he
was not the king of the country, and I determined to put
down Mr. Oshoria.

We cleaned our guns, and I prepared my revolvers,
and the next morning we set out, without waiting for
the return of the king's brother, greatly to the dismay
of Damagondai and of his peaceful people. But nothing must stop us. We must return to Washington. My
men swore that they would fight to the death.

When we came in sight of Guabuirri, I saw that some
of my fellows, who a short time before were going to be
so brave, began to show the white feather. I therefore
pointed to my revolver, and told them that I would blow
out the brains of the first man who failed to fight to the
last. They had a great respect for this wonderful revolver, and they immediately answered, "We are men."

So we pulled down the stream and soon came almost
opposite Oshoria's people. I gave orders to make for the
town. On the shore stood about one hundred and fifty
fellows armed with spears and axes, and led by ten men
who had guns. All of them were making a great noise.

My men were all well armed, and, if I remember well,
there were only sixteen of us. I had my revolver in one
hand, and a double-barreled gun in the other. The men
all had guns, which were placed beside them in such a
way that the natives on shore could see them. At this
piece of bravado Oshoria's men became very civil. They
retreated as we approached the landing; and instead of
continuing their war shouts and firing at us, they received
us peaceably, and shouted to us not to fire.

Damagondai's brother hurried down to meet me, and announced that there was no palaver: I must not kill any body. I was then led to where the quarrelsome Oshoria stood. Looking at him with a stern look, I reproached him for his conduct, telling him that if any body had been killed, the palaver would have been on his own head. He said he had been vexed that I did not stop to see him on my way up; and, after making farther excuses, added, "Aouè olomé," " thou art a man ;" an expression used in several ways, either to designate a smart man or a rascal, or, in the best sense, a very brave man I was content to accept it as an intended compliment.

I was presented with fruits and fowls, and we were presently the best of friends. To show them what I could do in the way of shooting, I brought down a little bird which sat on a very high tree. They all declared that I must have a very big shooting fetich ; and they reverenced me greatly.

The next morning I left Oshoria, and once more I glided down the placid waters of the Ogobai. I reached Washington in safety.

It was in the month of August, and the malaria of the Anengue marshes began to tell on me. I fell sick with dysentery, and symptoms of malignant fever. In three days I took one hundred and eighty grains of quinine, and thus happily succeeded in breaking the force of the fever, which was the most dangerous of the two diseases. I was ill from the 18th to the 31st of August, and I did not regain my strength till the 9th of September. The Commi waited patiently for my recovery before they would go through some of their ceremonies.

There was to be a *mbola ivoga* at Biagano, that is, an

16

end of the mourning time, to be celebrated with ceremonies and a terrible noise.

When any one of importance dies, the clan, or town,
or the relatives, cease to wear their best clothes, and make
it a point to go unusually dirty. No ornaments whatever, such as earrings, or bracelets, or beads, are worn.
This is the way they "mourn." Mourning lasts generally from a year to two years. The ceremonies at the
breaking up of this mourning are what I am now about
to describe.

The man who had died left seven wives, a house, a
plantation, several slaves, and other property. All this
the elder brother inherited; and on him, as the heir, it
devolved to give the grand feast. For this feast every
canoe that came brought jars of mimbo, or palm wine.
Sholomba and Jombouai, the heir, with his people, had
been out for two weeks fishing, and now returned with
several canoe-loads of dry fish. From his plantation a
large supply of palm wine was brought in. The women
and slaves had prepared a great quantity of food. Every
thing needful was provided in great abundance.

In the village the people all got ready their best clothes
and furbished up their ornaments. Drums and kettles
were collected for music; powder was brought out for the
salutes; and at last all was ready for the mbola ivoga.

The seven wives of the deceased seemed quite jolly,
for to-morrow they were to lay aside their widows' robes,
and to join in the jollification as brides. The heir could
have married them all; but he had generously given up
two to a younger brother, and one to a cousin. He had
already sixteen wives, and might well be content with
only four more. Twenty wives is a pretty good number

No wonder the widows were glad to see the time of mourning over. For two whole years they had been almost imprisoned in their husband's house, hardly ever going out.

At seven o'clock three guns were fired off to announce that the widows had done eating a certain mess, mixed of various ingredients, supposed to have magical virtues, and by which they are released from their widowhood. This was the first part of the ceremony. They then put on bracelets and anklets, and the finest calico they had. Some of the Commi women wear brass anklets on each leg almost as high as the knee, as you see represented in the picture. The weight must be between twenty and thirty pounds on each leg. Besides these anklets, they wear a few bracelets of the same material. On their necks they wear beads.

From early morning the guests had been coming, all bringing provisions and mimbo (palm wine) with them, and dressed in their best clothes. There were several hundreds in all. The guests that lived far away had come the day before. About nine o'clock all the guests sat down on mats, spread about outside of the house of the deceased, and along the main street. They were divided into little groups, and before each was set an immense jar of mimbo, and food was spread before them. All began to talk pleasantly, till suddenly the Biagano people fired off a volley of about one hundred guns. This was the signal for the drinking and eating to begin. Men, women, and children set to, and ate as much as they could, and from this time till the next morning the orgies were continued without interruption. They drank, they sang, they shouted, they fired guns, and load ed them so heavily when they got tipsy that I wonder the old trade-guns did not burst. They drummed on every thing that could possibly give out a noise. The women danced—such dances as are not seen elsewhere! You may imagine what they were when every woman was so furiously tipsy.

This mbola ivoga would have lasted probably for several days, but the victuals and palm wine finally gave out.

Next day, about sunrise, Jombouai came and asked me to assist at the concluding ceremony, for I had told him that I wanted to see every scene of the mbola ivoga. His brother's house, according to the custom, was to be torn down and burned—yes, burned to the ground, so that not a vestige of it would remain to remind the people that once there stood a house whose possessor was dead.

The people came around the house and fired guns; then, in a moment, as if they were an infuriated mob, they hacked the old house to pieces with axes and cutlasses; then they set fire to it. When the ruins were burnt, the feast was done.

This is the way they go out of mourning among the Commi. The widows were all married again, and, until another death should occur, every thing would go smoothly again.

Hardly were the rejoicings over when Ishungui, the man who had faithfully taken care of my house in my absence, lay at death's door. He had gone out on Jombouai's fishing excursion in order to catch fish for the mbola ivoga which I have just described. He caught cold, and had now a lung fever. The people called for me. I knew as soon as I saw him that he must die, and I tried to prepare his mind for the change. But his friends and relatives by no means gave him up. They sent for a distinguished fetich doctor, and under his auspices they began the infernal din with which they seek to cure a dying man. I am afraid the cure is worse than the disease.

One of the Commi people's theories of disease is that Obambou (the devil) has got into the sick man, and as long as the devil remains in the body there is no hope of curing the man. Now this devil is only to be driven out by noise, and, accordingly, a great crowd surround the sick man, and beat drums and kettles close to his head, fire off guns close to his ears, and in every part of the house they sing, shout, dance, and make all the noise they can. This lasts till the poor fellow either dies or is better; but I must say that he generally dies, unless the operators get tired out first.

Ishungui died. He left no property, and his brother buried him in the sand, without a coffin, in a grave so shallow (as is the custom) that, when I came upon it some days after, I saw that the wild beasts had been there and eaten the corpse.

The mourning was short in this case; it lasted only six days. There were no wives or property; there was no feast. The relatives of the deceased slept one night in his house as a mark of respect.

Among the Commi, it is the custom, when a man has died, to keep the *nchougou*. The nchougou is a feast that takes place generally, if not always, after the man has been dead six days. There is drinking, eating, and dancing; but the rejoicing is not so uproarious as the

ceremony of the mbola ivoga. Then the mourning begins. I think you will agree with me that the nchougou
is a most extraordinary custom.

After Ishungui had died, it became necessary to discover the persons who had bewitched the dead man; for
the Commi said, "How is it that a young man, generally
healthy, should die so suddenly?" This they did not
believe to be natural; hence they attributed his death to
sorcerers, and were afraid that the sorcerers would kill
other people.

A canoe had been dispatched up to Lake Anengue to
bring down a great doctor. They brought down one of
Damagondai's sons, a great rascal. He had been fore-
most in selling me the idol, or *mbuiti* of the slaves, of
which I spoke to you, and he was an evident cheat.

When all was ready for the trial, I went down to look
at the doctor, who looked really diabolical. I never saw
a more ugly-looking object.

He had on a high head-dress of black feathers. His
eyelids were painted red, and a red stripe, from the nose
upward, divided his forehead into two parts; another
stripe passed around his head. The face was painted
white, and on each side of the mouth were two round
red spots. About his neck hung a necklace of grass, and
also a cord, which held a box against his breast. This
little box is sacred, and contains spirits. A number of
strips of leopard's skin, and of skin of other animals,
crossed his breast, and were exposed about his person;
and all these were charmed, and had charms attached to
them. From each shoulder down to his hands was a
white stripe, and one hand was painted quite white. To
complete this horrible array, he wore around his body a
string of little bells.

He sat on a box. Before him stood another box containing charms. On this stood a looking-glass, before which lay a buffalo horn. In this horn there was some black powder, and it was said to be the refuge of many spirits. The doctor had also a little basket of snake-bones, which he shook frequently during his incantations, and several skins, to which little bells were attached. Near by stood a fellow beating a board with two sticks.

All the people of the village gathered about this couple. The doctor had, no doubt, impressed the people with his great power. His incantations were continued for a long time, and at last came to the climax. Jombouai was told to call over the names of persons in the village, in order that the doctor might ascertain if any of those named were sorcerers. As each name was called, the old cheat looked in the looking-glass to see the result.

During the whole operation I stood near him, which seemed to trouble him greatly. At last, after all the names were called, the doctor declared that he could not find any " witch-man," but that an evil spirit dwelt in the village, and many of the people would die if it continued there. I have a suspicion that this final judgment with which the incantations broke up was a piece of revenge upon me. I had no idea until the next day how seriously the word of one of these *ougangas* (doctors) is taken.

The next morning all was excitement. The people were scared. They said their mbuiti was not willing to have them live longer here; that he would kill them, etc. Then began the removal of all kinds of property, and the tearing down of houses, and by nightfall I was actually

left alone in my house with a Mpongwe boy and my little Ogobai boy Macondai, both of whom were anxious to
be off.

Old Ranpano came to beg me not to be offended; he
said that he dared not stay; that the mbuiti was now in
town. He advised me, as a friend, to move also; but
nobody wished me ill, only he must go, and would build
his house not far off.

I did not like to abandon my house and settlement at
Washington, which it had cost me a good deal of trouble
to build. I called a meeting of the people, and it was
with the greatest difficulty that I could get some of my
own canoe-boys and a few men to come and stay at my
place. These began immediately to build themselves
houses, and a little village was built, of which I was now,
to my great surprise, offered the sovereignty. I remembered how the new king was made in the Gaboon, and I
did not know but that the Commi had the same custom.
The thought of the ceremony which precedes the as-
sumption of royalty deterred me. Finally, the men determined to have me as their chief, next to Ranpano:
and with this my ambition was satisfied.

WOLF HUNTING.

CHAPTER XXX.

HUNTING IN THE WOODS.—THE MBOYO WOLF.—WE CATCH
ANOTHER YOUNG GORILLA.—HE STARVES TO DEATH.

EVERY thing went on smoothly among the good Commi. When I absented myself they took great care of my property. They seemed proud of their honesty; and, though it was a wild country, and they were a wild people, I felt very safe among them.

Now and then I left Washington to go and live entirely in the woods, and hunt, sometimes for gorillas, at other times for wild boars or buffaloes, or something else.

I was also very fond of hunting the *mboyo*, a very shy animal of the wolf kind, with long yellowish hair and straight ears. They are very cunning; and now and then you can see them in the grass, engaged in hunting for themselves. I have often watched these animals surrounding and chasing game. They run very well to-

gether in a drove; and as their policy is to run round
and round, they soon bewilder, tire out, and capture any
animal of moderate endurance. As they run round,
gradually their circle grows smaller and smaller; and of
course, the smaller it becomes, the more bewildered becomes their prey.

Often I have seen them prying about alone in search
of prey. How roguish they look! and I could only shoot
them at very long distances. I never was able to get
near one of them.

At times I went into the country where gorillas were
plentiful, and had a good deal of fun and plenty of excitement. This country was not far from the village of
a chief called Makaga Onne-jiou. This chief was affect-
ed with leprosy. He had already lost all the fingers of
his left hand, and two fingers of his right hand, besides
the big toe of his left foot. But Makaga was very kind
to me, and was much beloved by his people. His village
was small, but was a very dear little village to him. It
was surrounded by fields of sugar-cane, plantain-trees,
and little fields of ground-nuts; and now and then the
gorillas came and helped themselves to the good things
these people had planted. This made them very wroth,
and they were always glad to have me come and spend a
few days among them.

Early in the morning I could sometimes hear the gorillas, who then came quite near the village. Here I
found that I need not make long journeys in order to
reach the hunting-ground. But they are difficult of approach; the slightest noise alarms them and sends them
off. It is only once in a while that you can surprise an
old male, and then he will fight you.

While staying with Makaga Oune-jiou I captured a second young gorilla, and we had an exciting time, I assure you, before we got him.

We were walking along in silence, when I heard a cry, and presently I saw not far from me, in the midst of a dense foliage, a female gorilla, with a tiny baby gorilla hanging to her breast. The mother was stroking the little one, and looking fondly down at it ; and the scene was so pretty and touching that I withheld my fire and considered (like a soft-hearted fellow) whether I had not better leave them in peace. Before I could make up my mind, however, my hunter fired and killed the mother, who fell dead without a struggle.

The mother fell, but the baby clung to her, and, with piteous cries, endeavored to attract her attention. I came up, and when it saw me it hid its poor little head in its mother's breast. It could neither walk nor bite, it was such a tiny little baby gorilla. We could easily manage it ; and I carried it, while the men bore the mother on a pole.

When we got to the village another scene ensued. The men put the body down, and I set the little fellow near. As soon as he saw his mother he crawled to her, and threw himself on her breast. He did not find his accustomed nourishment, and perceived that something was the matter with his mother. He crawled over her body, smelt at it, and gave utterance from time to time to a plaintive cry, " hoo, hoo, hoo," which touched my heart.

I could get no milk for this poor little fellow. He could not eat, and consequently he died on the third day after he was caught.

AN INCANTATION SCENE.

CHAPTER XXXI.

GOING TO UNKNOWN REGIONS.—QUENGUEZA SENDS HIS SON
AS A HOSTAGE.—I TAKE HIM ALONG WITH ME.—RECEPTION
BY THE KING.—OUR SPEECHES.—QUENGUEZA AFRAID OF A
WITCH.—AN INCANTATION SCENE.

TIME passed on. It was several years since I left the
United States, but nevertheless I determined to set out
for the head waters of the Fernand-Vaz, and for countries undiscovered as yet by white men.

Quengueza had sent to me his eldest son, named Kom-
bé (the sun), with a present of ebony wood, and his young-
est son, a boy of ten, called Akounga; and he said I must
come, and leave Akounga in Ranpano's hands as a hostage for my safety. "You see," he sent word, "that I
am not afraid of you. You may trust me."

I had to take my big boat, because no canoe would

hold all the goods, powder and shot, guns, provisions, and medicines I took along. It was to be a very, very long journey. I was the first white man to venture up in this direction, and I was anxious to get as far as possible.

We were fifteen in all in my boat. Another canoe, with fifteen more men, followed us. Quengueza's little boy was with us too. I would never have thought of such a thing as keeping the poor little fellow away from his mother and father. I took also the brave little Maeondai, whom I had at first determined to leave behind, as being too small to stand the fatigues of such a journey. The little fellow entreated so much to be taken that I at last consented. He behaved like a man. Macondai grew fast as years went by, and I wish you could have seen him fighting by my side in Ashango land.

At last, after much fatigue and hard pulling, we reached the village of Goumbi, the residence of King Quengueza. Here I was received in the most triumphant manner. I could not make myself heard for the shouts and firing of guns. The whole population of Goumbi crowded down to the shore to see me, and I was led up in procession to an immense covered space, capable of holding at least a thousand people, and surrounded by seats. I found there strangers from various parts of the interior, who gazed at me, and especially at my hair, with the greatest wonder.

A large high seat was appointed for me, and another close to it was for Quengueza, who presently arrived with a face beaming with joy. He shook hands with me, and then seated himself.

There was a dead silence in the vast crowd before us. Quengueza was an old, white-wooled negro, very tall,

spare, and of a severe countenance, betokening great en-
ergy and courage, qualities for which he was celebrated
all over their country. When younger he was the dread
of all, but now that he had become the chief of his clan,
and was getting old, he had grown milder, and become
peaceful, to the great joy of the surrounding villages. He
was a very remarkable man for his opportunities. He
made haste to tell me that he was in mourning for his
eldest brother, who had died two years before, and left
him chief of their clan, the Abouya.

Quengueza had on a finely-knit black cap, and a grass
body-cloth, which was black also; both the cap and cloth
were of Ashira make, and were really beautiful. He had
no shirt; that article is not allowed to mourners; but he
wore an American coat which was too small for him.

After the king had done welcoming me, I called his
little son, Akounga. When he had come forward, I said
to the king in a loud voice, that the people might hear,
"You sent your son to me to keep, so that I might feel
safe to come to you. I am not afraid. I like you, and
can trust you; therefore I have brought your little son
back to you. I do not want him as a hostage for my
safety. Let him remain by the side of his mother."

At this there was tremendous shouting, and the people
seemed overjoyed.

The king rose to reply. There was immediately a dead
silence, for Quengueza was greatly reverenced by his people. The king said, "This is my *ntangani* (white man);
he has come from a far country to see me. I went down
to beg him to come up to me. Now he has come. Let
no one do harm to his people; for him I need not speak.
Give food to his people. Treat them well. Do not steal

any thing. If you do not do as I say, A BIG PALAVER WILL COME UPON YOU!" This last sentence he uttered in a tremendous voice.

Then he addressed himself to the Ashira and Bakalai, who were present, saying, "Beware! Do not steal my white man, for if you should make the attempt, I will sell you all."

Then loads of plantains and sugar-eanes, together with a hundred fowls, and several goats, were presented to me by the king, and this closed the ceremony.

The longer I staid with Quengueza, the more I loved him; I was only sorry that he was so curiously superstitious. For a year he had not passed down the street which led most dircetly to the water, but had gone always by a roundabout way, beeause, when he eame to the throne, this street was pronounced bewitched by a seeret enemy of his, and he was persuaded that if he passed by it he would surely die. This superstitious notion had originated in a dream of the king's, which had been interpreted in that way.

Several times efforts had been made by distinguished doctors to drive away the *aniemba* (witch) which there lay in wait; but the king, though he believed in sorcery, did not have much faith in the exorcisers or doctors. He thought that perhaps the aniemba had not gone, and that it was better to be on the safe side, which was not to go on the road at all. But his subjects felt very much troubled about this matter, for they wanted their king to pass through their street sometimes.

Onee more a last attempt was made to drive off the aniemba, or witch. A famous doctor from the far-off

Bakalai country had been brought down to perform this act. His name was Aquailai.

In the evening the people gathered in great numbers under the immense *hangar*, or covered space in which I had been received, and there lit fires, around which they sat. The space thus covered was one hundred and fifty feet long by forty wide, and was roofed with palm branches and leaves.

About ten o'clock, when it was pitch dark, the doctor commenced operations by singing some boastful songs, recounting his power over witches. Immediately all the people gathered into their houses, and with such great haste that two women, failing to get home, and afraid to go farther through the streets, took refuge in my house. Then all the fires in the houses were carefully extinguished, those under the hangar having been already put out; and in about an hour more there was not a light of any kind in the whole town except mine. They had only asked of me that I should shut my door. The most pitchy darkness and the most complete silence reigned every where. No voice could be heard, even in a whisper, among the several thousands of people gathered in the gloom.

At last the silence was broken by the doctor, who, standing in the centre of the town, began some loud babbling, of which I could not make out the meaning. From time to time the people answered him in chorus. This went on for an hour, and was really one of the strangest scenes I ever took part in. I could see nothing but the faces of the two women in my house, who were badly frightened, poor things, as, in fact, all the people were. The hollow voice of the witch-doctor resounded curiously through the silence; and when the answer of many mingled voices came through the darkness, the ceremony really assumed the air of a poet's incantation scene.

At last, just at midnight by my watch, I heard the doctor approach. He had bells girded about him, which he jingled as he walked. He went to every family in the town successively, and asked if to them belonged the aniemba (witch) that obstructed the king's highway. Of course, all answered no. Then he began to run up and down the bewitched street, calling out loudly for the witch to go off. Presently he came back and announced that he could no longer see the aniemba, which had doubtless gone never to come back. At this all the people rushed out of their houses and shouted, "Go away! go away! and never come back to hurt our king!"

Then fires were lit, and all sat down to eat. This done, all the fires were once more extinguished, and the people sung wild songs until four o'clock. Then the fires were lit again.

At sunrise the whole population gathered to accompany their king down the dreaded street to the water. Quengueza, I know, was brave as a hunter and as a warrior. He was also very intelligent about many things regarding which his people were very stupid; but the poor old king was now horribly afraid. He was assured that the aniemba was gone, but he evidently thought that he was walking to almost certain death. He hesitated; but at last he determined to face his fate, and walked manfully down to the river and back, amid the plaudits of his loyal subjects. So ended the ceremony; but Quengueza never went again on that road; his dread of it still remained.

17

CHAPTER XXXII.

GORILLA HUNTING. — MY COMPANIONS MOMBON, ETIA, AND
GAMBO.—ETIA KILLS A LARGE GORILLA.—WE MAKE UP
A LARGE PARTY.—CAMP STORIES ABOUT GORILLAS.—WE
CAPTURE A YOUNG GORILLA.—HER UNTIMELY DEATH.

QUENGUEZA had a slave named Mombon whom he
loved greatly. Mombon was his overseer, chamberlain,
steward, man of business, and general factotum, the man
whose place it was to take care of the king's private
affairs, set his slaves to work, oversee his plantations,
and who had the care of the keys of the royal houses.
Mombon was to see that I was made comfortable in
town.

Quengueza had also another slave named Etia. Etia
was his favorite hunter, and he gave him to me for a
guide in the bush. This Etia was a fine-looking old
man, belonging to a tribe far in the interior, who had
never heard that there was such a thing as a white man
in the world. He was living on a little plantation outside the town, where he had a neat house, and a nice old
wife, who always treated me in a kind, motherly way;
she always had something to give me to eat. Etia's business was to supply the royal larder with "bush meat,"
and he went out hunting almost every week for that
purpose.

Etia and I became great friends, and loved each other

GORILLA HUNTING.

much. I gave to Etia and to his wife many little presents, with which they always seemed very much pleased.
Around the house of Etia were arranged skulls of elephants, hippopotami, leopards, and gorillas, as trophies of
his prowess.

Among the numerous guests of Quengueza was an
Ashira chief, who had come on a visit to the king. He
had a son called Gambo, a noted hunter. Gambo was a
very ill-looking fellow, but he had a fiery eye, great courage, and a kind heart. I became very fond of Gambo,
and Gambo became very fond of me. Sometimes Quengueza could not help saying to his people, "See how
hunters love each other, no matter if they come from
different countries. See how my white man loves the
black hunters." In fact, we were always together.
I had never seen the Ashira tribe to which Gambo belonged.

One day we had been going through the woods about
three hours when at last we came upon fresh gorilla
tracks. Etia now set out alone, while Gambo and I
walked silently in another direction. The gorilla is
so difficult to approach that we had literally to creep
through the thick woods when in their vicinity. The
hunter can not expect to see his enemy till he is close
upon him. The forest is so thick and gloomy that even
when quite near the animal is but dimly visible. All
this makes hunting for the gorilla very trying to the
nerves; for it is in the hunter's mind that if he misses
—if his bullet does not go to the most fatal point—the
wounded and infuriated brute will make short work of
his opponent.

As we crept silently along, suddenly the woods re-

sounded with the report of a gun. We sped at once toward the quarter whence the report came, and there we
found old Etia sitting complacently upon the dead body
of the largest female gorilla I ever saw. The total
height of the animal was four feet seven inches. This
was a huge gorilla for a female, for they are always
much smaller than the males.

Another time we made up a large party. We were
to go a considerable distance to a spot where Etia gave
me hopes that we should catch a young gorilla alive. I
would have gone through any hardship and peril to get
one large enough to be kept alive, and to be sent to Europe.

Etia, Gambo, myself, and ten men composed our party. Each was armed, and laden with provisions for a
couple of days. The men were covered with fetiches.
They had painted their faces red, and had cut their
hands in more than fifty different places. This bleeding of the hands was done for luck. The fellows were
nearly naked; but this is their usual habit.

As for me, I had also made extra preparations. I had
blackened my face and hands with powdered charcoal
and oil; and my blue drilling shirt and trowsers and
black shoes made me as dark as any of them. My revolvers hung at my side, with my ammunition bag and
brandy flask; my rifle lay upon my shoulder. All this
excited the admiration of the crowd which assembled to
see us go out.

Quengueza was greatly delighted, and exclaimed,
" What kind of ntangani (white man) is this? He fears
nothing; he cares for neither sun nor water; he loves
nothing but the hunt."

The old king charged the people to take great care of his white man, and to defend him with their lives, if need be.

We traveled all day, and about sunset came to a little river. Here we began at once to make a fire and build leafy shelters for the night. Scarcely was the fire-wood gathered, and we were safely bestowed under our shelter, when a storm came up which lasted half an hour. Then all was clear once more. We cooked plantains and smoked some dried fishes.

In the evening the men told stories about gorillas.

" I remember," said one, " my father told me he once went out to the forest, when just in his path he met a great gorilla. My father had his spear in his hand. When the gorilla saw the spear he began to roar ; then my father was terrified, and dropped the spear. When the gorilla saw that my father had dropped the spear he was pleased. He looked at him, and then left him and went into the thick forest. Then my father was glad, and went on his way."

Here all shouted together, " Yes ; so we must do when we meet the gorilla. Drop the spear ; that appeases him."

Next Gambo spoke. " Several dry seasons ago a man suddenly disappeared from my village after an angry quarrel. Some time after an Ashira of that village was out in the forest. He met a very large gorilla. That gorilla was the man who had disappeared ; he had turned into a gorilla. He jumped on the poor Ashira, and bit a piece out of his arm ; then he let him go. Then the man came back with his bleeding arm. He told me this. I hope we shall not meet such gorillas."

Chorus—"No; we shall not meet such wicked go-rillas."

I myself afterward met that man in the Ashira coun-try. I saw his maimed arm, and he repeated the same story.

Then one of the men spoke up: "If we kill a gorilla to-morrow, I should like to have a part of the brain for a fetich. Nothing makes a man so brave as to have a fetich of gorilla's brain. That gives a man a strong heart."

Chorus of those who remained awake—"Yes; that gives a man a strong heart."

Then we all gradually dropped to sleep.

Next morning we cleaned and reloaded our guns, and started off for the hunting ground. There is a particular little berry of which the gorilla is very fond, and where this is found in abundance you are sure to meet the animal.

We had divided. Etia, Gambo, two other men, and I kept together, and we had hardly gone more than an hour when we heard the cry of a young gorilla after his mother. Etia heard it first, and at once pointed out the direction in which it was.

Immediately we began to walk with greater caution than before. Presently Etia and Gambo crept ahead, as they were expert with the net, and were also the best woodsmen. I unwillingly remained behind, but dared not go with them, lest my clumsier movements should betray our presence. In a short time we heard two guns fired. Running up, we found the mother gorilla shot, but her little one had escaped; they had not been able to catch it.

The poor mother lay there in her gore, but the little fellow was off in the woods; so we concealed ourselves hard by to wait for its return. Presently it came up, jumped on its mother, and began sucking at her breasts and fondling her. Then Etia, Gambo, and I rushed upon it. Though evidently less than two years old, it proved very strong, and escaped from us. But we gave chase, and in a few minutes had it fast, not, however, before one of the men had his arm severely bitten by the savage little beast.

It proved to be a young female. Unhappily, she lived but ten days after capture. She persistently refused to eat any cooked food, or any thing else except the nuts and berries which they eat in the forest. She was not so ferocious as "Fighting Joe," but was quite as treacherous and quite as untamable. She permitted no one to approach her without trying to bite. Her eyes seemed somewhat milder than Joe's, but had the same gloomy and treacherous look, and she had the same way as Joe of looking you straight in the eyes when she was meditating an attack. I remarked in her also the same manœuvre practiced by the other when she wished to seize something—my leg, for instance, which, by reason of the chain around her neck, she could not reach with her arm. She would look me straight in the face, then quick as a flash would throw her body on one leg and one arm, and reach out with the other leg. Several times I had narrow escapes from the grip of her strong big toe. I thought sometimes that when she looked at me she appeared cross-eyed, but of this I could not make certain. All her motions were remarkably quick, and her strength was very great, though she was so small.

A TRIAL BY ORDEAL.

CHAPTER XXXIII.

VOYAGE UP THE RIVER. — WE BUILD A VILLAGE NEAR
OBINDJI. — QUENGUEZA'S PLAN FOR KEEPING THE SAB-
BATH.—KINDNESS OF THE NATIVES.—A TRIAL BY ORDEAL.

KING QUENGUEZA accompanied me on my voyage up
the Rembo and Ovenga Rivers. We were followed by a
great many canoes, and by chiefs of the Ashira and
Bakalai tribes. We were going to the Bakalai country.
The weather was intensely hot ; even the negroes suffered ; and, though I had a thick umbrella over my head,
and sat quite still, I had frequently to bathe my head
and keep net handkerchiefs in my banana hat ; for I
feared a sunstroke.

The river was narrow and deep, flowing generally between high lands and hills, and now and then in the
midst of flats.

Every body complained except Maeondai. He was the most spirited little negro I ever saw—a real little hero. I tell you that many, very many, of these African boys have a good deal of pluck, although they are black.

Two days after starting we arrived, a little before sun-set, at the village of Obindji, a Bakalai chief who was a great friend of Quengueza. Wherever we passed a Bakalai village the people rushed down to the banks to see me. As we approached the village of Obindji, our men fired guns and sang songs. Obindji came down in great state, dressed in his silk hat, a shirt, and a nice cloth. He was ringing his *kendo*—a bell, which is the insignia of kingship there—a sort of royal sceptre. The high-crowned silk hat, also, as I have said before, is worn only by the chiefs.

I said to Obindji, " Why do you ring your kendo ?"

He replied, " Obindji's heart is glad, and he thanks his Mboundji (a spirit) that he has to-day come up higher than he ever stood before—a *ntangani* (white man) has come to see Obindji."

When we had landed, and the two kings and I were seated on the stools used in that country, the grand re-ception began. Quengueza gave to his friend Obindji, and to all the Bakalai who surrounded us, an account of his entire intercourse with me, from the time he came down to see me at the sea-shore to the present hour.

Then Obindji replied, giving, in like manner (in short sentences), a statement of his feelings when he heard that Quengueza was to bring a ntangani to see him. This closed the conference.

The village of Obindji was small, and was beautifully situated at the foot of a high hill, just on the banks of

the Ovenga. The Ovenga River belonged to Quengueza,
and, except at its head waters, it had been inhabited by
the Bakalai only since the time of Quengueza's eldest
brother, whom he had succeeded. These Bakalai are
very warlike; they are much dreaded by the other tribes.

The region of the Ovenga is a grand and wild country.
It consists of hills and mountains, covered with impenetrable forests, which teem with all kinds of insects.
Many animals, curious birds, and a great number of
snakes are found there, together with those extraordinary ants, the Bashikouay. There also are the chimpan-
zees and gorillas.

As I intended to remain some time I set about building another village. The men all went into the forest
to collect bark, palm leaves, and posts.

When Sunday came, I requested Quengueza to make
the men rest on this day, explaining to him that white
men do not work on the Sabbath.

The old man was puzzled for a moment, and then said,
" We are much hurried now. Suppose you put off the
Sunday for three or four weeks. Then we can have as
many Sundays as you want. We will keep four or five
days following each other as Sundays. It will be just
the same."

He seemed quite proud of his discovery, and was quite
disappointed when I told him it would not do.

I worked very hard in building my house. The labor
was the more trying because the heat was so intense;
there was not a breath of wind in this Bakalai country.
Besides, the fever had got hold of me again; but I did
not give way to it.

Obindji became very friendly to me. I may say that

all these negroes seemed to take a liking for me. I made quite a number of friends among the Bakalai. Two of them, indeed, were very dear friends of mine; they were called Malaouen and Querlaouen. I really do not know which of the two I liked the best. They were ready to do any thing I wished them to do. If I proposed a hunt, they immediately offered to accompany me; if they killed game, they presented me with the best piece. Their wives were sure to bring me, almost every day, sugar-cane, plantain, or something else. As for Obindji, he did all in his power to please me. Moreover, Quengueza was always close to me. He said that wherever I went he would follow me, and build his shed by the side of mine. I was now Quengueza's white man and Obindji's white man. They all seemed to take pride in me. I am sure I also tried my best to be kind to them. Above all things, I wanted them to believe my word implicitly. Hence, whatever I promised, I kept my word. They noticed this, and therefore no one doubted me. These poor people, though they had no word to describe " an honest man," know the difference between lying and truth-telling; and they appreciate truthfulness.

One day I saw a trial by ordeal performed. A little boy, a son of Aquailai, the doctor who had driven the aniemba, or witch, from the main street at Goumbi, reported that one of Quengueza's men had damaged a Bakalai's canoe. The owner demanded compensation for the injury. The Goumbi men denied that he had injured the canoe, and asked for trial. An Ashira doctor who was in the village was called. He said that the only way to make the truth appear was by the trial of the ring boiled in oil. Thereupon the Bakalai and the

Goumbi men gathered together, and the trial was at once made.

The Ashira doctor stuck three little billets of wood into the ground, with their top ends together; then he piled some smaller pieces between, till all were laid as high as the three pieces. A native earthenware pot, half full of palm oil, was set upon the wood, which had been set on fire; and the oil was set on fire also. When it had burned up brightly, a brass bracelet or ring from the doctor's hand was cast into the pot. The doctor stood by with a little vase full of grass soaked in water, of which he threw in, now and then, some bits. This made the oil blaze up afresh. At last all was burned out, and now came the trial. The accuser, the little boy, was required at once to take the ring out of the pot. He hesitated, but was pushed on by his father. The people cried out, "Let us see whether he lied or told the truth." Finally he put his hand in and seized the almost red-hot ring, but quickly dropped it, having severely burned his fingers. At this there was a shout, "He lied! he lied!" and the Goumbi man was declared innocent. I ventured to suggest that he also would burn his fingers if he touched the ring, but nobody seemed to consider this view of the subject.

MEETING THE GORILLA.

CHAPTER XXXIV.

THE KOOLOO-KAMBA.—THE GOUAMBA, OR MEAT-HUNGER.—
EXPLORING THE FOREST. — GORILLA-HUNTING. — WITHIN
EIGHT YARDS OF A LARGE GORILLA. — HE ROARS WITH
RAGE AND MARCHES UPON US.

WE established ourselves in a deserted Bakalai village
a few miles from the banks of the Ovenga, and about ten
miles above Obindji. I was glad that I had no olako to
build.

There were with me several Bakalai, among whom, of
course, were my good friends Querlaouen and Malaouen.
Gambo was also one of our party.

After our camp was arranged we went out to look for

gorilla tracks.   It was too late to hunt; besides, we were
too tired.   In the evening Malaouen came in after dark,
and said he had heard the cry of the kooloo, and knew
where to find it in the morning.

Of course I asked what this kooloo was, for I had not
the slightest idea of what he meant.   I had never heard
the name before.   I received, in answer, a description of
the animal, which threw me into the greatest excitement;
for I saw this was most certainly a new species of ape,
or man-like monkey—a new man of the woods, of which
I had not even heard as yet.   It was called kooloo-kamba
by the Goumbi people from its cry or call, "Kooloo," and
the Commi word *kamba*, which means "speak."   The
Bakalai call it simply *koola*.

I scarce slept all night, with fidgeting over the morrow's prospects.   The Bakalai said the kooloo-kamba was
very rare here, and there was only a chance that we
should find the one whose call had been heard.

At last the tedious night was gone.   At the earliest
streak of dawn I had my men up.   We had fixed our
guns the night before.   All was ready, and we set out in
two parties.   My party had been walking through the
forest about an hour by a path which led I knew not
where, when suddenly I stepped into a file of Bashikouay
ants, whose fierce bites nearly made me scream.   The
little rascals were infuriated at my disturbance of their
progress, and they held on to my legs and to my trowsers
till I picked them off.   Of course I jumped nimbly out
of the way of the great army of which they formed part,
but I did not get off without some severe bites.

We had hardly got clear of the Bashikouays when my
ears were saluted by the singular cry of the ape I was

after. "Koola-kooloo, koola-kooloo," it said several times. Only Gambo and Malaouen were with me. Gambo and I raised our eyes, and saw, high up on a tree-branch. a large ape. It looked almost like a black hairy man. We both fired at once, and the next moment the poor beast fell with a heavy crash to the ground. I rushed up, anxious to see if, indeed, I had a new animal. I saw in a moment that it was neither a nshiego mbouvé, nor a common chimpanzee, nor a gorilla. Again I had a happy day. This kooloo-kamba was undoubtedly a new variety of chimpanzee.

We at once disemboweled the animal, which was a full-grown male. We found in his stomach nothing but berries, nuts, and fruits. He had, no doubt, just begun to take his breakfast.

This kooloo-kamba was four feet three inches high. He was powerfully built, with strong and square shoulders. He had a very round head, with whiskers running quite round the face and below the chin. The face was round ; the cheek-bones prominent ; the cheeks sunken. The roundness of the head, and the prominence of the cheek-bones, were so great as to remind me of some of the heads of Indians or Chinamen. The hair was black and long on the arms, which, however, were partly bare. His ears were large, and shaped like those of a human being. Of its habits the people could tell me nothing, except that it was found more frequently in the far interior. I brought the skin of this kooloo-kamba to New York, and some years ago many people saw it.

On our return to Obindji we were overtaken by my good friend Querlaouen, who had shot a wild pig, of which the good fellow gave me half. The negroes feasted on

18

the kooloo meat, which I could not touch. So the pig was welcome to me, as indeed it was to Quengueza, whom we found almost crying with an affection which is common in this part of Africa, and is called *gouamba*, but for which we happily have no name. Gouamba is the inordinate longing and craving of exhausted nature for meat. For days, and sometimes for weeks, a man does not get any meat at all, and whenever other food is brought before him, you will hear him say, looking at the food with disgust, "Gouamba," which means, literally, " I am sick of food ; I have a craving for meat ; I care for nothing else."

I had some glorious gorilla-hunting while in the Bakalai country, in the upper regions of the Ovenga River. Malaouen, Querlaouen, Gambo, and I often started out together, and remained for days in the thickest part of the forest. Now and then we would return to Obindji to get a supply of plantain, and then would go off again. We roamed over the forest in all directions ; we explored some new regions ; and sometimes we got lost in the midst of impenetrable mountains, where often for days we killed nothing.

In these excursions we suffered sometimes a good deal, for we had to endure many hardships. We often had very poor fare, and fever sometimes prostrated me.

One day, I remember well, we were out for gorillas, which we knew were to be found thereabouts by the presence of a pulpy pear-shaped fruit, the *tondo*, of which the animal is very fond. I also am very fond of the subdued and grateful acid of this fruit, which is eaten by the negroes as well as by the gorilla.

We found every where gorilla-marks, and so recent

that we began to think the animals must be avoiding us. This was really the case, I believe, though I am not sure. At any rate, we beat the bush for two hours before, at last, we found the game. Suddenly an immense gorilla advanced out of the wood straight toward us, and gave vent, as he came up, to a terrible howl of rage, as much as to say, "I am tired of being pursued, and will face you."

It was a lone male, the kind which are always most ferocious. This fellow made the woods resound with his roar, which is really an awful sound, resembling very much the rolling and muttering of distant thunder.

He was about twenty yards off when we first saw him. We at once gathered together; and I was about to take aim and bring him down where he stood, when Malaouen stopped me, saying in a whisper, "Not time yet."

We stood, therefore, in silence, gun in hand. The gorilla looked at us for a minute or so out of his evil gray eyes, then beat his breast with his gigantic arms—and what arms he had!—then he gave another howl of defiance, and advanced upon us. How horrible he looked! I shall never forget it.

Again he stopped, not more than fifteen yards away. Still Malaouen said "Not yet." Good gracious! what is to become of us if our guns miss fire, or if we only wound the huge beast?

Again the gorilla made an advance upon us. Now he was not twelve yards off. I could see plainly his ferocious face. It was distorted with rage; his huge teeth were ground against each other, so that we could hear the sound; the skin of the forehead was drawn forward and back rapidly, which made his hair move up and down, and gave a truly devilish expression to the hide ous face. Once more he gave out a roar, which seemed to shake the woods like thunder; I could really feel the earth trembling under my feet. The gorilla, looking us in the eyes, and beating his breast, advanced again.

"Don't fire too soon," said Malaouen; "if you do not kill him, he will kill you."

This time he came within eight yards of us before he stopped. I was breathing fast with excitement as I watched the huge beast.

Malaouen said only "Steady" as the gorilla came up. When he stopped, Malaouen said "Now!" And before he could utter the roar for which he was opening his mouth, three musket-balls were in his body. He fell dead almost without a struggle.

He was a monstrous beast indeed, though not among the tallest. His height was five feet six inches. His arms had a spread of seven feet two inches. His broad brawny chest measured fifty inches round. The big toe of his foot measured five inches and three quarters in circumference. His arms seemed like immense bunches of muscle only; and his legs and claw-like feet were so well fitted for grabbing and holding, that I could see how easy it was for the negroes to believe that these animals, when they conceal themselves in trees and watch for prey, can seize and pull up with their feet any living thing, leopard, ox, or man, that passes beneath.

The face of this gorilla was intensely black. The vast chest, which proved his great power, was bare, and covered with a parchment-like skin. His body was covered with gray hair. While the animal approached us in its fierce way, walking on its hind legs and facing us as few animals dare face man, it really seemed to me to be a horrid likeness of man.

MEETING OF THE MBUISI.

CHAPTER XXXV.

WITH Quengueza I resumed the ascent of the River
Ovenga. We were bound to the town of a chief named
Aguailai. The place was called N'calai Boumba.
We left Obindji early in the morning. On the way
we passed several Bakalai villages, the largest of which,
Npopo, I afterward visited. The river banks, all the
way up, were densely wooded, but very sparsely inhabited by beasts. We saw no animals the whole day except
one monkey and a few birds.

Aguailai, who was one of the vassals of Quengueza, and a powerful Bakalai chief, and whom I had met at Obindji's, received us well.

Aguailai's town is the hottest place I ever saw in Africa. N'calai Boumba was set in a hollow, and the houses were so small and close as to be quite unendurable to me. The village was only a little more than a year old. The people had come lately from the interior. Plantations of plantains were very abundant.

Toward the end of April I was brought down to my bed with fever. This was the severest attack I had yet experienced in Africa. It entirely prostrated me. I looked like a corpse. Not a single particle of color could be seen on my face. I had no strength. I could not eat. I could not walk.

For three days I had violent returns of the fever. The blood rushed to my head, and my mind wandered at times; so the natives told me. Of course I can not remember what I said. I only know that my head burned like fire, and that I was almost mad with pain. Between the attacks of fever I really thought I should die, and I commended my soul to God.

While I lay sick, people came and entreated me not to hunt so much and so constantly. They said, "Look at us; we hunt one day; we rest two. When we hunt three days, we rest for many days after it. But you go out every day."

I thought to myself, they are right, and I shall follow their rule hereafter. But it was hard to do so; for I felt that no one else was in the field; that in such an unhealthy climate no one can live very long, and I wanted to do as much work as I could. I wanted to bring

all the wonders of that part of the world to light; and
I felt that I was getting older and older, and there was
yet very much work to be done. So I prayed God to
give me strength for the work that was intrusted to my
hands.

I shall never forget the kindness of those native wom-
en to me while I was sick. Poor souls! they are sadly
abused by their task-masters. They are the merest slaves.
They have to do all the drudgery. They receive blows
and ill usage. And yet, at the sight of suffering, their
hearts soften, just as women's hearts soften in our own
more civilized lands. No sooner did sickness attack me
than these kind souls came to nurse and take care of me.
They sat by me to fan me; they brought more mats for
my bed; they bathed my burning head with cold water;
they got me refreshing fruits from the woods. At night,
when I woke up from a feverish dream, I used to hear
their voices, as they sat around in the darkness, pitying
me and contriving ways to cure me.

When I think of these things I can not help thanking
God for them; that, wherever I have gone, He has made
human hearts tender and kind to me; that, even under
the black skin of the benighted and savage African, He
has implanted something of His own compassionate love.

Aguailai and Quengueza were sadly alarmed at my
illness. Aguailai accused his people of wickedly bewitching me. One still night he walked up and down
the village, threatening, in a loud voice, to kill the sorcerers if he could only find them. I had to get up and
tell Aguailai that I was sure his people and the Bakalai
loved me too much to wish me to be sick, whereupon
they all shouted at once, " It is so; it is so."

After a few days I was able to walk again a little, and I went and lived in the forest, where I suffered less from the heat than in our little houses.

How sorry I often felt that these kind-hearted negroes were given to superstitions which led them to commit the most horrid cruelties. A little boy, about ten years old, had been accused of sorcery. On being examined, he confessed that he had made a witch. Thereupon the whole town seemed to be seized with the ferocity of devils. They took spears and knives, and actually cut the poor little fellow to pieces. I had been walking out, and returned just as the dreadful scene was over. I could not even make the wretched men feel shame at their bloody act. They were still frantic with rage at the thought that this little fellow had made a witch to kill some of them, and they were not quiet for some hours after.

I felt so badly that I went into the woods, and took the path that led to the village of Npopo, which was not far distant from N'calai Boumba. I wanted to see if the people had returned; I wanted to see Aguailai the chief. He was the doctor who had come to Goumbi to drive off the aniemba. When I went down to Npopo the first time I found the people all gone into the bush. Every thing was open and exposed to thieves; chickens and goats were walking about; and I wondered to see such carelessness in the village. But in the centre, looking down on every thing, stood the *mbuiti*, or god of Npopo, a copper-eyed divinity, who, I was informed, safely guarded every thing. It seemed absurd; but I was assured that no one dared steal, and no one did steal, with the eyes of this mbuiti upon him.

This uncommonly useful idol was a rudely-shaped piece of ebony, about two feet high, with a man's face, the nose and eyes of copper, and the body covered with grass.

At last we started for the ebony woods. Our new location was about nine miles from the river, on the side of a long hill, and close by where a cool sparkling rivulet leaped from rock to rock down into the plain, making the pleasantest of music for me as I lay, weak and sick, in the camp. Five huge ebony-trees lifted their crowned heads together in a little knot just above us. All around were pleasant and shady woods. It was a very pleasant camp, but proved to have one drawback—we nearly starved to death. I sent out the hunters immediately on our arrival. They were gone two days, but brought back nothing. Game was very scarce there; and, without an *ashinga*, or net, such as many Bakalai villages have, not much was to be got.

CHAPTER XXXVI.

HUNTING FOR FOOD.—WE KILL A FEMALE NSHIEGO MBOUVÉ.
—A YOUNG NSHIEGO WITH A WHITE FACE.—HE BECOMES
MY PET TOMMY.—HIS AFFECTION FOR ME.—HIS STEAL
ING PRANKS.—TOMMY GETS DRUNK.—HIS BEHAVIOR AT
MEALS.—HIS SUDDEN DEATH.—CONCLUSION.

At last I got better. I could not stand hunger and
gcuamba any longer, and determined to make up a regular hunting-party, and stay out till we got something to
eat. Malaouen told me that if we went off about twenty
miles we should come to a better game country. So we
started in the direction he pointed out, and where he
thought we should find the gorilla, or perhaps the nshiego
mbouvé.

The men were covered with greegrees, or fetiches, and
had cut their hands for luck. Aguailai told me that his
ogana (idol) had told him that to-morrow the heart of
the *otanga* (the white man) would be made glad, for we
should kill game.

For some hours after we started we saw nothing but
old tracks of different wild beasts, and I began to think
that Aguailai's ogana had been too sanguine. Finally,
toward twelve o'clock, when we were crossing a kind of
high table-land, we heard the cry of a young animal,
which we recognized to be a nshiego mbouvé. At once
all my troubles left me. I no longer felt either sick or
hungry.

A YOUNG NSHIEGO MBOUVE WITH A WHITE FACE.

We crawled through the bush as silently as possible, still hearing the baby-like cry. At last, coming out into a little place where there was very little undergrowth, we saw something running along the ground toward where we stood concealed. We hardly dared to breathe for fear of awakening the animal's suspicions.

When it came nearer, we saw it was a female nshiego mbouvé, running on all-fours, with a young one clinging to her breast. She was eagerly eating some berries, while with one arm she supported her little one.

Querlaouen, who had the fairest chance, fired, and brought her down. She dropped without a struggle. The poor little one cried " Hew! hew! hew!" and clung to the dead body, sucking her breasts, and burying his head there, in alarm at the report of the gun.

We hurried up in great glee to secure our capture. I can not tell my surprise when I saw that the nshiego baby's face was as white as that of a white child.

I looked at the mother, but found her black as soot in the face. What did it mean?—the mother black, the child white! The little one was about a foot in height. One of the men threw a cloth over its head, and secured it till we could make it fast with a rope; for, though it was quite young, it could walk. The old one was of the bald-headed kind, of which I had secured the first known specimen some months before.

I immediately ordered a return to the camp, which we reached toward evening. The little nshiego had been all this time separated from its dead mother, and now, when it was put near her body, a most touching scene ensued. The little fellow ran instantly to her. Touching her on the face and breast, he saw evidently that some great change had happened. For a few minutes he caressed her, as though trying to coax her back to life. Then he seemed to lose all hope. His little eyes became very sad, and he broke out in a long, plaintive wail, "Ooee! ooee! ooee!" which made my heart ache for him. He looked quite forlorn, and as though he really felt his forsaken lot. All in the camp were touched at his sorrows, and the women especially were much moved.

All this time I stood wonderingly staring at the white face of the creature. It was really marvelous, and quite incomprehensible. A more strange and weird-looking animal I never saw.

While I stood there, up came two of my hunters and began to laugh at me. "Look, Chaillie," said they, calling me by the name I am known by among them, "look at your friend. Every time we kill gorilla, you tell us look at your black friend, your first cousin. Now, you see, look at your white friend." Then came a roar of laughter at what they thought a tremendous joke.

"Look! he got straight hair, all same as you! See white face of your cousin from the bush! He is nearer to you than the gorilla is to us!"

Then they roared again.

"Gorilla no got woolly hair like me. This one straight hair like you."

"Yes,' said I; "but when he gets old his face is black; and do you not see his nose, how flat it is, like yours?"

Whereat there was a louder roar than before.

The mother was old, to judge by her teeth, which were much worn; but she was quite black in the face; in fact, her skin was black. Like all the nshiego mbouvé, she was bald-headed.

Now I must give you an account of the little fellow who excited all this surprise and merriment. He lived five months, and became perfectly tame and docile. I called him "Tommy," to which name he soon began to answer.

Three days after his capture he was quite tame. He then ate crackers out of my hands, devoured boiled rice and roasted plantain, and drank the milk of a goat. Two weeks after his capture he was perfectly tamed, and no longer required to be tied up. He ran about the camp, and, when we went back to Obindji's town, he found his way about the village and into the huts just as though he had been raised there.

He had a great affection for me, and used to follow me about. When I sat down, he was not content till he had climbed upon me, and hid his head in my breast. He was extremely fond of being petted and fondled, and would sit by the hour while any one stroked his head or back.

He soon began to be a very great thief. When the people left their huts, he would steal in, and make off with their plantains or fish (for he could then eat any thing). He watched very carefully till all had left a house, and it was difficult to catch him in the act. I flogged him several times, and, indeed, brought him to the conviction that it was *wrong* to steal; but he could never resist the temptation.

From me he stole constantly. He soon found out that my hut was the best supplied with ripe bananas and other fruit. He also discovered that the best time to steal from me was when I was asleep in the morning. At that time he used to crawl slowly and carefully on tiptoe toward my bed, and look at my closed eyes. If he saw no movement, with an air of great relief he would go and pick up several ripe plantains. If I stirred in the least he was off like a flash, and would presently re-enter for another inspection.

If my eyes were open when he came in on such a predatory trip, he would come directly to me, with an honest face, and would climb upon me, and caress me ; but I could easily detect an occasional wistful glance toward the bunch of plantains.

My hut had no door, but was closed with a mat. It was very funny to see Tommy gently raising one corner of this mat, and popping his head in to see if I was asleep. Sometimes I feigned sleep, and then stirred just as he was in the act of taking off his prize. Then he would drop every thing, and make off in the utmost consternation.

He kept the run of meal-times, and was present at as many meals as possible ; that is, he would go from my breakfast to half a dozen others, and beg sometimes at each. But he never missed my own breakfast and dinner, knowing by experience that he fared best there.

I had a kind of rude table made, on which my meals were served, in the open part of my house. This was too high for Tommy to see the dishes, so he used to come in before I sat down, when all was ready, and climb up on the pole that supported the roof. From here he would attentively survey every dish on the table, and having determined what to have, he would descend and sit down at my side. If I did not immediately pay attention to him he would begin to howl, " Hew ! hew ! hew !" louder and louder, till, for peace sake, his wants were satisfied. Of course I could not tell what he had chosen for dinner of my different dishes, and would offer him first one, then another, till the right one came. If he received what he did not want, he would throw it down on the ground with a little shriek of anger and a stamp of his foot, and begin to howl, and this was repeated till he was served to his liking. In short, he behaved very much like a spoiled child.

If I pleased him quickly, he thanked me by a kind of gentle murmur, like "hoohoo," and would hold out his hand to shake mine. He knew perfectly how to shake hands. He was very fond of boiled messes, particularly boiled fish, and was constantly picking the bones he found lying about the village. He wanted always to taste of my coffee, and when Macondai brought it, would beg some of me in the most serious manner.

I made him a little pillow to sleep on, and he became very fond of it. After he was accustomed to it, he would never part with it, but dragged it after him wherever he went. If by any chance it was lost, the whole camp knew it by his howls. Now and then, on some forest excursion, he would mislay it, and then I had to send people for it in order to stop his noise. At other times the people would hide it, just to tease him. He slept on it, coiled up in a little heap, and only relinquished it when I gave him permission to accompany me into the woods.

As he became more and more used to our ways, he grew more impatient of contradiction, and more fond of being caressed; and whenever he was thwarted he would howl in his disagreeable way. Now and then I gave him a flogging to teach him better manners.

19

As the dry season came on it became colder, and
Tommy began to wish for company when he slept, to
keep him warm. The negroes would not have him for
a companion, for he seemed too much like one of themselves. I did not like to have him in bed with me. So
poor Tommy was reduced to misery, as he seemed to
think nobody would have him. But soon I found that
he waited till every body was fast asleep at night, and
then crawled in softly next to some of his black friends,
and slept there till the earliest dawn. Then he would
get up and get away undiscovered. At other times he
felt too warm and comfortable to get up, and was caught
and beaten, but he always tried it again.

He showed an extraordinary fondness for strong drink.
Whenever a negro had palm wine Tommy was sure to
know it. He had a decided taste for Scotch ale, of which
I had a few bottles, and he even begged for brandy. Indeed, his last exploit was with a brandy bottle. One day,
before going out to the hunt, I had carelessly left the
bottle on my chest. The little rascal stole in and seized
it; and, being unable to get out the cork, in some way he
broke the bottle. When I returned, after some hours'
absence, I found my precious bottle broken in pieces!
It was the last; and to an African traveler brandy is as
indispensable as quinine. Master Tommy was coiled up
on the floor amid the fragments in a state of maudlin
drunkenness. When he saw me he got up, and tried to
stagger up to me; but his legs tottered, and he fell down
several times. His eyes had the glare of human drunkenness; his arms were extended in vain attempts to reach
me; his voice came thick; in fact, he looked disgusting-
ly and yet comically human. It was the maudlin and

sentimental stage of human drunkenness very well represented. I had seen men looking exactly as Tommy
did, and I wished these drunkards could have seen him;
they might then, perhaps, have become so disgusted with
themselves that they would have given up their horrid
vice. I gave him a severe thrashing, which seemed to
sober the little toper somewhat; but nothing could cure
him of his love for liquor.

He was also very fond of tea and coffee, but wanted
both to be well sweetened. He could drink out of a
cup. Sometimes, to tease him, I would not put in any
sugar; then he would throw down the cup and begin to
howl, and he would make the whole place resound with
his noise.

He had a great deal of intelligence; and, if I had had
leisure, I think I might have trained him to some kind
of good behavior, though I despaired of his thieving dis-
position. The older he grew, the greater thief he became.

He lived so long, and was growing so accustomed to
civilized life, that I began to have great hopes of carry
ing him alive to America.

Sometimes he would come round the fire where my
men were, and warm himself with them. How comical
he then look d! At other times, when they took their
meals, and ate out of a common dish, Master Tommy
would join the party; and when they would all put their
hands into the dish, he would put his in also, and take a
little handful of cooked and smoked fish. In fact, he
kept time with them.

But alas! poor Tommy! One morning he refused his
food, seemed downcast, and was very anxious to be pet-

ted, and held in our arms. I got all kinds of forest berries for him, but he refused all. He did not seem to
suffer, but he ate nothing; and next day, without a struggle, he died. Poor fellow! he seemed sorry to leave us.
I was grieved; and even the negroes, though he had
given them great trouble, were mournful at his death.
He had hardly expired when the news spread through
the village that little Tommy was no more. They all
came to see him; he looked as if he were asleep.

It seemed as if we had lost a friend. We missed his
mischief and noise; and for many days we all mourned
for Tommy, and wished him back among us.

Tommy turned darker as he grew older. At the time
of his death he was yellow rather than white. If he had
lived to be old, he would, no doubt, have become black,
like his mother.

And now, young friends, for the present I have done.
I have told you many things about Africa, about its
strange animals, its terrible gorillas, its savage Cannibals; and all that I have told you is true, for it is what
I have seen with my own eyes.

But I have not told you all that I saw and heard in
that far-distant country. I have many more singular
sights to describe, and queer adventures to recount to
you.

So I will not bid you farewell; I will say to you "*Au
revoir!*" That means, "Good-by till I come again."

THE END.

MACAULAY'S ENGLAND. The History of England from the Accession of James II. By THOMAS BABINGTON MACAULAY. 5 vols., in a Box, 8vo, Cloth, with Paper Labels, Uncut Edges and Gilt Tops, $10 00; Sheep, $12 50; Half Calf, $21 25. (*Sold only in Sets.*) Cheap Edition, 5 vols., 12mo, Cloth, $2 50; Sheep, $3 75.

MACAULAY'S MISCELLANEOUS WORKS. The Miscellaneous Works of Lord Macaulay. 5 vols., in a Box, 8vo, Cloth, with Paper Labels, Uncut Edges and Gilt Tops, $10 00; Sheep, $12 50; Half Calf, $21 25. (*Sold only in Sets.*)

HUME'S ENGLAND. History of England, from the Invasion of Julius Cæsar to the Abdication of James II., 1688. By DAVID HUME. 6 vols., in a Box, 8vo, Cloth, with Paper Labels, Uncut Edges and Gilt Tops, $12 00; Sheep, $15 00; Half Calf, $25 50. (*Sold only in Sets.*) Popular Edition, 6 vols., in a Box, 12mo, Cloth, $3 00; Sheep, $4 50.

THE WORKS OF OLIVER GOLDSMITH. Edited by PETER CUNNINGHAM, F.S.A. 4 vols., 8vo, Cloth, Paper Labels, Uncut Edges and Gilt Tops, $8 00; Sheep, $10 00; Half Calf. $17 00.

THE RISE OF THE DUTCH REPUBLIC. A History. By JOHN LOTHROP MOTLEY, LL.D., D.C.L. With a Portrait of William of Orange. 3 vols., in a Box. 8vo, Cloth, with Paper Labels, Uncut Edges and Gilt Tops, $6 00; Sheep, $7 50; Half Calf, $12 75. (*Sold only in Sets.*)

HISTORY OF THE UNITED NETHERLANDS: From the Death of William the Silent to the Twelve Years' Truce—1548–1609. With a full View of the English-Dutch Struggle against Spain, and of the Origin and Destruction of the Spanish Armada. By JOHN LOTHROP MOTLEY, LL.D., D.C.L. Portraits. 4 vols., in a Box, 8vo, Cloth, with Paper Labels, Uncut Edges and Gilt Tops, $8 00; Sheep, $10 00; Half Calf, $17 00. (*Sold only in Sets.*)

THE LIFE AND DEATH OF JOHN OF BARNEVELD, Advocate of Holland. With a View of the Primary Causes and Movements of the "Thirty Years' War." By JOHN LOTHROP MOTLEY, LL.D., D.C.L. Illustrated. 2 vols., in a Box, 8vo, Cloth, with Paper Labels, Uncut Edges and Gilt Tops, $4 00; Sheep, $5 00; Half Calf, $8 50. (*Sold only in Sets.*)

GIBBON'S ROME. The History of the Decline and Fall of the Roman Empire. By EDWARD GIBBON. With Notes by Dean MILMAN, M. GUIZOT, and Dr. WILLIAM SMITH. 6 vols., in a Box, 8vo, Cloth, with Paper Labels, Uncut Edges and Gilt Tops, $12 00; Sheep, $15 00; Half Calf, $25 50. Popular Edition, 6 vols., in a Box, 12mo, Cloth, $3 00; Sheep, $4 50. (*Sold only in Sets.*)

A DICTIONARY OF THE ENGLISH LANGUAGE. Pronouncing, Etymological, and Explanatory: embracing Scientific and other Terms, Numerous Familiar Terms, and a Copious Selection of Old English Words. By the Rev. JAMES STORMONTH. The Pronunciation Revised by the Rev. P. H. PHELP, M.A. Imperial 8vo, Cloth, $5 00; Half Roan, $6 50; Full Sheep, $6 50.

A MANUAL OF HISTORICAL LITERATURE, comprising Brief Descriptions of the most Important Histories in English, French, and German, together with Practical Suggestions as to Methods and Courses of Historical Study, for the Use of Students, General Readers, and Collectors of Books. By CHARLES KENDALL ADAMS, LL.D. Third Edition, Revised and Enlarged. Crown 8vo, Cloth, $2 50.

ART AND CRITICISM. Monographs and Studies. By THEODORE CHILD. Richly Illustrated. Large 8vo, Cloth, Ornamental, Uncut Edges and Gilt Top, $6 00. (*In a Box.*)

THE SPANISH-AMERICAN REPUBLICS. By THEODORE CHILD. Illustrated by T. DE THULSTRUP, FREDERIC REMINGTON, WILLIAM HAMILTON GIBSON, W. H. ROGERS, and other Eminent Artists. Large 8vo, Cloth, Ornamental, $3 50.

ILIOS, the City and Country of the Trojans. A Narrative of the Most Recent Discoveries and Researches made on the Plain of Troy. By Dr. HENRY SCHLIEMANN. Maps, Plans, and Illustrations. Imperial 8vo, Illuminated Cloth, $7 50; Half Morocco, $10 00.

TROJA. Results of the Latest Researches and Discoveries on the Site of Homer's Troy, and in the Heroic Tumuli and other Sites, made in the Year 1882, and a Narrative of a Journey in the Troad in 1881. By Dr. HENRY SCHLIEMANN. Preface by Professor A. H. Sayce. With Wood-cuts, Maps, and Plans. 8vo, Cloth, $5 00; Half Morocco, $7 50.

HISTORY OF THE UNITED STATES. By RICHARD HIL-
DRETH. FIRST SERIES: From the Discovery of the Continent
to the Organization of the Government under the Federal Con-
stitution. SECOND SERIES: From the Adoption of the Federal
Constitution to the end of the Sixteenth Congress. Popular
Edition, 6 vols., in a Box, 8vo, Cloth, with Paper Labels, Uncut
Edges and Gilt Tops, $12 00; Sheep, $15 00; Half Calf, $25 00.
(*Sold only in Sets.*)

RECOLLECTIONS OF PRESIDENT LINCOLN and His Ad-
ministration. By LUCIUS E. CHITTENDEN. With Portrait.
8vo, Cloth, Uncut Edges and Gilt Top, $2 50; Half Calf,
$4 75.

MEMOIR OF THE LIFE OF LAURENCE OLIPHANT and of
Alice Oliphant, his wife. By MARGARET OLIPHANT W. OLI-
PHANT. 2 vols., 8vo, Cloth, Uncut Edges and Gilt Tops, $7 00.
(*In a Box.*)

EPISODES IN A LIFE OF ADVENTURE; or, Moss from a
Rolling Stone. By LAURENCE OLIPHANT. 12mo, Cloth, $1 25.

HAIFA; OR, LIFE IN MODERN PALESTINE. By LAURENCE
OLIPHANT. Edited, with Introduction, by CHARLES A. DANA.
12mo, Cloth, $1 75.

CONSTITUTIONAL HISTORY OF THE UNITED STATES
from their Declaration of Independence to the Close of their
Civil War. By GEORGE TICKNOR CURTIS. Two Volumes.
Vol. I., 8vo, Cloth, Uncut Edges and Gilt Top, $3 00.

OUR ITALY. An Exposition of the Climate and Resources of
Southern California. By CHARLES DUDLEY WARNER. Illustrated. 8vo, Cloth, Uncut Edges and Gilt Top, $2 50.

LONDON LETTERS, and Some Others. By GEORGE W.
SMALLEY, London Correspondent of the *New York Tribune.*
Two Volumes. Vol I. Personalities—Two Midlothian Cam-
paigns. Vol. II. Notes on Social Life—Notes on Parliament—
Pageants — Miscellanies. 8vo, Cloth, Uncut Edges and Gilt
Tops, $6 00.

LIFE AND LETTERS OF GENERAL THOMAS J. JACKSON
(Stonewall Jackson). By His Wife, MARY ANNA JACKSON.
With an Introduction by HENRY M. FIELD, D.D. Illustrated.
8vo, Cloth, $2 00.

*POLITICAL HISTORY OF RECENT TIMES (1816–1875). With Special Reference to Germany. By WILLIAM MÜLLER. Translated, with an Appendix covering the Period from 1876 to 1881, by the Rev. JOHN P. PETERS, Ph.D. 12mo, Cloth, $2 00.

THE LIFE AND LETTERS OF LORD MACAULAY. By his Nephew, GEORGE OTTO TREVELYAN, M.P. With Portrait on Steel. 2 vols., 8vo, Cloth, Uncut Edges and Gilt Tops, $5 00; Sheep, $6 00; Half Calf, $9 50. *Popular Edition*, two vols. in one, 12mo, Cloth, $1 75.

THE EARLY HISTORY OF CHARLES JAMES FOX. By GEORGE OTTO TREVELYAN. 8vo, Cloth, Uncut Edges and Gilt Tops, $2 50; Half Calf, $4 75.

WRITINGS AND SPEECHES OF SAMUEL J. TILDEN. Edited by JOHN BIGELOW. 2 vols., 8vo, Cloth, Uncut Edges and Gilt Tops, $6 00 per set.

MEMOIRS OF JOHN ADAMS DIX. Compiled by his Son, MORGAN DIX. With Five Steel-plate Portraits. 2 vols., 8vo, Cloth, Uncut Edges and Gilt Tops, $5 00.

THROUGH THE DARK CONTINENT; or, The Sources of the Nile, Around the Great Lakes of Equatorial Africa, and Down the Livingstone River to the Atlantic Ocean. 149 Illustrations and 10 Maps. By H. M. STANLEY. 2 vols., 8vo, Cloth, $7 50; Sheep, $9 50; Half Morocco, $12 00.

THE CONGO and the Founding of its Free State, a Story of Work and Exploration. With over One Hundred Full-page and smaller Illustrations, Two Large Maps, and several smaller ones. By H. M. STANLEY. 2 vols., 8vo, Cloth, $7 50; Sheep, $9 50; Half Morocco, $12 00.

HISTORY OF THE ENGLISH PEOPLE. By JOHN RICHARD GREEN, M.A. With Maps. 4 vols., 8vo, Cloth, $2 50 per vol. Volumes sold separately. Complete sets, Sheep, $12 00; Half Calf, $19 00.

THE MAKING OF ENGLAND. By JOHN RICHARD GREEN. With Maps. 8vo, Cloth, $2 50; Sheep, $3 00; Half Calf, $4 75.

THE CONQUEST OF ENGLAND. By JOHN RICHARD GREEN. With Maps. 8vo, Cloth, $2 50; Sheep, $3 00; Half Calf, $4 75.

A SHORT HISTORY OF THE ENGLISH PEOPLE. By JOHN RICHARD GREEN, M.A. Revised and Enlarged. With Colored Maps and Tables. 8vo, Cloth, $1 20.

THE LAND OF THE MIDNIGHT SUN. Summer and Winter Journeys in Sweden, Norway, Lapland, and Northern Fin-
land. By PAUL B. DU CHAILLU. Illustrated. 2 vols., 8vo,
Cloth, $7 50; Half Calf, $12 00.

CYCLOPÆDIA OF UNITED STATES HISTORY. From the
Aboriginal Period to 1876. By BENSON J. LOSSING. Illus-
trated by 2 Steel Portraits and over 1000 Engravings. 2 vols.,
Royal 8vo, Cloth, $10 00; Sheep, $12 00; Half Morocco, $15 00.

PICTORIAL FIELD-BOOK OF THE REVOLUTION; or, Illustrations by Pen and Pencil of the History, Biography, Scenery,
Relics, and Traditions of the War for Independence. By BEN-
SON J. LOSSING. 2 vols., 8vo, Cloth, $14 00; Sheep or Roan,
$15 00; Half Calf, $18 00.

PICTORIAL FIELD - BOOK OF THE WAR OF 1812; or,
Illustrations by Pen and Pencil of the History, Biography.
Scenery, Relics, and Traditions of the last War for American In-
dependence. By BENSON J. LOSSING. 8vo, Cloth, $7 00;
Sheep or Roan, $8 50; Half Calf, $10 00.

ENGLISH MEN OF LETTERS. Edited by JOHN MORLEY.
The following volumes are now ready:

JOHNSON. By L. Stephen.—GIBBON. By J. C. Morison.—SCOTT. By R. H.
Hutton.—SHELLEY. By J. A. Symonds.—GOLDSMITH. By W. Black.—HUME.
By Professor Huxley.—DEFOE. By W. Minto.—BURNS By Principal Shairp.
—SPENSER. By R. W. Church.—THACKERAY. By A. Trollope.—BURKE. By
J. Morley.—MILTON. By M. Pattison.—SOUTHEY. By E. Dowden.—CHAUCER.
By A. W. Ward.—BUNYAN. By J. A. Froude.—COWPER. By G. Smith.—POPE.
By L. Stephen.—BYRON. By J. Nichols.—LOCKE. By T. Fowler.—WORDS-
WORTH. By F. W. H. Myers.—HAWTHORNE. By Henry James, Jr.—DRY-
DEN. By G. Saintsbury.—LANDOR. By S. Colvin.—DE QUINCEY. By D. Mas-
son.—LAMB. By A. Ainger.—BENTLEY. By R. C. Jebb.—DICKENS. By A.
W. Ward.—GRAY. By E. W. Gosse.—SWIFT. By L. Stephen.—STERNE. By H.
D. Traill. — MACAULAY. By J. C. Morison.— FIELDING. By A. Dobson.—
SHERIDAN. By Mrs. Oliphant.—ADDISON. By W. J. Courthope.—BACON. By
R. W. Church.—COLERIDGE. By H. D. Traill.—SIR PHILIP SIDNEY. By J. A.
Symonds.—KEATS. By S. Colvin. 12mo, Cloth, 75 cents per volume.

Popular Edition. 36 volumes in 12, Cloth, $12 00; Half Leath-
er, $21 00.

HISTORY OF THE INQUISITION OF THE MIDDLE AGES.
By HENRY CHARLES LEA. 3 vols., 8vo, Cloth, Uncut Edges and
Gilt Tops, $3 00 per vol.

THE MIKADO'S EMPIRE. Book I. History of Japan, from 660 B.C. to 1872 A.D. Book II. Personal Experiences, Observations, and Studies in Japan, from 1870 to 1874. With Two Supplementary Chapters: Japan in 1883, 1886, and 1890. By W. E. GRIFFIS. Copiously Illustrated. 8vo, Cloth, $4 00; Half Calf, $6 25.

A SHORT HISTORY OF THE ENGLISH COLONIES IN AMERICA. By HENRY CABOT LODGE. With Colored Map. 8vo, Half Leather, $3 00.

THE LAND AND THE BOOK. Biblical Illustrations drawn from the Manners and Customs, the Scenes and Scenery, of the Holy Land. By WILLIAM M. THOMSON, D.D., Forty-five Years a Missionary in Syria and Palestine. In Three Volumes. Copiously Illustrated. Square 8vo, Ornamental Cloth, per volume, $6 00; Sheep, $7 00; Half Morocco, $8 50; Full Morocco, Gilt Edges, $10 00.
    Volume I. SOUTHERN PALESTINE AND JERUSALEM.—Volume II. CENTRAL PALESTINE AND PHŒNICIA.—Volume III. LEBANON, DAMASCUS, AND BEYOND JORDAN.
    Also, Handsome *Popular Edition* in Three Vols., Cloth, $9 00 per Set; Half Leather, $12 00. (*Sold only in Sets.*)

THE INVASION OF THE CRIMEA: its Origin, and an Account of its Progress down to the Death of Lord Raglan. By ALEXANDER WILLIAM KINGLAKE. With Maps and Plans. Six vols. 12mo, Cloth, $2 00 per vol. ; Half Calf, $22 50 per set.

FIFTY YEARS AGO. By WALTER BESANT. With a Portrait and Characteristic Illustrations by Cruikshank and others. 8vo. Cloth, $2 50.

THE TSAR AND HIS PEOPLE; or, Social Life in Russia. Papers by THEODORE CHILD, EUGÈNE MELCHIOR DE VOGÜÉ, CLARENCE COOK, and VASSILI VERESTCHAGIN. Illustrated. Square 8vo, Cloth, Uncut Edges and Gilt Top, $3 00.

THE CAPITALS OF SPANISH AMERICA. By WILLIAM ELEROY CURTIS. With a Colored Map and 358 Illustrations. 8vo, Cloth, $3 50.

JINRIKISHA DAYS IN JAPAN. By ELIZA RUHAMAH SKID-MORE. Illustrated. Post 8vo, Cloth, Ornamental, $2 00.

LIFE OF BISHOP MATTHEW SIMPSON, of the Methodist Episcopal Church. By George R. Crooks, D.D. Illustrated. 8vo, Cloth, $3 75; Gilt Edges, $4 25; Half Morocco, $5 25. (*Sold by Subscription.*)

SERMONS BY BISHOP MATTHEW SIMPSON, of the Methodist Episcopal Church. Edited by George R. Crooks, D.D. 8vo, Cloth, $2 50.

LITERARY INDUSTRIES. By Hubert Howe Bancroft. With Steel-Plate Portrait. Post 8vo, Cloth $1 50.

CURIOSITIES OF THE AMERICAN STAGE. By Laurence Hutton. With Copious and Characteristic Illustrations. Crown 8vo, Cloth, Uncut Edges and Gilt Top, $2 50.

STUDIES IN THE WAGNERIAN DRAMA. By Henry E. Krehbiel. Post 8vo, Cloth, $1 25.

HISTORY OF MEDIÆVAL ART. By Dr. Franz von Reber. Translated and Augmented by Joseph Thacher Clarke. With 422 Illustrations, and a Glossary of Technical Terms. 8vo, Cloth, $5 00.

HISTORY OF ANCIENT ART. By Dr. Franz von Reber. Revised by the Author. Translated and Augmented by Joseph Thacher Clarke. With 310 Illustrations and a Glossary of Technical Terms. 8vo, Cloth, $3 50.

OUTLINES OF INTERNATIONAL LAW, with an Account of its Origin and Sources, and of its Historical Development. By George B. Davis, U.S.A. Crown 8vo, Cloth, $2 00.

CYPRUS: its Ancient Cities, Tombs, and Temples. A Narrative of Researches and Excavations during Ten Years' Residence in that Island. By L. P. di Cesnola. With Portrait, Maps, and 400 Illustrations. 8vo, Cloth, Extra, Uncut Edges and Gilt Top, $7 50.

THE ANCIENT CITIES OF THE NEW WORLD: Being Voyages and Explorations in Mexico and Central America, from 1857 to 1882. By Désiré Charnay. Translated by J. Gonino and Helen S. Conant. Illustrations and Map. Royal 8vo, Ornamental Cloth, Uncut Edges, Gilt Top, $6 00.